THE
RULE
OF
ONE

THE RULE OF ONE

ASHLEY SAUNDERS

+

LESLIE SAUNDERS

SKYSCAPE

SKYSCAPE

Text copyright © 2018 by Ashley Saunders and Leslie Saunders
All rights reserved.

Published by Skyscape, New York
www.apub.com

Amazon, the Amazon logo, and Skyscape are trademarks of Amazon.com, Inc., or its affiliates.

ISBN-13: 9781503953161 (hardcover)
ISBN-10: 1503953165 (hardcover)
ISBN-13: 9781503953178 (paperback)
ISBN-10: 1503953173 (paperback)

Cover design by David Curtis
Author photo by Shayan Asgharnia

Printed in the United States of America

First edition

For Mom and Dad, always

PART I
THE SECRET

Mira

I am falling. The darkness is claustrophobic, like I'm buried underground. I drop through air, the wind shrieking in my ears, slapping my long red hair across my face like tiny, fiery whips.

My stomach flips and I feel sick. I try to open my mouth to vomit or scream, but I cannot move. I am made of stone, a statue hurtling deep down into the dark void.

Something brushes against my right wrist. Dozens, hundreds of fingers suddenly claw at my body, hands tearing at my clothes, clamping tight to my neck and feet.

My mind wild, but my body immobile, I desperately will my limbs into action. In a blind panic I fight to break free, but my arms and legs remain bound and rigid, helpless to the hands that threaten to pull me apart. To bury me.

My strength fades away just as a woman's voice cracks open the silence. Her beautiful, warm voice rises and falls in a song, and I remember. *My mother.*

My darting eyes know only the black void, but her voice intensifies and surrounds me. With all the power I have, I struggle to reach out for my mother through the crushing fingers and darkness. Finally, my arms yank loose from the iron hands, and I feel myself ascend.

I jolt awake.

Breathing heavily, I find that I am sitting up in our twin bed inside the basement below our backyard, my muscles sore, my teeth and jaw aching. Ava touches me soothingly on the shoulder, but I'm unable to look at her, embarrassed I woke her again.

"Nightmare?" Ava asks. I nod stiffly, and she lowers her eyes like she understands. But she doesn't. Not fully.

I look at the time. 6:30 a.m. "We're late."

Ava leaps out of bed and tears through the dresser before finally slipping on a pair of our white slacks.

"Where's the clean—"

Careful not to wrinkle it, I toss her our structured linen top. Like a sash, a royal-purple line stretches diagonally across the front from heart to hip, the only break in the pure all-white uniform.

She rips off her T-shirt and continues to dress for school as I turn to the desk beside the stairs. I place our small tablet into our satchel and watch in the mirror as Ava takes great care to brush down her bangs that stop just above her green eyes. The same green eyes as mine.

I grab the concealer from a drawer inside our desk and look up to find myself face-to-face with the lifelike portrait of our mother. Images from my sleep rush over me, the terror of those hands gripping me in the dark more a memory than a dream. Popping the knuckles of my thumbs, I walk over to Ava standing in front of the mirror and try to forget. To shake off the lingering impression.

I know it's no use. I will remember everything. After all, our entire lives are owed to mastering the most minute details. If we don't remember, we don't survive.

Placing the square compact in her waiting palm, I look up at my sister. My twin. With quick taps she skillfully applies the concealer over a star-shaped scar on her neck. When we were in the eighth grade, she tripped and fell into a patch of prickly pears in the greenhouse. Father was furious, but Ava reminded him that it was an accident and that we can't control everything. No matter how hard he tries.

The scar now hidden, she smiles at me in the glass. "There. Now we're the same person," she says. I smile back and analyze our identical reflections. I am her and she is me. One soul in two bodies.

Without thinking, I touch my right wrist, where a microchip should be. A permanent reality of being the second-born in a Rule of One America: *I don't really exist.*

"I wish it was your day at school," says Ava. "You would have no problem getting us a perfect score." I swing our satchel over her shoulder, and together we move up the stairs that lead to the long, empty wall.

"Just keep a clear head during our Spanish oral, and you'll do fine, Ava. We studied all night."

She emits a doubtful sigh, and I pull her forehead to mine. "Tú puedes hacerlo." *You'll do great.*

Ava grins and lifts her hand to the wall. Two soft knocks and the wall recedes, revealing a secret passageway that leads to our house. "See you soon," she tells me.

She turns and half jogs down the tunnel. I hover at the opening until the last flame of her red hair disappears in the dark. I already feel her absence. Half of me is gone.

I close the passageway and descend the stairs in three light steps. I return to our bed.

And wait.

AVA

Starting the day off our usual routine has my nerves on edge, and I have to hurry through the tight underground passageway to make up for being late. As I charge past the concrete walls and up a second set of stairs, I shift my mindset into being above ground; once I step outside our house, I submit to a world with no privacy. Cameras and watchful eyes will monitor my every move. I have to be ready.

It is a precious secret that the two of us exist.

Father had five years to train his little girls in the art of deception before we left the safety of his protection and attended primary academy. Rules were drilled into Mira and me since before we could speak. Knowing this would be the key to our survival, he made following these rules into a game that was fun for us to play. The reward of his honest praise meant everything to me. One of my very first memories is reciting Father's most important governing principle: *We must be perfect. If one of us slips and reveals the secret, we will all lose the game entirely.*

I knock twice on the smooth wall, and it instantly slides open, unveiling our pristine living room. The wall sealing into place behind me, I race into the house and move for the front door. In my distracted haste, I plow unexpectedly into my father standing in the entrance hall. He holds my sleek lunch pail in his hands, a stern look in his eyes.

My own eyes go wide with shock. "It's six forty-five . . . Why aren't you at your office?"

He narrows his lids into thin slits. I carefully grab my lunch from his grasp and stuff it into my bag. The fridge is stocked with premade lunches for each day of the week; everything about our lives is diligently regimented to the point of extreme annoyance.

My father's continued silence pressures me to add, "We won't do it again, I promise."

"No. *I* promise. That was the last time. You cannot spend the night together—it is simply too dangerous."

Father isn't the sort of man whose glare you want aimed in your direction. A high-ranking government official—Director of the Texas Family Planning Division—he exudes authority and breathes schedules. In his sharp military uniform, he cuts a dignified figure, but there's a slight bend in his shoulders this morning that I recognize as the heavy weight of responsibility.

I try to lighten the load by breaking into a grin.

"We're learning a new song in choir today. Mira and I could sing it for you tonight after dinner," I say.

His furrowed brow finally smooths over. "I would like that," he says, straightening. He kisses my forehead lightly. "Keep your guard up, and always stay alert."

"You have a good day too, Father," I say over my shoulder as I head out the door.

Time to play the game.

I practice aloud softly for our Spanish oral exam as I walk through our densely populated neighborhood lined with neat sustainable homes. In the distance, muted behind the careful order of rock yards and community gardens, lies the bloated metropolis of Dallas. The mighty capital of Texas.

Our father's status allows us to live in the city's outer ring, designed for the privileged class. This grants us the luxury of slightly better air quality and the rare advantage of being able to call a piece of land our own. Most of the populace live crammed on top of one another in gigantic billboard-laden skyscrapers, the incessant advertisements from neighboring towers flashing into their windows day and night. Their lives are spent fighting each other for more space, more resources, more everything. Neighbor will kill neighbor over a new pair of shoes. There's never enough of anything to go around.

A mass of cyclists whips past me, weaving through the commuters that crowd the broad avenue leading downtown. Mira and I rarely, if ever, leave the Trinity Heights district; the university is a safe mile up the road from our house. Every day one of us spends an hour walking to and from school, eight hours in the classroom, and the rest of the evening completing coursework and relaying the details of another repetitive day to each other before we separate and go to bed. One of us in the basement, one of us in the upstairs bedroom we call "Ava's room." Wake up and the other repeats. Our days are miserably reliable and monotonous.

I stare at my feet, studying the faded lines on the pavement that was once solely utilized for vehicle traffic. To stimulate my mind I try to imagine the noises and smells of what a fifty-car traffic jam used to be like, when a loud honk blares on a connecting road ahead. It's as if my imagination—minus the forty-nine other cars, but still worth my attention—manifests itself right in front of me for my own entertainment. No one takes note of the lone car hopelessly attempting to cross through the endless mob but me.

The army of walkers pushes me closer to the car, and I peer through the tinted windshield to see a richly dressed businesswoman talking loudly to herself, presumably leading some meeting she is late for. The air-conditioning blasts her hair around her face like she's caught in a picturesque windstorm. It's old-fashioned and perfectly psychotic to commute to work in a private vehicle. The only reason anyone uses a car in the pedestrian-congested city is to wave their prosperity flag pompously to the masses.

I hate inefficiency. Traffic jams must have been an infuriating waste of time. I shake my head, wipe my sweating brow, and continue my own short commute to school by foot. My preferred method of travel.

As I penetrate another half mile into the city, it's hard to see the sky at all, with tower after looming tower dominating the horizon. A sign of progress, the government says. A sign of power. The sky is not enough—we will have to keep building up, up, up and conquer space itself before we will ever be satisfied.

I reach campus five minutes behind schedule and take a shortcut through the Great Lawn, passing the statue of Stephen F. Austin holding a massive Texas flag high above his head. The air is dead and windless, but the Father of Texas would never be allowed to wave a limp flag, especially in his adoptive capital. Hidden air currents blow underneath the lone-starred cloth, producing elegant red, white, and blue ripples that welcome students onto campus.

Strake University is one of the nation's most prestigious colleges; great things are expected of you if you walk its hallowed halls. When the Family Planning Policy—known to the public for what it really is, the Rule of One—passed into law, the ideology of American society shifted dramatically. No more living for oneself; the American independent spirit is dead. We live now for the family. There's just one chance for parents to make their only child a success, to carry on their name with pride and accumulate an income large enough to provide for the aging generations who will rely on their support. Because of this, adolescence has become a cutthroat competition, and Strake offers the appropriate training to compete in an overpopulated world where the weak do not last long.

I'm surrounded by thousands of students dressed in the same white linen uniform as I am, identical except for the strips of color that identify which placement level each student tested into. Although Mira and I are only eighteen, we've been placed in the most advanced rank of sophomore year, entitling us to the color purple. Flashes of the various tiers race across the lawn: purple, blue, red, green, and the lowest, yellow. What rank you graduate with determines the rest of your life. A purple diploma lays the world at your feet.

I make a swift right toward the eastern side of the quadrangle and observe that most of my peers have color-coded umbrellas covering their prudently coiffed heads, either to block out the Texas heat or to shield themselves from the prying surveillance cameras that line every corner.

I arrive at my destination, Tower Hall. Before I enter the ivy-covered building, I quickly close my own umbrella and turn on my smile in anticipation of the Facial Recognition System scanners.

The unavoidable surveillance cameras inspect every person entering any building on campus. The cameras can sweep through a crowd of a thousand people and know in an instant if a face doesn't belong there. No need to scan individual wrists for security—that only happens if you draw attention to yourself.

In the corner of the entrance hall, a uniformed Texas State Guard scrutinizes the system's monitors. I peer at the screens as the cameras connect my face with my name, which is programmed in the database. "Ava Goodwin—Approved" flashes across the monitor, and I mentally send out a small thanks to the universe that Mira and I share identical features.

Two sharp bells ring from the speakers, and I dutifully fall in line with the crowd that leads into the main hall.

Choirmaster Dashwood paces up and down a raised platform, his arms fervidly moving to the music as if possessed. He leads the mass of students—we only vaguely deserve to be called a choir—with a passionate focus that I find admirable. My own heart slightly racing, I close my eyes tight as I sing the slow, impassioned song, not needing the large hologram projection that broadcasts the lyrics.

Mira and I grew up watching hologram recordings Father gave to us of our mother singing at her piano. Sometimes he'd watch with us, sitting on the floor and leaning against our twin bed in the basement, captivated as our mother performed a private concert. The four of us, together, a secret family that can only exist inside a basement.

I've memorized everything about her—she seems so real in them. As children we became obsessed with music, less out of a desire to mimic what our mother loved and more out of a need to be closer to her. That longing ache of desperately wanting something I never actually had in the first place, I'm learning, is the pain of true disappointment.

"And move to the chorus. Louder!"

I sense a change in the room and crack my eyes open to find Halton entering the doorway. His carriage not quite straight, his gawky shoulders nevertheless yearn to be elegant underneath his impeccably neat white uniform with its bold purple line slashed across his body. His dark hair has a slight oily sheen to it, although I'm certain he washed it this morning. Despite all his attempted grandeur, he can't keep his real self from seeping out.

He walks irritatingly slow, taking his time, knowing his tardiness will go unremarked.

The choir continues to sing while he finds his place next to me, forcing another student to slide down the riser. His bodyguard, Special Agent Hayes, falls in line beside him, attempting to blend into the choir by wearing a school uniform. Mouth firmly closed, the middle-aged man isn't fooling anyone.

"Ava," Halton says to me with a formal nod. His stare lingers, as if he expects me to pick up a conversation in the middle of the song.

I close my eyes again, pretending not to notice.

It's seen as a great honor to have Halton's favor, and he damn well knows it. *I don't care how powerful your family is.* Power won't win my attention.

The heat of his gaze on my face becomes too much. I open my eyes again and turn to face him. Usually he'd have backed off by this point, but Halton just stands there staring at me in his quiet, privileged aura, not bothering to sing with the rest of us.

What do you want? I challenge with my eyes.

The choirmaster gives a loud *clap clap clap* in my direction. "Goodwin, eyes to the front!"

Angry with myself for being publicly reprimanded, I snap my head around just as the music abruptly cuts from the speakers with a wave of the choirmaster's hand.

"Thoroughly unremarkable. If that performance is to enlighten the Texas Legislature on the importance of art programs, I pray you are all geniuses at math and science. Memorize by tomorrow. Dismissed."

For the first time in half a century, Strake is reestablishing its choir program. The performing arts were deemed an unessential use of money while millions of people were starving to death and dying from superstorms. Singing belonged to the past.

This year is different. In an unprecedented, lavish affair, Governor Howard S. Roth, the influential leader of Texas, envisions a grand spectacle for the Seventy-Fifth Anniversary Gala commemorating the Rule of One. Our youthful voices raised in unified song will surely lull the people into forgetting we are celebrating that we are controlled to the point we can't even choose how many children we have.

The governor will spare no expense. Next week distinguished delegates from every state will all converge onto Dallas to celebrate, including the president himself. The Lone Star Network speculates this momentous occasion will culminate in the president announcing his support for Roth's own presidential bid next year.

Roth is the longest-serving governor in Texas history, and he rules his state with an iron fist. Despite his controversial methods, leaders all over the world have taken note of Texas's prosperity. The world is so warped you now need iron instead of air to stay afloat.

My classmates silently depart the stage in an orderly single-file line, their concentration already jumping to the next round of grueling classes as they move out the auditorium doors. I hang toward the back, enjoying the stillness of an empty room.

Lingering a few moments in the quiet, I nod respectfully to Choirmaster Dashwood before facing the overcrowded hallway that leads to my next scheduled stop. Since it's illegal to cover identifiable marks on your body, Mira or I visit the same bathroom every day so I can privately reapply concealer to the star-shaped scar on my neck.

Head down—we always stare at our feet—I push my way through the Great Lawn and up to the second-floor hallway of the Union. I enter the women's restroom and sit in the stall farthest from the entrance, but as I pull out my makeup compact, there's suddenly a shout from above.

"Using unauthorized makeup? Oh dear."

Startled, I jump from my seat and look up to find a girl staring down at me from the top of the other stall. Recognizing her face, I rapidly search my brain for her name, but it's hard to memorize and identify tens of thousands of classmates.

"I'm going to have to report you to the Dean." She clicks her tongue disapprovingly, and her head disappears.

Terrified, I burst from the stall. "Please, you can't report me!" I plead. "I just—" My appeal is abruptly cut short when a group of influential girls with famous last names erupts into loud, stinging laughter.

"You're such a prig, Goodwin," another girl bites. Smiling, she joins their leader (*What is her name?*) in front of the mirror. High-ranking purple and blue are blazed across their uniforms.

"Whatever you're trying to cover up," she continues, "it's not working."

In the mirror I see the girls move, not to primp their perfect hair, but to place square patches on each other's chests, just above their cleavage.

Tape. The chosen drug of the rich.

"If you're going to break the rules, Goodwin, do try and live up to the possibilities."

One of the girls holds out a patch of Tape for me on the tip of her middle finger, bending her finger back and forth in a welcoming gesture. She winks. Another girl attempts to pull up my shirt, but I throw my head down and push my way out of the bathroom to another onslaught of laughter.

I proceed directly to the crowded dining hall, their laughter still ringing in my ears, and sit at my usual bench by the window with only Rylie Sparks for company. There's an unspoken understanding between us that while we both prefer to eat alone, it's better to have someone across the table than not.

I wish I could have friends. I wish I could feel a real connection with others and discover the different types of love that exist in this world, but I've built up such high walls to keep our secret—to keep us safe—that it's impossible for anyone to get close to me. I'm alone inside my own defenses. Except for Mira. I'll always have my sister. If she were to die before I do, I know she'd search through all of time and space to find me again. And I her.

I shake these thoughts away and scan the long line of students queued up in front of the glossy 3D printing machine. The next person in line scans his wrist and chooses the item he desires from the menu. A tray consisting of a simple, lean protein paired with a side of steaming vegetables pops out instantly in front of him. The girl behind him selects her item, and her plate—the same ingredients but prepared in a vastly different way—appears ten seconds later. I pull out my home-cooked meal from my lunch pail—Tuesday is lemon chicken and broccoli—shove a hearty bite into my mouth, and set to work on my tablet.

I have half an hour before advanced chemistry. Mira already perfected our assignment last night, so I have this free time to get a head start on the physics homework assigned in my first class this morning. The workload is immense, but my fingers glide nimbly across the screen as I easily solve complicated equation after complicated equation.

My single-minded focus is broken when I hear a shout from a machine. "Insufficient ration credits, Mr. Wallace!"

I raise my head to see Aden Wallace, clothed in his faded white uniform with its telltale yellow stripe, attempt to scan his wrist again. A student's color rank curiously tends to correlate with their family's economic status.

"Are you sure? I haven't used all my rations, I know it," he implores.

"Insufficient credits, Mr. Wallace. Leave the line at once."

With his shaky chin held low, the thin boy begs for his meal, muttering, "Please. I'm hungry." But the machines do not care how empty people's bellies are. Insufficient credits are insufficient credits.

Aden doesn't look to anyone for help—he knows no one is likely to share. When he sees a Texas State Guard coming to escort him from the line, he withdraws from the dining hall to judgmental whispers and pointing.

I return my attention to my physics equations and catch Halton observing me from a nearby table.

He's surrounded by purples and blues, at the center of his personal court, but no one talks to him. He sticks out among his brawny, handsome peers, with their easy, charming laughter and smiles. It's clear he inherited these so-called friends instead of earning their friendship on his own merit.

Mckinley Ruiz, the sinewy, raven-haired freshman sitting across from Halton, turns to face me. She swivels and finds Halton's eyes finding mine. Anger flashes in her eyes.

He's mine! she silently screams at me across the large room.

She's a known rank-climber. A thin blue sash cuts across her uniform, and I know all she wants is to turn her blue blood purple. Not by earning better grades, but through marriage. Halton is her ladder.

Aggravated at being forced into the middle of their romantic theatrics, I place my hand over my forehead, hoping to shield myself from view.

In a sprawling public square outside campus, two bustling paths filled with evening commuters split in opposite directions.

Façades of the surrounding skyscrapers project a simulated sunset on massive screens, the artificial light casting spectacular oranges and pinks across the broad walkway. My heart instantly lightens. Although I know the images are deliberately designed to manufacture powerful feelings of well-being, they're still beautiful.

As I continue my walk home, the calming sunset is replaced with a PSA of a smiling couple and their single daughter. Huge flashing text screams at the crowd, "One Child, One Nation."

I ignore the propaganda by looking at my feet. I try to visualize the exact positions of every surveillance camera stationed in the area. There's a camera inside the watchful eyes of the longhorn statue in the square's center, and two in the bank tower on my right.

A sudden flurry of motion distracts me, and I snap my head up as a fair-haired woman wrenches a bottle of water from an unsuspecting student's hands.

"Thief!" the young man screams at the top of his lungs.

The woman rushes through the alarmed mass of people, coming straight at me, but I can't seem to move.

A loud, crushing *boom*, and the woman drops to the ground, convulsing. Three more violent spasms and her body goes limp.

The water bottle lies forgotten a few feet away, its precious contents pooling wastefully on the hot concrete. A man emerges unnoticed from the crowd, quickly grabs the stolen plunder, and disappears safely into the herd of pedestrians.

Holding his twelve-gauge shotgun taser, a robust Texas State Guard approaches the woman and stops, the point of his boots stepping on the tips of her fingers.

Half the evening commuters have stopped to watch the scene play out. Some of them linger for pure entertainment, but others look on with barely concealed rage.

I go against all my conditioning and remain in this suddenly charged moment. I should be removing myself calmly from the situation, careful to not draw the Guard's attention, but instead I stand immobile next to the woman sprawled out motionless on the ground.

I feel the energy of the crowd burn hot and angry. A shout rings out, loud and clear.

"Enough!"

Three voices pick up the rallying cry, creating a fiery echo.

A handful of protesters try to push their way to the Guard holding the taser, causing a small skirmish to ripple across the square. An entire unit of State Guards immediately floods the area.

"Disperse immediately, or you will be arrested!"

One of the soldiers lifts a sonic weapon into the air and fires without hesitation. Everyone in a hundred-yard radius collapses incapacitated to the ground, hands pressed desperately to their ears.

I fall hard on the pavement and clamp my palms tight against my head. The overwhelming sound ruthlessly invades my brain, and I can't make it stop. I curl into a fetal position and stare at the arrested woman next to me. The look she sends me is desperate and wild, but all I can do is stare at her in my own helplessness.

The Guard, spared from the auditory assault by his earplugs, roughly pulls out the woman's twisted wrist from underneath her body and scans it with a small device. Microchips not only monitor food rations but also contain everything about you: arrest records, blood type, social security number, addresses, credit card information, insurance. Everything. It took several generations for the public to accept being microchipped, but it happened.

It's not control, they say; *it's for our own safety. Microchips save lives.* We've all been conditioned to believe this. But I don't believe it. Microchips led to my mother's death.

"On your feet!" the Guard screams. "Move!"

I struggle to comply, the painful pounding in my ears throwing off my balance, making me feel sick.

"Do you have a problem, young lady?" The Guard scrutinizes me from above, singling me out.

"No sir," I manage.

"If you continue to loiter on my walkway, I will arrest you next," he threatens. He holsters his taser before bending down to zip-tie the woman's hands behind her back.

The protesters swiftly subdued, orderly lines are already reforming on the street. In a daze I stand and join them.

It's impossible to fight back; the government made sure of that long ago. Civilians are not allowed to own weapons—only the Guard has that authority. The people can fight solely with their raised voices, and I've only ever heard them silenced.

The ones with the guns always win.

MIRA

I must keep active. Spending twenty-four unbroken hours confined in an eighteen-by-fifteen basement four days a week feels like a prison. Ava and I exercise regularly to keep our endorphins high and our depression low. We both favor jumping jacks. I'm up to twenty minutes straight.

My heart still beats like drumfire in my chest as I recharge on the floor, my back against the foot of our bed.

"E-book database," I say to the empty room. A hologram pops up before me, and I cross my legs, settling in. I raise my forefinger in the air and swipe through the long list of nonfiction e-books Ava and I have purchased over the years. We both share a childlike fascination for the landscapes and cultures of the outside world. Places that seem to only exist in the three-dimensional images in front of me. Or in my imagination.

We've never met someone from outside the United States, of course. And it's as unaffordable as it is unthinkable for an American citizen to travel to the few countries that still allow foreign visitors. The threat of death—or worse, of being taken captive for a ransom the US government simply can't afford to pay—is a risk not many take. It's funny. Just when technology shrank the world, making every*where* and every*one* accessible, it's all never felt more out of reach.

4:43 p.m. Ava's late.

"Hologram off," I say as I head up the stairs. I pace the polished concrete floor, my gaze fixed on the security camera projections in the corner of the room. Eight turns around the landing later, my heart rate picks back up when I see Ava appear on the monitors.

She lowers her umbrella and swipes her fingerprint to unlock the front door. My eyes shift to the second monitor to follow her progress through the living room. Her lips move in a quick, silent command, and the clear glass wall behind her darkens to gray, sealing the room in privacy. She approaches the false wall and knocks twice.

I wait the ten seconds it takes for her to move through the passageway, then the wall slides open and Ava stands before me.

"Why are you so late?" I know from the haunted look in her eyes that something happened.

As she moves past me down the steps, I see the stain on her right lower leg. The scuffs and small tears on her right elbow. It's difficult to keep a white uniform white in a polluted, bustling city. We've always achieved it, of course, because it is expected of us. But Ava seems calm. So I keep calm.

"Did something happen?" I say, as tranquil as I can manage.

Ava plops down hard on the bed, sliding off her shoes with her toes. "Just let me appreciate the AC for a moment."

I join Ava on the bed and catch the sharp scents of sweat and sunlight. The lingering traces of being in the open air. I scoot closer to her, feeling nearer to the sun by proximity. Five hours and sixteen minutes until it's my turn above ground.

"I finished our English paper," I finally say.

"I saw. Why do you insist on correcting my drafts in red? It makes it look like our assignments are covered in blood."

I smile, amused.

"I'm just going to get this out of the way," Ava says, sighing heavily. "I got an A minus on our Spanish oral."

"That's all right . . ." I wonder if this is really the most damning news of the day. "I'll make up for it on the exam next week."

Ava nods, thoughtful. She lies down across the bed, her head finding the corner of a pillow. She pops the knuckle of her thumb, and I fold my hands in my lap and wait for her to speak. I should give her time to decompress.

"A girl caught me in the bathroom stall with the unapproved makeup," she says, finally. "I looked her up—her name is Tifani Cheng."

My mind goes straight to the worst-case scenario. We've been expelled.

"But Tifani just laughed it off and let Jocelyn Wood slap a patch of Tape on her skin right in front of me. Morgan Vega was there too," Ava continues. "I recorded more details about what was said in the journal."

I roll my eyes, annoyed at the girls' arrogance. "Stupid. They're going to get arrested. Your last name only goes so far."

The government takes the war on drugs very seriously. If Tifani gets caught using, she faces a minimum ten years of hard penal labor in a local prison farm.

"Halton was creepier than usual today," Ava continues. "He would not stop staring at us in choir and again in the cafeteria."

I jerk up, sending Ava bouncing on the mattress.

"Shit!" I say. "He's going to ask us to the Gala!"

Instantly realizing I'm right, Ava lurches forward. "Disgusting!" She shakes her body in exaggerated distaste. "I hope he asks when it's your day at school!"

With a mischievous smile, I shove Ava back down on the bed, and we both erupt into the same deep laughter.

I swallow a few muffled snorts, already strategizing how best to avoid Halton's advances, when I suddenly register that Ava has gone quiet. She stares stiffly at the ceiling above, her mind faraway. My smile disappears.

"What else happened?"

"A woman was tasered on my walk home. For stealing water." Ava pauses and slowly turns her head toward me, her bangs a tangled mop on her forehead. "It nearly caused a riot."

My heart sinks. Not for the woman, but for us. "They'll increase security on campus now. Father won't be pleased."

Ava attempts to shove her bangs behind her ears and sits bolt upright.

"Mira, she stared right at me while it was all happening. The crowd started screaming *'Enough'* to the Guards, and I just stood there," she says rapidly, locking my hand in hers. "I can't shake seeing the fear in her eyes. The absolute fear."

I remember those old airline safety videos we used to watch when we were younger. We wanted to be ready in case we ever got to fly. *In the event of an emergency, always put on your own mask first before helping others near you.*

"You couldn't do anything for her." In truth, Ava should have left the scene sooner, but I decide not to press.

Ava tightens her grip on my hand, her expression both earnest and drained. She squares her shoulders and looks me straight in the eyes.

"Will you go up for dinner?" she asks.

Startled at the suggestion, I pull away, separating our linked hands. *Why would she ask this of me?* Especially tonight.

"My head is still pounding from the damn Scream Gun the Guard fired off to control the crowd," Ava urges, placing her hand to her right temple. "I don't want Father to see. He'll make a big deal of everything like he always does."

My fingers brush my right wrist. "Father would be furious with us. It's your day up, and we can't break the schedule."

"He probably won't even notice." Ava reaches out again for my hand, forcing me to listen. "I don't have the energy to play the game tonight, and I'm sick of always having to follow rules. We're eighteen, Mira. We should be able to make our own decisions."

"I don't know. It's an important dinner, and you're the one with the microchip." I shift in my seat. "It's dangerous."

"It's not like I'm asking you to try and cross the US border," she retorts. "It's dinner at our own house!"

I scoff at her attempt to make her request sound simple. "Yes, but it's *who* is invited for dinner that you're failing to acknowledge here."

"Why can't you just help me and tag team?" She lets out a long sigh. Her voice softens. "Today was crazy, Mira."

"Crazy is all the more reason to stick to the rules."

Our eyes lock: Ava's insistent, mine unwavering. "I'd do it for you," Ava throws at me. She rises from the bed and storms up the stairs.

"Ava!" I call after her. She doesn't respond, simply knocks twice on the wall to open the passageway. I surge to my feet on pure instinct—from the guilt of never wanting to upset her, from never wanting to disappoint.

"Fine. I'll go up."

Ava stops and turns. Our eyes meet, and we understand one another with just a glance.

I walk to the desk in the corner and open the bottom drawer. I take out a small box that contains strips of Ava's fingerprints. Ava approaches and helps me carefully apply the prints to each of my fingertips. "The only part of me that you don't have," she says.

We smile at each other, our bond quiet and absolute.

There's something about emerging from a bath that makes me feel like I can do anything. It's a blank slate, a renewal. A transformation into Ava.

I softly shut the door to Ava's bedroom, where we each sleep when it's our turn to play the game, and stride down the hallway, gaining confidence with each step. As I descend the long staircase to the dining room, I press down on the frills and embellishments of my dress, hoping to make them disappear. Or at least make them less noticeable. Ava and I prefer comfort and simplicity, but Father expects us to wear our finest on an occasion such as this. To show respect for our guests.

We can do this.

I clasp my hands into a stiff ball and place them behind my back, so as not to focus on my microchipless wrist. Out of sight, out of mind.

The empty, useless capsule implanted beneath my skin was designed by my father to help make me feel "normal." But it's all just for show. After all these years venturing above ground without a real chip, I've grown accustomed to the unsettling sensation of feeling publicly naked and exposed. Convinced a thousand eyes are on me and know what I really am.

There's no other way. An individual's microchip is impossible to duplicate. And Father spent years researching ways Ava and I could trade the chip, like taking it out of her wrist and putting it into mine when it was my day to go up. But this proved equally impossible. The older Ava and I get, the more the possibility of mutations in our DNA grows, altering our identical genetic information. The microchip would detect the unregistered DNA instantly, setting off the alarm. The only way for me to have a life outside the basement is to walk around with an imitation microchip. And nerves of steel.

I make my way into the dining room and hit a wave of aromas escaping from the kitchen. My mouth waters. All-natural beef tenderloin.

Thirty years ago, the Isolation Act was imposed, banning all foreign trade, mostly in an effort to keep American-grown food in American-born mouths. It still wasn't enough. Today, ninety-five percent of our country survives on lab-grown meat and genetically modified crops. Real beef is especially scarce and extremely expensive. By hosting a dinner party with this rare cut of meat, Father is aiming to impress.

Expansive glass walls dominate the room, affording a perfect view of Dallas in the distance. Light pollution from the vast skyline handsomely illuminates our large dining table, set formally with five-piece place settings.

"Good evening, Miss Goodwin," Gwen greets me, folding a cloth napkin into a fan.

"The table looks beautiful," I say as I watch her place the intricate design carefully atop a small porcelain plate. I realize five places have been set for dinner. Not four.

"Why is there an extra—" I start to ask, but the sharp click of boots announces Father's arrival, and Gwen stiffens as he enters, marvelous in his crisp uniform.

I, too, feel my body tighten. *This is it.*

If Ava and I were standing side by side, Father would be able to know the difference right away. But when we are separated, it's much harder for him to identify who is who. Your eyes register what your brain expects to see. Father expects to see Ava, so I am Ava. The foundation of our success.

"Thank you for helping us tonight, Gwen," Father says warmly, analyzing her work. Her tense demeanor melts away as she notes my father's relaxed manner.

"I'm grateful for the work, Dr. Goodwin," she says, still finding it difficult to look him in the eyes.

Gwen is from the inner city. When she was a student, she was chosen from thousands of applicants by my father's Equal Future Scholarship Program to receive full financial aid to a top-ranked university. And look where her degree got her. Ten years of serving food and cleaning houses.

"Be sure to prepare a plate for yourself and your husband before you leave," Father adds, thumbing through the countless urgent work messages on his tablet. Finally, he turns to me and gives me a quick once-over. He nods in approval.

I allow myself a small smile. He didn't notice.

"Your favorite thing about today, Ava?" he asks, pocketing his tablet and devoting his full attention to me.

He asks this question every night at dinner. We usually eat down in the basement, the three of us crowded around a small card table sharing reheated food Gwen leaves for us in the fridge. Some days I think he asks as some sort of test, like there's a particular answer he's looking for.

"Dreaming about that chocolate cake," I say lightheartedly, fishing for a laugh. He chuckles, watching Gwen move the dessert a safe distance away from my grasp.

The doorbell rings, and we both shake off our candid smiles, hardening ourselves for the present. With a well-rehearsed urgency, Gwen moves toward the front hall.

Confidence high, I position myself next to my father as Gwen opens the door to the formidable Governor Roth. He stands tall and dignified, just like on TV, his uniform practically sagging from the weight of his medals. Mrs. Roth, all big lips and big hair, holds a petite portable fan to her face. Special Agent Hayes follows behind.

The agent sweeps the premises with trained eyes, his mouth like a ventriloquist's as he whispers into his mouthpiece, "All clear."

I catch movement behind the courtly party, and my eyes land on their grandson, Halton. I push back the unhappy surprise of his presence by stretching my fake smile even bigger. He stands awkwardly dwarfed behind his grandparents, and for some reason the sweat on his shiny face annoys me.

"Governor Roth, it is an honor to have you in our home," Father says as he steps forward, inviting them out of the heat. Gwen moves aside to enable the governor to pass, but he remains outside the entryway, glowering at the surrounding houses.

Offensively modest, I know he's thinking. Governor Roth has never agreed with Father's choice of neighborhood. He firmly believes it is too common and unfit for a man of Father's position. Yet we live in one of the premier communities of the entire Dallas–Fort Worth metroplex. *I* firmly believe the governor has lost touch with reality. We can't all live in mansions.

"We will be needing refreshments directly," he announces finally. "Mrs. Roth is feeling overheated." Gwen rushes into the kitchen as if from the crack of a whip.

We proceed into the dining room, and Mrs. Roth greets me with a handshake. "Nice and strong. Good, good."

She turns to her grandson, the strength of her grip still stinging my hand. "Halton, doesn't Ava look stunning tonight?" she asks, admiring my necklace while Halton admires me.

"Captivating," he answers, forcing me to give a polite smile in acknowledgment.

Gwen appears with a tray laden with glasses of ice water, saving us from further conversation. She hands a dripping glass to Mrs. Roth, who downs its contents in three loud gulps.

Our circular dining table allows no place for a head of the table, a fact that must be glaringly obvious to the governor. But Father courteously leads Roth to a chair to the right of his own, offering our honored guest a superior view of the city he rules.

"Oh, what lovely flowers, Darren!" says Mrs. Roth, positively lighting up when she spots the beautiful centerpiece of fresh yellow flowers.

Father pulls out her chair next to mine, inviting her to sit. "Yes, they're black-eyed Susans from the neighborhood greenhouse. Ava tends to them devotedly."

The governor shakes out his napkin as he watches his grandson disapprovingly. "Halton, it is very rude not to pull Miss Goodwin's chair out for her. You are her guest."

Halton's embarrassment shows red on his face. It spreads in odd splotches as he approaches me, not daring to catch my eye. Mortified, I try to help him tuck in my chair, and after several fits and stops, the metal of my chair shrieking painfully against the oak wood, we finally achieve it. I whisper a soft thank-you, wondering what shade of scarlet my cheeks elected.

Gwen fills the wine glasses from a rare bottle of Napa Valley cabernet before serving the first course of cold cucumber soup.

"To the governor and his family," Father toasts simply.

Before my lips touch my glass, Mrs. Roth begins her interrogation. "Darren tells me you are a very clever young woman, Ava. And what have you decided as your career path after university?"

I place my full wine glass back down on the table. Best to keep a clear mind. "Well, I really—" I begin to say before Father cuts me off.

"I am very pleased to say it is Ava's wish to continue her medical school education at Strake University," he answers for me. "She hopes to soon serve her great state under the Family Planning Division."

That is not my wish. That is our future chosen by my father. I stare down at my napkin, letting my anger show for a fraction of a second.

"Just like her father," Mrs. Roth says to me. I turn and match her beaming smile, tooth for tooth.

"Strake is the finest institution our country has ever built," Governor Roth growls, half his wine already drained. His own grandmother founded Strake, naming the university after a part mounted on aircraft that improves aerodynamic stability. Meaning students are simply parts on a machine to make Texas soar. Not individuals or anything.

I sit back, thoroughly aware he's about to dig into one of his long-winded speeches. I take the opportunity to dig into my soup.

"Our promising youth should stay here, where they were born and raised. The time and resources we've invested into these students' futures—what benefit is there for us if the child leaves? All that potential and promise gone, given to some other state, when their skills should be utilized here, aiding in the prosperity of Texas. Not wasted on some drowning coastal city in Florida or in the Carolinas that should have been cut from our country like a useless limb."

Like Texas severed Houston. Roth was the first governor to refuse aid to one of his own cities, setting a precedent. His Gulf Coast citizens either migrated inland or succumbed to a watery grave.

I half-listen to Father's agreeable response and focus instead on Halton sitting across from me. He looks stuffy and cramped inside his high-collared blazer, the purple buttons on his shirt glossy and blinding. He barely touches his soup, and like the governor, he favors the wine.

"Of course, our Halton will follow in his grandfather's footsteps as well," says Mrs. Roth. "He's ranked number two in his year."

It has long been believed Halton earns his grades through fear. Not fear of him, of course. Fear of his last name.

"We are so proud," she says, a smile plastered on her face. Governor Roth hardly glances up to acknowledge his grandson.

Halton downs the rest of his cabernet like a shot and lifts his glass for another. Gwen answers promptly with the bottle, eliciting a glare from Mrs. Roth that says, *Cut him off.*

Flawlessly, Gwen aborts midpour and begins clearing away the dishes for the main course.

With an air of familiarity, Mrs. Roth places a heavily jeweled hand on my right wrist, continuing her assault. "Have you chosen your date for the Anniversary Gala, Ava?"

I pause before answering, wondering if Father will let me speak. "I will be attending the celebration with my father."

Mrs. Roth clasps her hands together, pleased. "Nonsense. Halton will be your partner." Free from her grasp, I lightly brush my wrist and force another smile as I lock eyes with Halton.

"Agent Hayes, send in the photographer!" Mrs. Roth shouts, clapping with the excitement of a child on Christmas morning.

Before I understand what's happening, a large woman with a tiny camera is yelling at me to stand and move closer to Halton.

I look to Father, who takes this unexpected intrusion in stride, keeping his manner light. "Now, Mrs. Roth, you know how much Ava despises having her photo taken."

"I've never been very photogenic," I force out as our go-to excuse.

"You Goodwins are so camera shy! But think what these two will look like together as an advertisement on the side of a skyrise! The prince of the Gala and his princess."

"Scoot closer!" the photographer orders, winking at me like she's giving me a gift.

Halton's arm slips behind my back, his hand hovering above my waist. He seems to think better of it and moves his hand up to higher ground, landing on my shoulder.

My skin crawls. I can't move, but out of the corner of my eye, I see him staring at my bracelet. Or is he staring at my wrist? With enormous effort, as if moving through quicksand, I ball my hands into fists behind my back, shielding my right wrist from view.

"Your own child as the face of the Gala, Dr. Goodwin? The public will be fawning over her!" the photographer adds with eager adoration as her camera's shutter fires off with rapid *click click click*s.

Governor Roth emits a low growl at this, a Rottweiler claiming his territory. The Gala is his. Dread fills the room, waiting for his bark, but Mrs. Roth clears the air by shooing the silly woman away. I break away from Halton and return stiffly to my seat with my artificial smile.

"And who will be your partner, Darren?" Mrs. Roth continues smoothly.

As Director of the Texas Family Planning Division, Father is expected to attend with a proper guest. Mrs. Roth parrots my thoughts aloud and turns to her husband for reinforcement.

"I'm certain you agree, dear?"

Governor Roth takes a hearty sip of his wine and reviews the lavish piece of beef tenderloin set down in front of him, unimpressed.

"I'm afraid my duties will occupy my attention during the com- memoration, Mrs. Roth," says Father, ending the debate.

"Your duties . . ."

The governor does not raise his voice but speaks quietly, forcing the smallest of noises to settle before he continues.

"What is the old phrase with which they've christened you, Darren?"

No one offers up the phrase, knowing he means to say it himself. He holds the silence for emphasis, and I shift in my seat, uneasy. The pleasantries are over.

"Ah, yes. The People's Champion . . . *the people*." His last words ring with displeasure. He throws a side-glance at Gwen, provoking my temper. The governor has always been envious of my father's ability to win the praise and hearts of the public. The people may vote for Roth, but they will never love him.

Gwen approaches Roth's left side, almost bowing as she delicately serves bourbon-glazed carrots from a silver dish. With shocking speed, Roth grabs Gwen's arm and grips it so tightly she drops her spoon.

"I did not tell you I wanted those. Remove them," he snaps. "Now." He glowers at her like she's a piece of trash polluting his air.

"Gwen, that will be all for tonight, thank you," says Father, trying to take control of the situation. To save her.

"The girl stays," Roth commands with a booming ferocity.

Gwen is a full-grown woman, not a girl. It's this sort of power play that tests my father's composure. But I mimic him and keep a neutral face. Inscrutable.

"All the work I do, Governor, I do for the betterment of Texas," Father says, his voice uncharacteristically strained. He sets down his fork and faces the governor. "For your name and your legacy."

"My legacy." The governor taps his empty wine glass with a dispar- aging smile. With a discreet nod from Mrs. Roth, Gwen rushes to refill it, her eyes shiny with tears.

"Texas has always been the Lone Star this country has looked to for guidance. A symbol of preservation. And the rest of the world wants in."

Mrs. Roth's delicate nostrils flare at the possibility.

A bulging vein appears on the governor's left temple. It seems to swell and expand with every new word he spits out.

"Have you read the latest DHS report?"

He doesn't wait for Father's answer.

"Four million. Four million of these filthy Gluts have already attempted to get through our Big Fence this year—more than half that number attacking our own Texas walls."

Gluts. Surplus. Those considered the unwanted overflow in our overpopulated world.

"And these parasites are not the only filth trying to get in. My State Guard locates and destroys hundreds of tunnels a day dug by Mexican cartels trying to infest our country with their cocaine, meth, and latest dirty drugs. And from the sky, Moscow, Beijing, and Riyadh repeatedly threaten to target Dallas and Washington with their missiles if the US does not open our borders to trade."

Nuclear warfare. A polite dinner topic for modern polite society. Father stares at the governor soberly, his untouched plate of food turning cold.

"America can no longer attack our enemies—we can only defend. And what my wall cannot defend, I make damn certain my soldiers and my drones protect, because if the outside world succeeds, they will bring with them disease, starvation, lawlessness, and war. And though these Gluts will never get through, they will keep trying. Desperation is a hard foe to fight against, because the desperate never stop."

I keep my head down and concentrate on cutting my meat. To my left I note Halton's gaze lingering over portraits of Ava and my father, our perfect two-member family. I guess he doesn't have an opinion on these matters. I'm unsure if I do either. Famine breeds war, and humankind will always raid before they starve. But can we blame the desperate?

I didn't do anything special or have a say in the matter—I was just lucky enough to be born in a land still capable of growing food. Most political issues are so black-and-white, but I live in the gray. I *am* the gray.

"America idolizes you for your overwhelming success in protecting the Texan borders against the dangers that lie outside our walls. But what of your citizens who are here, inside your own Big Fence, starving and sick with no hope for aid?" Father says.

Stunned, I have trouble swallowing my steak. Trouble digesting my Father's brazenness. I can count on one hand the times he's let slip criticisms of Roth or his policies to me and Ava. He would never reproach the governor to his face. No one does.

"The lazy, useless degenerates that do nothing but suck up our state's resources, begging for handouts? Waging riots and violence when they don't get what they want? Are these your *people*, Darren?"

Amazingly, Father keeps pushing. "These people are your own citizens, Governor, simply fighting for survival. With no foreseeable solution, the global climate crisis has our country balancing on the edge of a tipping point. As the temperatures continue to rise, so too will the tensions between the elite and the lower classes. We must adapt and adjust our model, or the United States will collapse. And until leaders with your power start to listen, riots like the one that nearly erupted outside Strake are just the beginning."

Governor Roth cuts a large piece from his bloody steak, taking his time to chew. The tension is like sitting next to a bomb, anticipating the blast.

"You would have our country buried under lowlifes and filth?" the governor begins in a calm voice. Unnaturally calm. "You're a doctor . . . Take a gunshot to the belly, for instance. When a body is bleeding, you must find the source, the cause. It is messy and violent as you dig and search, but then you finally see it. The bullet. The cause of all this turmoil. The threat to life. And so you expel it, you seal up the wound. There is no more blood, and the body heals."

I dare to sneak a glance at the governor and discover the vein on his temple has disappeared. The cool, sterile look he gives my father causes every hair on my skin to rise.

"I will protect the body of Texas and drive out all who threaten to kill it."

The governor sits back, allowing his allegory to sink in.

"The great Han and Roman Empires fell in the end because of their weak and shortsighted leaders. That will not be my legacy."

My father turns to me, face cordial and composed. "Ava, why don't you show Halton the neighborhood greenhouse and pick a bouquet of fresh flowers for Mrs. Roth to bring home?"

Before turning back to his sparring match, he gives me a double take. It's quick and subtle, but through his politician façade, I can see his anger.

We're caught. *He knows I'm Mira.*

"Yes, Father." I rise from my chair dutifully, wondering if Ava has been watching from the basement. I hope she's formulating a better excuse than the one she gave me.

Governor Roth gives a small nod to Agent Hayes, who stands forgotten in the corner. Hayes falls in behind Halton, becoming his shadow as I lead the way out the front door.

I escort a brooding Halton along a path of leafy greens and vegetable vines, ignoring the patches of yellow flowers we pass. My mind still solidly in the dining room, I have little patience to play the cordial tour guide. I grip my basket and shovel with white knuckles, a thousand thoughts racing through my head. I try hopelessly to grab hold of only one.

How did Father realize it was me . . . does he really believe the United States will collapse . . . he dared to criticize . . . my father is the bullet the governor will expel . . .

"We're passing all the flowers," Halton says, jolting me back into the present.

"They're black-eyed Susans," I say, not slowing my pace.

I note Halton's heavy feet, stumbling slightly as he follows me. A neighbor from two houses down attempts to blend in with a line of bell pepper plants as he watches us from three rows over. His eyes fall nervously on our surly chaperone standing guard at the back entrance. Just get this done quick.

A classical piece of music plays softly overhead, encouraging the plants to grow. Jules Massenet's "Meditation" from the opera *Thaïs*. The solo violin rings across the greenhouse, and it's as if I can actually see every plant reach out its limbs to be nearer to the speakers.

"How do you get the flowers to grow here? Do you cheat your water rations?" asks Halton.

I roll my eyes, careful he doesn't see. "They're drought tolerant."

I turn to find him no longer following me, but staring fixedly at the golden flowers. Black-eyed Susans are best known as wildflowers. This is probably the nearest he's ever been to anything wild in his life.

"They are also a pioneer plant," I continue as he leans in to study them closer, his body bent forward like a broken stem. "If a fire burns down part of a forest, this plant will be one of the first to grow again."

He grabs hold of a single flower with his thumb and forefinger.

"No! Don't touch them!" I hear myself shout. Before he can pluck the stem, I rush toward him, forgetting myself.

Halton stiffens at my words, all at once sobering up. He shoots an embarrassed glance toward Agent Hayes before shifting his gaze to my hapless neighbor. The man gives a perceptible jump and rushes for the front exit.

Immediately recognizing my misstep, I produce a charming smile, ignoring the sudden tension. "I apologize if I spoke out of line, but the flowers are very special to me. My mother planted them."

I gesture amiably toward the eagle's claw cacti. "How many do you think Mrs. Roth will wish to take home?"

Halton's mouth turns down in aversion. "None."

Well, these are the only ones I'm giving you, so how can we make this easy?

"I think they have an unassuming beauty," I say, trying to sell him. He displays a shy smile, reading into my words. "They personify the people of our state. Strong and resilient," I add for good measure.

Halton nods in approval, buying my bullshit.

I pull on a pair of gloves and begin to dig up the roots of the barbed plant with my shovel. I sense his eyes on me, analyzing my every move. He wets his lips and steps closer to me.

"They say you weren't born in a hospital but in your home. That's very uncommon."

"My mother wanted a natural home birth, and my father is a prominent doctor. The governor granted them his consent."

Should I ask you about your own missing parent? His mother passed away from skin cancer when he was five, but what happened to his father? The details are murky, filled with holes and dark spots. The entire country acts as if Halton's father had never been born.

"Still. That's unusual," he presses. "And never allowed again after what transpired."

My mother's death. She died in our basement giving birth to her illegal twin daughters. A uterine rupture. Father couldn't save her.

But she saved me.

I angrily thrust the shovel in the soil and throw the first plant into the basket. I take deep breaths to calm myself and begin on a second cactus.

"You still live at home."

Jesus, he's the same as his grandparents: his grandfather and his wine, his grandmother and her questions.

"Most students in the city live with their family, including you," I say.

"I live in the Governor's Mansion," says Halton, believing this somehow does not count. "Your father's wealth would enable you to live on your own. It's unusual you would not take that opportunity."

"I think two cacti should do it," I say, my patience gone. *What is he playing at?*

I stab at the soil, heedless of the cacti's roots, still feeling the burn of his gaze on my neck. The silence presses down on me, and a shiver flashes through my body.

"I've been watching you, Ava," says Halton.

I keep my face carefully composed—the Goodwin way—and hide my growing panic.

He takes a step toward me.

"Every morning before you enter Tower Hall, you hesitate, just for a second, as you switch on that bright smile of yours before marching off to physics class. In choir you close your eyes for the last verse of every single pointless song. In the dining hall you chew your lower lip, working furiously away on your tablet as you eat your homemade meal. Protein first. Sides last. You pop the knuckle of your thumb when you're anxious before Spanish, toss your bangs when you're flustered before advanced chemistry. You whisper aloud to yourself on your walk home, your head always down, careful never to draw attention to yourself. I could go on . . ."

He pauses, as if expecting me to say something. Does he think this fanatical attention is some form of flattery?

"Of course, no one would notice these little things but me." He takes another step forward. "You have to be watching."

I slowly rise to my feet and peel off my dirt-stained gloves. Sweat drips freely from my brow, but I do not move to wipe it.

"Why are you watching me?" I say, surprised how thin my voice sounds.

"It's like clockwork—your habits," he almost coos. An impish smile plays on his lips. "But recently, for the past few months, I've seen you touch your right wrist when you get nervous. You touch your microchip. But you don't do it every day like all your regular habits. Just every other day. You didn't do it today in choir or at lunch . . . yet you touched your wrist at dinner and again just now."

Did I? I clench my hands into tight fists, my fingernails digging into my palms.

"That throws off the clock. Puzzling." The harsh yellow lights from above hide Halton's eyes beneath two dark pits, and I can't tell where he's looking. But it feels like my very core.

"My grandfather has ordered more soldiers outside campus starting tomorrow. You were right in the middle of the incident, weren't you? What did that man steal?"

He's testing me.

The greenhouse seems to shrink, the glass walls pushing in, the ground threatening to open up and swallow me.

"The thief was a woman. She was shot with a taser for stealing a bottle of water," I manage to say.

Halton takes another step forward, and I maneuver the wicker basket between us. "I'm sure they're expecting us at the house," I say and turn to move down the row, preventing any more questions.

"My grandparents mean to make a match of us. For marriage."

The words hit me like a physical blow. *No. Never!* I think to myself, or did I scream the words out loud?

I keep my back turned and my feet moving, entirely focused on getting to the front exit. Suddenly he's behind me, reaching for my arm.

"My grandfather wants—"

I strike down his approaching hand with a sharp slap.

"I don't care what your grandfather wants!" I cry.

Red splotches appear on Halton's cheeks, this time from anger. I place my hand over my mouth, blocking any more words from slipping out. He stares at me, wide eyed, and I'm sure I look the same. A deer in headlights just before impact.

"Like I said, my grandmother would rather have these instead." With an arrogant leer, he stoops to roughly tear an entire handful of black-eyed Susans from their roots. Something in me snaps, and I break into a run and tackle him from behind.

Our bodies slam into each other in what feels like slow motion. We drop hard to the concrete. Our weight lands heavily on Halton's arm, and his hold loosens on my mother's flowers. They scatter crudely across the pavement, and with tunnel vision I crawl to them, but Halton's strong grip on my dress stops me. He drags me closer and wraps his fingers around my wrist like a noose, pulling tighter the more I fight.

"Let go of me!" I scream. I struggle madly to pull away, but Halton keeps his grasp right where my microchip should be.

The taser gun aimed at my lower neck shocks me back into reality. Halton releases his hold on me, and I lift my hands in the air, thinking this is the end.

"Stand down, Agent," says Halton, eerily calm, the way his grandfather speaks when he's calculating. Agent Hayes lowers his weapon, but his eyes show that he wants to shoot. He's just waiting for a reason.

Halton stands, taking his time to straighten his clothes. He smooths back his greasy hair and brushes the dirt from his jacket. He bends down so there are only a few inches of air between us. "You shouldn't have done that," he whispers.

He seizes a handful of flowers from the ground and marches with his bounty down the row, Agent Hayes following in his wake.

I sit paralyzed, a small figure in the large, empty garden. He can't know.

He can't.

AVA

Father stands in front of us like a drill sergeant about to scold his troops. His piercing gaze scans Mira before it falls on me, dripping with disappointment.

Mira and I usually have time alone together before our nightly family meetings, but Father followed Mira into the basement directly after dinner. He didn't want to give us a chance to formulate a defense justifying our switch.

I can't hear a thing through the soundproof walls, but I saw Roth strong-arm Gwen and the surprise photo shoot over the surveillance video. Not good at all. Father must be livid.

I need just one glance from Mira to reassure me she managed it all fine, but she won't give it to me.

"Did you honestly think you could trick your own father?" he finally says.

"We've done it before," I say in defense. And we have.

Last year, I found an illegal bottle of Japanese Nikka whisky buried in the tomato garden I was tending in the greenhouse. Hidden in one of the cameras' blind zones, I made certain no one saw me take it. I couldn't resist surprising Mira with such a rare delicacy—the government can't stop *all* contraband from being sold on the black market. Mira ended up drinking so much celebratory whisky the night we found out our placement level results at Strake, she spent the entire next morning vomiting. I went to school that day in Mira's place; Father still doesn't know it was me.

"Your life is not a game, Ava! How could you take such a childish risk on a night like this?"

I hate when he refers to us like we are still children. And our life *is* one endless game.

"Do you hold no fear for Governor Roth or his agents? Do I need to remind you what he is capable of?"

No, it's perfectly clear to me what Roth is capable of: anything. Defiant, I keep my head held high, but I can see Mira's eyes shift to the floor. Why is she backing down?

"Nothing happened," I say, because she doesn't.

He gives me an incredulous look. "Routine has gotten us this far, and it is the only reason you two have survived these eighteen years. You are growing too reckless. The odds are already against us without the both of you messing up our schedule. The moment we get comfortable is when everything we've worked so hard to keep will be taken from us. Have you completely forgotten what is at risk—"

"Have *you*?" Mira cuts Father off. "You dared to speak out against Governor Roth during dinner. Threatening him with our society's collapse . . . threatening him with riots! Why would *you* go against the rules *you* made and take such a risk?"

I look from Father to Mira, taken aback not only by what my sister's saying, but also by her anger. What the hell happened at dinner?

Father rubs a hand hard over his face and opens his mouth for a rebuttal, but Mira can't keep her words from pouring out.

"And how long have you known Roth's intention to marry us to Halton? How does that fit into the plan?"

My mouth drops open.

"What?" I turn to Father, expecting him to deny Mira's revelation straightaway.

"I was just made aware of his intention to do so tonight. I will deal with it when the time comes," he says. "As I will deal with the Anniversary Gala. Your face will not be on a skyrise."

It's my turn for words. The truth is boiling hot inside of me like lava primed to explode. Feelings I've never admitted out loud, much less expressed to my father.

"*You* will deal with it when the time comes. We must always stick to the plan that *you* made for us. But it's *our* life, Father, and this is all happening right now, not in some far-off future. We aren't just pieces of some mapped-out strategy."

I take a step toward him. "We can't go on forever like this. We aren't children anymore—something has to change. We agreed to continue at Strake for our medical degree, but we have to be allowed our own apartment in the city next semester."

"Absolutely not," Father says. "We cannot afford to make careless decisions. The safest place for you both is here with me."

"We can't spend our entire life living in our father's basement!" Mira shouts.

"That's enough!" Father yells back, raising a trembling hand for silence.

Mira and I flinch. I've never seen Father lose his carefully controlled temper so completely. We stand side by side, shaken and quiet, eyes fixed to the ground. We pushed too far. I quickly glance up and notice lines on my father's face that weren't there before.

"It's getting late," he says in a gentler tone. He takes a long, deep breath. "You have exactly one hour to finish debriefing each other on your day." He addresses Mira. "Afterward, you are to go straight upstairs to Ava's room for the night. I will be checking."

Later, when Father leaves the basement, he will sit motionless on the living room couch for hours. A hologram of our smiling mother, so realistic and detailed, will float in front of him. He likes the video of her simply walking around our house the best. She'll wander through the kitchen, giving a tour of our newly built home, before Mira and I were born. She'll laugh and hold out her hand, eyes playfully saying to him, "I love you."

But right now Father reaches out to wrap his arms around Mira, then gathers me into the embrace against his chest. He hugs us tight, his palms resting protectively on the tops of our fiery heads.

"We were lucky tonight," he says.

Mira's face now forced next to mine, I see something I don't understand in her eyes. More happened than what she's revealed to father, but I can't read what it is.

Our father glances at his watch and pulls away, smoothing out the wrinkles our bodies created on his stately uniform. He turns, lifts his heavy shoulders, and walks, formal and composed, from the basement.

He must miss Mother—with her same blazing-red hair and stubborn green eyes—every time he looks at us.

Mira sits on the piano bench absently playing the melody of the song from choir. I sit close beside her, a frown creasing my brows. "Did you learn a new verse today?" she asks me.

The question is a diversionary tactic. She feels closed off and distant in a way that makes me feel angry and hollow in the pit of my stomach. Secrets never separate us.

I reach over and place my hand on hers, stopping the music. "Tell me what else happened at dinner." My skin immediately tingles with the curious vibrating sensation, like a field of energy, that sometimes happens when we touch. In these random, fleeting moments, I can physically feel the inexplicable bond between us.

Mira's eyes lock onto her right wrist. I've seen her do this several times recently, and I'm about to ask if her imitation chip is bothering her when she admits all at once, "I shoved Halton in the garden. He stole Mother's flowers, and I shoved him to the ground."

I close my eyes, taking in her surprising confession with a sort of numb disbelief. "You laid hands on the governor's grandson?"

Mira looks up at me for the first time. "I know it's serious. Halton's agent aimed his taser at me, Ava."

I rise from the piano bench, and we both stare at the security screen projecting a picture of our front lawn. Astonishingly, all is well.

Why wouldn't the agent report an assault on such a valuable charge? Recently people have been taken away for much less. Last month, a neighbor was arrested for filming a State Guard beating a man on a public street. No one has seen him since.

"Halton stopped his agent from arresting me," Mira says.

I turn away from the screen to look at her. "Why?"

She lifts her shoulders in a half shrug. "It might be because of the governor's plan to marry him to us. To *you*."

"An arranged marriage," I say. "There's no way in hell we are agreeing to such a disgusting political move."

I pace the room restlessly, the heated feelings from earlier bubbling back up to the surface. Right now I want to run uncontrolled and wild like a big cat in the Serengeti of the past. In the history videos I watch with Mira, I've seen the creatures roam free through the vast grasslands. I have no sense of what that sort of freedom must feel like. I've lived in a congested urban sprawl my entire life. I've never even stepped foot on open land. I wish I could find some for us, and that I could keep Mira there, safe.

Father's words burn past my throat and erupt off my tongue: "Keep quiet. Keep hidden. Don't stand out; blend in."

I circle the room, round and around our cage. "We must *always* follow the rules. But not Father. He can do whatever he wants."

"And say whatever he wants. Even to the governor," Mira interjects.

Governor Roth and our father have always had a give-and-take relationship, because they need each other. But the leash the governor has around Father's neck is short, and he can only go so far without being pulled back. From the look in Mira's eyes, I'm afraid tonight Father may have cut the cord entirely.

A memory flashes unbidden into my mind of my father and me strolling through the gardens at the Governor's Mansion. In the middle of Father's reelection ceremony, a beaming Governor Roth led an impromptu tour of his enormous renovated grounds. Mira could not attend the lavish high-security event, even though it was her day up. Too many Guards and chances for a microchip scan.

I imagine no one in the world has more luxurious personal gardens than Roth. He modeled them after Versailles in the classical French style: imposing order over nature. The precise symmetry and regality of his gardens scream wealth and power, especially when most things outside the mansion grow yellow or barren. I still remember the tight line of Father's mouth that barely held in his disdain for such an arrogant display of riches, but he *did* hold it in. Afterward, he swore a solemn oath to protect and uplift Texas and its people, the governor adding the sixth Texas Public Health Service badge to Father's uniform cordially, even affectionately.

The two men ended the ceremony with respectful salutes. Yet something in the way Roth's stare lingered before he firmly turned on his heel was a silent threat: *Remember who is really giving you this honor—the man with enough power to build an Eden in the middle of a wasteland.* Why would Father risk breaking such a carefully constructed relationship?

I emerge from my musing to find Mira staring at the monitors. Still sensing nervousness, I eye her critically. "What are you thinking about, Mira?"

"Should we tell Father I pushed Halton?"

"Of course not. We are on a tight enough leash as it is," I say without hesitation.

We don't have much time left before she has to go upstairs and prepare for her day at school tomorrow, but a nagging feeling tells me I should ask again, "Did anything else happen in the greenhouse that I need to know?"

Mira looks straight into my eyes. "No."

I give a confident nod. "Stop worrying about Halton. If he were going to tell his grandfather, he would have done so straight off. And he'd never admit weakness to the governor."

I rejoin her at the piano, turning my back on the video surveillance. "But we should stay away from him."

"What about the Gala?" Mira asks.

"Either Father will find a way to get us out of it, or I will."

The bench emits a soft creak as I move closer to my sister, a wicked smile tugging at the corners of my lips. "Did you at least get a punch in?"

She manages a half smile but hides it by saying, "Teach me the new verse."

"Right. The entire song must be memorized. Then we'll go over our chemistry and Spanish before I finish detailing the day in our journal."

I begin the first verse on the piano and both our faces gradually settle into concentration. Our unified voices blend together perfectly, singing to celebrate One Child, One Nation.

MIRA

My mind hangs in the space between consciousness and sleep. I toss fitfully in the large queen bed in Ava's room, the covers entangling me like chains. Exhausted, I kick them off, giving up any hope of rest. I open my eyes and find the room as dark as my mind.

It did not happen. There's no way he knows. Before I left the greenhouse, I repeated these words like a mantra. After the two-hundred-and-forty-fifth time, the words rolled easily off my tongue, and I reentered the dining room fully believing it. It was all just a miscommunication, a fabricated memory born from my own paranoia.

It did not happen. There's no way he knows, I repeat to myself again now.

A layer of sweat coats my body, gluing the thin bottom sheet to my skin. I reach out for the nightstand and curl my fingers around a tall glass of water. I drip the water, still cold from the AC, onto my neck and wrists before taking long sips to soothe my raw throat. Light from the streetlamps—or maybe the moon—sneaks through the blinds, creating strange shapes on the ceiling. I concentrate on a pattern of mismatched polygons slanted just above the door and settle back onto the platform bed.

His fingers were on my wrist for just a second in time. A single moment.

I close my eyes and focus on breathing from my abdomen—my gut, which I keep alternately ignoring and fighting. I don't know how much time goes by like this, but when I open my eyes again, still restless and on edge, the light has transformed and reshaped itself along the wall.

I sit up and throw my damp hair behind my ears, then into a messy bun. Dragging my hands over my face, I rest my forehead on my knees. Again I reach for the glass of water, and as I lift my heavy head, I see my reflection in the floor-length mirror across the room.

Alone, in the small hours of the morning, the truth stares me straight in the face.

He knows. I don't know how, but he knows. It's as clear as the empty glass in my hand.

I look at the clock. 1:26 a.m.

Filled with an overpowering urgency to tell Ava everything, to confess, I slide out of bed and walk to the door. I turn the handle but find it unwilling to budge. Father locked me in.

I quiet my rising temper and grab my tablet from the dresser. I enter a passcode and attempt the handle a second time, but the door remains firmly secured. *Shit.* Pressing my head against the door in exasperation, I will a solution. *Think.*

For every locked door, there is a window.

Rallying, I stride quickly to the line of casement windows, unlock one, and push the glass open. I pop my head out and find no obvious watchers. The sleepy streets are dark and empty.

Barefoot, I step onto the first-floor roof and carefully approach the ledge. A five-yard drop. Doable if I roll on my landing. I turn, then push my feet off with a small grunt and hang from the roof by my fingertips.

Suddenly, bright lights illuminate the far end of our street.

My body reacts instantly, and I fall to the ground like a rock. I swallow back a cry, taking in the pain of landing through clenched teeth.

The headlights from the approaching cars grow closer, and I hurl myself forward, limping and stumbling, to hide behind our neighbor's fence. I reach it just as a black military SUV stops yards in front of me, glaring spotlights from its roof aimed directly on our house.

Oh my God.

Three Texas State Guards exit the first vehicle, head to toe in riot uniforms. With the sight of their raised guns, I become sickeningly aware of exactly what those fingers on my wrist, just a second in time, have done.

Hands trembling, I type a short passcode into my tablet to set off a warning and turn to sprint for the shadows.

Father. Ava. I'm sorry.

AVA

I wake violently from a deep hum vibrating the basement. It's the emergency alarm that signals Mira to hide below ground.

I rush up the concrete steps to the security screens in the corner and see soldiers flooding the exterior of the house, spotlights engulfing the lawn from large military vehicles. *"Oh my God,"* I exclaim, breathless.

The vibrating cuts off all at once, and I hear the wall recede from the passageway. I charge through the narrow tunnel, up the stairs, and stop cold. It's not Mira who faces me—it's our father.

Terrified, I look for my sister. "Where is she?"

He pulls me into the living room, the wall sealing behind us. Probing spotlights continue to pierce through the windows.

"What is happening?" I ask.

A loud pounding erupts from the front door. "This is the Texas State Guard!" The impatient fist strikes over and over. "Open the door immediately, or we will break it down!"

Father turns to me and quickly says, "Don't do anything unless I tell you to."

We've practiced this moment in trial drills, yet it's somehow altogether different when it's actually happening in real life. My blood feels like it has been set on fire, leaving my limbs with a light, useless sensation.

Father moves to unlock the door, shielding me behind him. I'm grateful—I need a moment to gather myself before the invasion. Oh God, are they here to arrest him?

Calm down. Just breathe.

The door opens with a bang, and a captain flanked by two State Guards burst into the house. They are tall and terrifying in their dark riot gear, the Texas seal reflecting bright on their chests from the spotlights.

"Dr. Darren Goodwin and Ava Goodwin, you have been accused of criminal activity on this property," the captain formally recites. "Move aside for our inspection."

Father all but shakes in his fury. "Who authorized this military sweep? I demand to see the warrant."

My heart stops beating entirely when I hear Governor Roth's voice. "I don't require a warrant."

The soldiers in the doorway part, allowing the governor to stand face-to-face with my father. Fear flashes in his eyes, but dies in an instant.

"Hold out your wrists," Roth orders.

"Governor, as a respected member of your staff, I ask why a military sweep has been authorized on my home?"

A foreboding pause lingers after the question. The governor wants us to crack under his heavy silence, which presses down on our nerves and gives us time to imagine all the terrible reasons he is here right now.

He turns away from my father.

"I'm not here to give explanations."

He nods, and the captain takes an aggressive step toward me. "Hold out your wrist," he commands.

I look apprehensively to Father. Does he want me to comply? This is an odd request, usually only done to identify an unknown person.

"Do not look to your father, girl. Look at me," the governor snarls, almost foaming at the mouth.

Mira lied. Something else happened in the greenhouse. Roth only has eyes for me.

I step out from behind my father and expose my wrist to the waiting captain. Whatever they are looking for, they won't find it in my microchip.

The captain scans my chip, and a sharp *ping* emits from his small device. The governor swiftly examines the information that appears on the screen next to my photo: "Name: Ava Goodwin. Age: 18. Occupation: Student, Strake University. Ration Credits: 5,000. Blood Type: AB+."

Impatient, he turns away from the device, not bothering to read the rest. With terrorizing swiftness, he bears down on me, blocking me from my father. His soldiers stand behind him, poised and ready. "Is there anyone else in this house?" he demands.

Father makes a move toward me, but the soldiers hold him back. "Governor—"

"It's just the two of us," I answer rapidly, setting my features into the very picture of innocent confusion. "I don't understand. Who else would be here, sir?"

The governor studies me for a long moment, the hallway settling into another suffocating silence.

I stand there paralyzed, unable to breathe.

"Search the house."

The two soldiers plow through my father, forcing themselves into the living room. All we can do is stand and watch as one soldier begins to shove the furniture over while the other barrels up the stairs to our room. I lift my head to the ceiling, following the deafening trail of footsteps from above.

Are you still up there, Mira?

The remaining soldier lifts up a large rug and sweeps a ground-penetrating radar around the living room floor. The governor looks over the Guard's shoulder and scowls when the radar detects nothing but solid ground.

"The kitchen," the governor orders the soldier.

The captain pushes past me through the entranceway to place a small contraption on the front door. A beam of light scans the handle and frame, checking for fingerprints. Our names, Ava Goodwin and Darren Goodwin, hover above the detected prints in little spheres.

"Scan every surface," the governor orders as he advances to our computer. He inserts a thin strip into the hard drive, and thousands of our private files are copied in an instant.

The captain covers our house with his contraption's penetrating white light. Tables, windows, stairs, cabinets, floorboards, walls, silverware—every object produces spheres that float around us like someone just wished on a dandelion. Ava Goodwin, Darren Goodwin, Governor Howard Roth, Victoria Roth, Halton Roth, Gwen Meyer.

But not a single petal reveals an unregistered print.

I move closer to my father when a frustrated Governor Roth approaches the space dangerously close to the hidden basement entrance. He presses his ear against the wall, and my nerves suddenly start to fracture.

Using his balled fist as a hammer, he strikes the wall, searching for hollow spaces. Panic floods my mind at the thought of discovery. My legs scream to flee, but I am also consumed with the deranged desire to attack the governor and protect my family. I do neither of these things, however. I simply stand silent next to Father, disciplined by my training.

My hand finds Father's. *Do something,* my fingers beg.

"Governor, if you tell me what you are looking for, I can lead you to it without having my house further destroyed," Father says, advancing toward him.

Distracted, the governor turns around, his hand dropping to his side before he can strike twice. His gaze, filled with unchecked disdain, lands on Father. "If you try to impede this investigation again,

I will have my soldiers escort you to the military car in handcuffs, Dr. Goodwin."

Darren. The governor always honors my father by addressing him by his given name. The leash has been unquestionably cut.

The captain approaches the governor and speaks quietly into his ear. Roth nods, revealing nothing. He scans the house a final time, his cold eyes targeting me.

With the awkward sound of stretched leather, Governor Roth straightens to his full height and walks stiffly to my father. He steps over the broken glass frame that contained the hologram of my mother.

"My men will clean up the mess," the governor says with no hint of apology.

"That will not be necessary, Governor," Father says. He opens the front door and stands there firmly, his body language demanding an immediate exit.

"Report to my office in the morning, Dr. Goodwin," the governor says before slamming the door shut.

I finally exhale and breathe.

Spotlights gone, we are left in darkness.

"Room, lights on—" Father presses his hand over my mouth before I can finish the command.

"The lights must stay off," he whispers hot in my ear. He grabs his tablet and sends out a signal that spreads across the room like a blue wave. I watch unnerved as it invades every cavity and corner, searching.

"You think they bugged the house?" A heavy ball of terror forms in my stomach.

Father's title as the head of the Texas Family Planning Division requires him to supervise and administer all public healthcare, but his most difficult and important task is to uphold the country's one child law. He is responsible for ensuring no couple has illegal multiple children in the State of Texas. If it were revealed that the Division Director himself, a member of the inner circle, has been hiding an illegal twin daughter for almost two decades, Governor Roth would be humiliated. His entire political career would be threatened.

There's a secret place—somewhere in the darkest part of me—that has been waiting for this moment all my life. The moment Mira and I are caught and separated, taken away screaming to our reckoning.

I glance anxiously out the living room window and see the captain hand-launch a surveillance drone before getting into the driver's seat of the governor's black luxury car and pulling away, two military vehicles following behind. A few brave neighbors observe the scene from their lawns, and I wonder fleetingly if they stand there out of concern or for the show.

The tablet gives a high-pitched *ping.* All clear.

Intent, Father moves up the staircase, and I instantly follow him like he's my lifeline. Again he sends out the wave of light in the hall. *Ping.* All clear.

I linger in the doorway and take in our ransacked bedroom. This space is just for show, merely a piece in the game. Our true selves do not adorn these four walls—that is reserved for the basement we share. But it doesn't prevent the heat that suddenly surfaces when I see our raided room.

The covers are a twisted mess on the floor, the mattress flipped over and cut. The dresser is hurled onto its side, the drawers tossed open, piles of our panties thrown across the ground. A quiet rage burns through me. Rage that the soldier touched our personal things without my permission. Rage at how vulnerable it makes me feel. How powerless.

"Father, where is she?" I ask again.

"Pack the essentials. We must be ready by the time she comes back," he answers.

I hug my trembling body, on the verge of outright panic. It's all happening too fast. "But they left. We can stay, Father! They found nothing . . . There's no proof!"

He seizes me by the shoulders, forcing me to focus on his face. "Ava, listen. My division hasn't found a case of hidden multiples in sixty years. The very idea of eighteen-year-old twins is inconceivable. But someone reported us. Someone knows."

I shake my head, disbelieving.

"The governor will return, and he will be relentless in his attempts to find the truth. Do you understand what I am saying?"

"We will be more careful. I'll finish out the semester, and Mira will just stay hidden," I insist.

"They won't stop until they discover our secret, Ava. We don't know who tipped them off, how many eyes could be watching us. And after failing tonight, the governor will certainly add many more to that number. We have to leave."

Father grabs a knife from his pocket and places it into my hands. "Wait for me downstairs. I'll need to cut out your microchip. They'll be tracking you now."

The National Security Agency would not usually waste resources monitoring the college-age daughter of a prominent government official. There are millions of high-risk targets more pressing than a seemingly average young girl, so unless you give them a reason to flag you, they will not track you. Father could access the system to know for sure if I've been flagged, but his refusal to listen to my pleas tells me we are beyond that now.

The weight of the heavy blade rests in my open palm and it's like he's just handed me the key to a forbidden room. I know I will open the door to a dark, cavernous space, and I will have to walk through it blindly. I lock eyes with my father.

I must have courage. "No. I'll do it myself."

With a stiff nod, he moves out the door to continue his search. Another *ping* rings through the air. All clear.

But nothing seems clear at all.

MIRA

I crouch, patient and still, poised to run.

Pressed against a neighbor's fence, I scan the streets once more. I've verified numerous times that no Guards or agents remain in the area. All spectators have gone inside; all lights are out. Yet I remain rooted to my hiding place.

I spare a quick glance at my tablet. 2:50 a.m. *You can't hide from our fate. Move.* I take one step and then another, choosing my path carefully but swiftly behind the row of quiet houses, using the darkness as my cloak.

My right ankle throbs with each slap of my naked feet against the hard concrete, but I keep moving. Our two-story home comes into view, and the pain of what waits for me inside that dark and silent house outweighs any physical pain. *Did the Guard take them?*

Oh God.

I hear the constant hum of a small surveillance drone overhead, patrolling the neighborhood from the sky. As it moves to circle our house once more, I hug the line of shadows that edge the fence and race toward the back of the greenhouse.

I smuggle myself into the community garden positioned just outside the glass complex, sticking to the path I know is blind to the cameras—two rows down, six up—and stop in the very back corner.

I collapse to my knees in front of the raised bed of newly ripened egg-plants and dig my hands into the soil, my fingers yanking the lobed leaves of the fruit in my haste.

The letter *X*, so microscopic one would have to know it's there to see it, appears beneath the mulch and manure. I place my index finger over the symbol and listen for the subtle click of the latch unlocking. The *X* radiates a blue light under my fingerprint, and a small shoulder-width door appears in the dirt.

Lifting the handle, I slip into the opening and shut the hatch softly above me. I slide down the ladder, hobble through the emergency tunnel, enter our basement, and climb the stairs to the empty wall.

With two knocks I push into the passageway. *Please let them be on the other side.* Two more knocks and I stagger across the living room, and find myself in the kitchen.

My body freezes when I see her.

Ava sits alone at the dinner table under the dim glow of a small work light, two stuffed rucksacks on the bench beside her. She must not have heard me enter, because she doesn't look up.

She makes a clean incision in her inner right wrist. Gasping in pain, she glides the tip of a blade into the open cut, and with a steady hand and a brutal flick, the microchip lands casually beside her, slick with red. We both stare transfixed at the metal capsule, unmoving.

"Are we running?" I say.

Ava jumps at the sight of me, her eyes somber and afraid. The cold, numb wall of strength I built up comes melting down, pouring out through burning tears. *Forgive me.*

She presses a bandage to her wound and moves to embrace me, hard. "Where were you?" she whispers. I don't answer. She doesn't care where I was. Just that I'm here now.

I feel Father before I see him. I keep my chin buried in Ava's shoulder and lift my swollen eyes to find him watching us from the staircase.

"We have to hurry," he says, steady and calm. His expression holds no anger. No blame.

"It was Halton," I confess. Tears fall freely down my cheeks, washing me clean. "He grabbed my wrist in the greenhouse and somehow knew my chip is an imitation."

Ava lets go of me and stands back. "Why didn't you tell me?"

I try to move toward her, to make her understand, but the agony of my twisted ankle prevents me. Deep purple and blue bruising has already spread across my inflamed foot. A mark of my penitence.

"Girls, we don't have time for this," Father says. He turns off the work lamp and approaches the back window, trusting the smart glass to conceal him. His eyes penetrate the black of the outside world, searching for leftover patrols.

Ava and I have never once been above ground together. Being in the kitchen with her now feels vulnerable and unbalanced. I need her to look at me, to tell me it's okay, but I'm too afraid to speak. *Ava!* I shout in my head. But she holds her focus on the glass wall facing the empty street.

Satisfied we are alone, Father takes my tablet and punches in several codes to destroy all our data. "You can't bring any devices in case you're monitored." He sets my tablet on the counter beside his own, which displays a running timer. *He's going to detonate the basement.*

"We leave in five minutes," he says, climbing the steps to the second floor.

Shoes. I need to put on shoes. I grasp for practicality, for something I can control. I walk heavily to the rucksacks and see Ava has already placed a pair of black boots on the chair for me. Pulling them on gingerly, I keep the laces of my right boot loose to fit my swelling ankle. When I look up I find Ava examining me, and our eyes meet like they always do, communicating a myriad of thoughts and emotions with just one glance.

Father glides down the staircase and in two long strides stands before us, a plastic box in his hands. His manner now earnest, he holds it out to Ava and opens his mouth to explain, but the words die in his throat.

The pulsating sound of the house alarm cuts through the room, sinking my heart and paralyzing my brain. Father suddenly surges forward, arms out, trying to block Ava and me just as a camera flash goes off, freezing the moment in time.

It takes several maddening seconds to blink out the spots in my vision, and when my eyes finally adjust, I see a single figure in the hallway. The slinking silhouette of Halton Roth.

He stands hypnotized, eyes raking over the two of us cowering behind our father's arms.

"Twins," he says, breathless. "I knew it."

Father explodes and charges for Halton, who lets out a loud squeal and turns to run. But Father catches him easily and with no hesitation punches him hard along the jawline. He drops to the ground like dead weight.

"Oh my God, oh my God," I repeat, my fear all-consuming. My eyes scan the room for evidence of broken glass, but I find nothing. *Did he crack our security codes?*

"The picture," Ava says, rushing past Halton's unconscious body to his fallen tablet. "Did he send it?"

Father turns off the alarm and grabs the tablet. He swipes Halton's finger across the screen to activate the sensor. I want to turn away, to not know the answer, but I force myself to look. To face our fate.

The picture pops up, and both Ava's face and my face stare back at us. Dumbstruck, terrified. Identical. "Shared" flashes bright in the bottom corner.

Father slams the tablet to the ground, shattering it into pieces. Before I can say anything, he leads us to the kitchen. "Listen to me. You have to run." He pushes the plastic box into Ava's protesting arms. "Take this and open it when you're safe outside the city."

I shake my head, uncomprehending, and my eyes dart to Father's right wrist. The skin is smooth and untouched, his microchip still intact. Ava sees it too.

"You're not coming with us," Ava voices my thoughts out loud. She says it as a statement, resigned to its inevitability.

"Why?" I say, taking a desperate step toward him.

"If the governor has me, there's a chance they won't come after you. I can convince them you two are not a threat, but you will prove them wrong."

"No!" I shout. "We're not leaving without you!"

"Where do we go?" Ava says evenly, reaching for her rucksack.

"Get out of Dallas before sunrise," Father says, ignoring the muffled groan from Halton on the floor. "Stick to the crowds and take the rail to Amarillo before they can find you on the surveillance system. There are more instructions in the box." He shoves it safely into the bottom of Ava's bag before placing the heavy rucksacks on each of our shoulders.

I hear the faint scream of sirens in the distance.

"You have to move," he says. "If you don't go now, this will have all been for nothing. Survive. Survive for me and your mother." Forcing a light smile, he pulls both of us closer. He touches our cheeks with great care, and I know he is memorizing our faces.

"You were born tied together forever," he says, folding my hand into Ava's. "Never leave each other."

I cling to my father like a child. Ava lets out a soft cry and wraps her arms around him, her hand still linked to mine. "I love you," he whispers to us. His voice cracks, and the pain is too much to bear. His words are so final, and with overwhelming clarity I understand this is our last good-bye.

The sirens grow louder, and Father gently lets go of us. I see tears in his eyes. I see strength.

"Now run."

PART II
THE TRUTH

AVA

Sirens rip through the air, overpowering all my senses. The alarm penetrates my ears and my eyes, its piercing touch invading my skin and overtaking my ability to smell anything but fear. I can taste the hot sound inside my mouth, and it tastes like blood and danger.

Mira and I escape through the underground passage in the garden, Father's voice screaming inside my head, fighting through the sirens: *Take the rail to Amarillo before they can find you on the surveillance system.*

An explosion erupts from our house, the blast shaking the ground. The basement. It's been destroyed.

I grab Mira's hand, and we sprint toward a winding path that leads through the neighborhood, avoiding the streets.

"The umbrellas," I say as we charge over a fence and through a backyard covered in tiny stone pebbles. Mira finds the two black umbrellas in my rucksack, tosses one to me, and we quickly throw them up above our heads to shield our faces.

The wailing cries grow faint in the background as we continue to flee away from our home, away from our father.

Roth is arresting him right now.

I push this thought to the back of my mind and focus on the flashing lights of the metropolis ahead. Breathing heavily, Mira falls behind.

I notice that she's running with a slight limp, and I know she must be hurting, but there's no time for sympathy.

"We have to keep moving," I say and press forward, forcing her to keep pace.

The TXRAIL station that will take us to Amarillo is in the heart of Dallas. I immediately see Father's plan: the Guard won't anticipate our running toward downtown, into an area with so much surveillance. They will expect us to hole up and hide in the fringes of the city until we are rooted out.

But how do we get on the rail undetected? And why Amarillo?

My chest heaves painfully by the time we throw ourselves into an alleyway sandwiched between two large glass buildings. Mira shoots her eyes up the side of the skyscraper.

"I don't see any cameras," she whispers. Regardless, we both continue to hold our umbrella shields firmly over our heads, the paranoia of surveillance deep-seated and constant.

Digging through my rucksack, I pull out a small bag of makeup and several articles of scent-eliminating clothing to shield us from the Scent Hunter drones. I motion for Mira to stand in front of me and apply a thick black line along her lower and upper lids with a wax pencil. She drapes a knee-length hooded vest over her shoulders to cover her nightclothes, and I place a dark beanie over her head, pushing her bangs off her face by tucking them into the cap. I step back to observe the effect.

Hidden beneath the beanie and makeup, she is not recognizably "Ava." This makeshift disguise will have to do.

I search through the clothing pile once more and pick out a loose-fitting gray jacket for myself.

"The jacket will make my frame look bigger than yours," I say as Mira grabs a tube of lipstick from the bag. She applies the stain to my lips, her unsteady hand making me wonder if more than my mouth is ending up red.

I peer over my shoulder at the massive TXRAIL station across the street. Large white sheets that look like sails from a luxurious yacht cover the tracks, designed to give mercy from the sun. Despite the early hour the platform is completely congested with people hoping to beat the even bigger morning rush at sunrise. The glaring streetlights allow for no shadows, no places to hide. Father thinks it's safer for us to hide within the crowds, but right now I am not so sure.

"Are you sure we should risk it?" Mira whispers.

I turn back to find her staring at the station with intense apprehension, and I remember she has never been on a rail before. All public transportation requires a microchip scan, and without a real chip, Mira has never been permitted to travel. I myself have traveled using public transportation within the Dallas limits only to the market or to accompany Father on his campaign tours. We walk or bike everywhere else.

When I don't answer, she gives me a worried look, but I have no white lies to comfort her. It will be a risk to expose ourselves on the station platform. Sealing ourselves into the railcar will be an even bigger one.

Get out of the city before sunrise. Survive.

We must have confidence that our temporary camouflage will be enough to deflect unwanted attention. Trust that the early morning commuters will glance upon us with dull eyes, not knowing they just witnessed the first sighting of identical twins in generations.

All I know is we have to keep moving. I throw up the hood of my linen jacket, cloaking my face in shadow.

"Are you ready for this?"

Mira vigorously shakes her head no.

I take a deep breath and hear my Father's words with every frantic beat of my heart.

You will prove them wrong.

I press my forehead fiercely against my sister's. "Mira, we can do this."

Closing our eyes, we hold our breaths, and for a moment our thundering hearts are quiet.

We exhale, and our breathing syncs as one.

Mira and I crowd behind the metal railings that barricade us from the station platform, our umbrellas carefully angled to block our faces from the cameras that are installed in every corner. An alert Texas State Guard patrols through the impatient mass of people, and we drop our heads low.

"How are we supposed to get in without a microchip?" Mira whispers in a tone so soft only a twin could hear.

I don't have the answer. I keep searching around me, trying to find the key. But I find only closed-off gates that require a microchip scan, and my heart falls into my stomach.

All I want is to protect Mira, but I know I'm not in charge. If someone came for my sister, I have nothing to fight them off except hands that have no special training and a knife I've never once used as a weapon.

A blinking green light above the gates signals more people are allowed to enter the platform. The barrier lifts, creating a small pathway, and straightaway a small young man wearing a wide-brimmed hat reaches out and scans his right wrist to a device at the entrance of the gate. A flash of blue light. *Ping.*

The mob behind follows suit, and it's like we're a thousand grains of sand fighting our way through an hourglass. The light flashes yellow—time is running out, and our small window of opportunity is closing. The frenzied crowd pushes Mira and me forward, desperate to get through the gate and onto the next rail.

Amid the messy free-for-all, a ragged old vagabond artfully squeezes himself through the multitude of people, and with a stealth I didn't think possible, slips through the doors without scanning his chip and strolls onto the platform undetected.

Chaos. The master key.

I grab Mira's hand and press tight against a lady holding a red parasol. As the woman swipes her wrist, I lunge through the gates, dragging Mira beside me.

I am elated with triumph for a single moment before an elbow connects with my temple. Mira and I are roughly shoved into the center of the moving herd jostling to get closer to the edge of the platform. Inside the gates I feel even more like cattle trapped inside a stockyard.

An anxious energy spreads through the crowd. Some people stand on the balls of their feet, ready to pounce at the first sign of the rail's arrival. Students, businesspeople, and the homeless all mix together, almost everyone using a cover of some kind in an attempt to protect their identity. Mira and I blend easily into the crowd. *You were right, Father.*

A group of youth in front of us wears elaborate, high-collared jackets, their hoodies transforming them into their public avatars. I note a bright-pink bear and a dark medieval knight. The corporate woman next to me wears a beautiful silk scarf around her head like a Golden Age movie star. The poor use dirty rags and makeshift cardboard masks wrapped around their faces. Only a brave few stand proud and bare, open to the prying cameras.

A heavyset Guard stalks the edge of the platform, forcing people to make a wide path. "Umbrellas, sunglasses, hats—off!"

He rips a pair of reflective shades from a man's face and throws them at his feet. The man bends down to retrieve the glasses and falls to his knees when an aggressive woman jockeys forward to take his place in the prized front row.

With a dizzying suddenness the rail barrels onto the tracks, and in unison hundreds of people surge forward to the edge of the platform in a stampede that crushes the fallen man. The doors of the newly arrived railcar open, and a handful of passengers manage to fight their way out before the onslaught of commuters begin to bulldoze their way in. I tug Mira's hand hard, indicating that we must do the same.

A loud *beep* announces the rail's impending departure. Body upon body presses determinedly against us as we force our way up to the car's closing doors. A Guard attempts to push away additional passengers trying to enter the car, but we duck and he drives back a man gripping his adolescent son instead.

"The doors are closing. I'm going to push!" I hear someone yell behind me.

Strange hands shove me into the resisting mass of people already stuffed into the car. The doors attempt to close, but there are just too many people. Hands wrap around Mira, pulling her away from me through the doors.

In a blind panic I thrust hard on the chest of the woman next to me, sending her flying out of the car. I'm sorry the moment I see her swallowed up by the hungry mob, but Mira bursts through the sleek metal doors that finally shut with a soft thud behind her.

The railcar lurches forward, instantly gaining high speed. Mira loses her balance and slams into a woman in a flattering dress.

"My apologies," Mira says. The woman glares down suspiciously at Mira's beanie and dark clothing before she checks her pockets for anything stolen.

Mira and I shift away from the woman and see the sign above the door at the same time. A warning reads "No Open Umbrellas Inside Car" next to a flashy ad for Texas lab-grown beef.

I lock my eyes on the floor and shove my way toward a row of seats in the back. I have to lift my umbrella high above people's heads in order to slide the runner closed, eliciting angry scowls when I accidently scrape the tips of the canopy against their faces.

Clasping her own umbrella stiffly to her side, Mira throws her hood low over her eyes and pushes her way to stand near the back of the car.

I manage to find a small opening in the handrail attached to the ceiling. My knuckles turn white with my grip, all my tension manifesting itself in my closed fist. *We'll be in Amarillo soon. Just keep your head down.*

A knee brushes against my thigh.

"You can sit in my lap if you don't want to stand," a young man offers, admiring me unabashedly. I don't respond and turn away just as the railcar is enveloped in a breaking newscast from the Lone Star Network.

The ceiling, floor, and all four walls of the car project the towering image of Governor Roth standing behind a podium in the garden of the Governor's Mansion. He clears his throat and begins to speak in the low, distinct way that forces everything around him to fall silent. And causes every nerve down my spine to shudder.

"I am both saddened and angered to inform the American people of Dr. Darren Goodwin's arrest made early this morning at his home in Trinity Heights. The Director of the Texas Family Planning Division has been charged with treason against the State of Texas."

The man beside me lifts his hand to his mouth in astonishment, and two women shake their heads in open disapproval of my father.

I feel dizzy, a hot nauseous ball reeling inside my stomach, and it's hard to remain still, to not shout out that my father is innocent. *But he's not innocent. Hold it in. Keep your face blank.*

Suddenly my father surrounds me. Adorned in a prisoner's uniform, wrists bound in handcuffs. His image is paraded on every wall. I snap my head up, fighting to get a better view of the damning headline that flashes across his body: "Traitor Awaits Sentencing."

My God.

"Darren Goodwin was elected by you, the people, with the sworn promise to uplift and protect our great state," Roth continues with a politician's poise. "But he has callously betrayed those he was chosen to serve, and with his egregious acts of treason has sought to sabotage our progress and our future."

I close my eyes to blindfold myself in darkness, waiting for Roth's final blow announcing the existence of Dr. Goodwin's illegal twins. I harden myself against the reactions of an outraged public who will soon demand we answer for our great sin of threatening humanity's right to survive.

If Father is a traitor, then we are traitors too.

"Thanks to the efforts of my grandson, Halton, justice will be served." My eyes remain closed, and I imagine Halton's lips stretching into a proud smile as he stands beside his grandfather. *You bastard.*

A loud murmur ripples throughout the car. Reluctantly leaving my dark hideout, I slowly open my eyes and see holograms of myself pop up all across the railcar.

The word "Wanted" flashes red and bold across my school uniform.

"Ava Goodwin, daughter of Dr. Darren Goodwin, has been charged as an accessory to his crimes. The fugitive has fled the scene but is still believed to be at large in the city."

Alarmed, I scan the passengers around me. Outrage, disapproval, hostility—their sentiments are marked clearly on their faces.

Then it hits me. The governor didn't mention the one word that would set the people into a mob. Twins.

"Let it be known that any persons providing illegal aid to Ava Goodwin will be immediately arrested."

So this is how you're going to play it. Keep the truth tucked under the bullshit blanket of vagueness. Shift the attention to finding me so you can withhold the reason for my father's arrest.

"I speak now directly to Ava Goodwin."

I lock eyes with Roth, who glares straight into the news camera, every bit the formidable general he used to be.

He still only has eyes for me.

"Turn yourself in. You will be caught, and you will pay for your crimes."

I want to look at Mira so badly, to share this terrorizing moment with her.

"The severity of your own punishment depends upon your next move," the governor finishes, never once breaking his stare.

The newscast cuts to black, and my hand begins to shake. I quickly cover it, Roth's last three words echoing in my mind with a terrifying urgency.

What is our next move?

MIRA

The repetitive purr of the high-speed rail creates a soothing lull, making it difficult to fight sleep.

Only ten other passengers remain in our car. A few idly watch the happy sitcom now projected on the wall where Governor Roth's face dominated an hour before, but most stare at nothing, eyes glazed and vacant. I stare through the glass doors of the car in front of me, eyes moving, always watching.

Anticipation is the worst part. I know something's coming. Someone will recognize us, the cameras will register our faces despite the concealment of our hoodies, the railcar will slow before reaching its designated stop, a full military unit will swarm the tracks, and Ava and I will be captured.

I can smell my fear. I'm drenched in it. Hiding my entire life behind the guise of Ava is nothing like the terror of being hunted. We've been unmasked. We're a bull's-eye. And now I'm trapped in a steel box, and I find it hard to sit still.

Adrenaline burns through me and I want to run, but I know the rail is cutting through Texas, closer to where Father wants us to go, at three hundred miles per hour. I just need to stay seated, stay inconspicuous.

My eyes on fire, I allow myself a brief moment of rest. My lids hurt when I close them, but it only takes a few seconds before I feel the heavy pull of sleep.

Loud cackling erupts from a woman beside the sitcom projection, stinging my insides and jerking me alert.

Nerves shot, my gaze immediately lands on Ava. Five rows in front of me, she holds her arms with a slight stiffness as she slides her body forward to the end of her seat and gives a small nod toward the car behind me. I dare a glance over my shoulder and spot a single Texas State Guard scanning the aisles of the neighboring car.

There he is. I feel strangely better now that I can see him. My hunter. I hold my stare long enough to witness the soldier approach a teenage girl sleeping against the grimy window, unceremoniously grab her wrist, and scan her microchip.

I turn back to my sister. She rises, slowly, so as not to attract attention, and moves to the doors opposite the Guard. I rise and do the same.

Survival mode kicks in, fueling me, and I somehow know exactly what to do. I search the walls and floor as I follow a safe distance behind Ava to the adjacent car, sizing up everything as a possible weapon.

We make it through the walkway and halfway into the next car when Ava stops short, which can only mean she detects another Texas State Guard ahead. I examine the car, counting only five commuters, backs all turned, focusing on their various devices. Ava turns to me, and with that single look, we both drop to the floor.

She crawls between a row of benches, dives under the seats, and motions for me to join her. My hands slip on the tile beneath my sweaty palms, so I use my knees and feet to drive me forward, thankful my right ankle has gone numb. *I know I'll pay for this respite later.*

Clearing the aisle, I make it to Ava just before the doors open and a thick black pair of boots enters the car.

Seven brisk strides and the Guard bears down on the young woman seated four rows up to the right. With her blonde hair and tan skin, she looks nothing like us, but the Guard was no doubt ordered to scan any woman under the age of thirty. The young woman wisely puts up no fight, and I hear the sharp *ping* of his device meeting her microchip.

Cautiously Ava sneaks her head out from beneath the seat as the Guard examines the chip's information. Ava's eyes scour the car left and right, searching for the screen that shows the rail's progress, but she tucks herself back into our hiding space shaking her head, her face pale and slack. She doesn't know when the rail will stop.

The Guard presses forward down the aisle, his thundering steps syncing with the hammering beat of my pulse.

Ten more steps and it's over.

Ava grips a knife in her hand.

There's a knife in the front pocket of my bag, but I can't reach it crushed between the bench and floor . . . There's a soda bottle three feet from me—if I can grab it, I can throw the liquid in the Guard's eyes before he sees us, and Ava can use her knife on him . . . *Oh God* . . . I'll be able to take his taser and gun, then we can sprint down the line of cars, holding off any pursuing Guards until the doors finally open . . . My mind races through all the various scenarios in the span of two swift steps of the Guard's boots. *It won't work. Nothing will work.*

Ava grabs my hand, her lips mouthing, "We have to run."

Where? Run where? I ask with my eyes. In either direction we face a State Guard. Panic threatens to take over.

Six more steps.

Ava points at the approaching Guard, then points to herself. She will go first. "Charge him," she mouths.

Her eyes fearless, she gives my hand a tight squeeze before turning to face the soldier. I ready myself and move into position to follow, but just as Ava prepares to launch herself—to sacrifice herself—I pull her back. From nowhere, a man slides into view under the seats across the aisle, his mouth split open in a rotting smile.

Four more steps.

He crawls into the opening between the empty benches and pulls himself into a crouching stance. I see his haggard face clearly and identify him as the older vagrant who snuck onto the station platform in Dallas.

His sleeve pulled up, I spot the faded ink of a tattoo on his right wrist. I've never seen anyone marked with a tattoo before. The ink distinguishes you, makes you an easier find for the cameras. Something most citizens avoid.

He waves his index finger in a deranged greeting, then moves it to his lips in a *shh* signal.

Before Ava and I can do anything, the man pops out from his hiding place and shouts, "Present your wrist for authorization! You must be scanned or you will seize!" He twists his arms and legs in sickening convulsions and moves away from the soldier toward the doors of the adjacent car. The Guard rushes past us, taser gun aimed at the crazed man.

"Present your wrist immediately!" the Guard screams as he simultaneously fires off his taser.

The electric current hits the door just as it closes, and I hear the continued shrieking of the ragged man. "You will seize; you will seize!" The Guard barrels through the doors, shouting at his comrade to fire.

The rail mercifully slows to a stop, and we launch ourselves toward the exit doors just as the muffled sound of a second taser goes off. And then a third.

I close my eyes, imagining the volts finding their target, feeling the electric pain that stuns the resisting old man into submission. Why did he help us? Did he recognize Ava?

He'll be locked away for years.

Don't think. Move.

A handful of other passengers exit behind us, removing themselves from the scene. It takes all the discipline I have not to sprint, to match my speed to Ava's and blend in.

Finally we reach the end of the platform and slip into the shadows of the early morning dawn.

Ava opens her umbrella, turns her head, and looks back, but I'm afraid to look behind me. I keep my eyes straight ahead—to the dangers that wait for us next.

The land is shriveled and bleached, marked by miles of crude leftover fences. The air is dry, blowing up a constant wind that tugs the canopy of my umbrella, throwing dirt into my eyes and mouth.

The gleam of the tracks serves as our guide as we move farther northwest toward Amarillo. The lines have been quiet—no railcars have sped past since we fled. Still, we keep a safe distance, afraid to get too close.

We don't talk. If we speak our thoughts aloud, the more real they become. I don't want Ava to confirm that we have no idea what we're doing, that we're all alone, and that we should be scared. I survive from moment to moment. If I let my mind linger on how long this nightmare will last, it's unbearable. I will break. I focus only on my sister and finding a safe shelter where we can open Father's box.

To the east I discern mounds of debris and devastation stretching parallel to our path. I swing the strap of my bag off my left shoulder, ignoring the dramatic relief this gives my upper back, unzip it, and pull out a pair of binoculars. Through the lens I witness the flattened remains of an entire town.

Hundreds of leveled strip malls and homes litter the area like land-fill, their wooden carcasses twisted with furniture, streetlamps, automobiles, and waste. I remember hearing the news of a record three tornados hitting the Texas Panhandle one summer five years ago. All three counties were the victims of a Category F5.

I zoom in and spy several scavengers picking through the ruins. I track a lone woman who looks to be in her fifties, her gaunt body red and peeling from the sun. She tosses aside a tennis shoe that appears two sizes too big and holds up a piece of cloth torn from either an old window or shower curtain. She wraps her new find around her small frame as if she's creating a protective barrier between her and the threats surrounding us, continues her hunt for a few more paces, then stops. Her expert hand dives into a pile of junk and emerges triumphant with a can of green beans. No smile for her victory, the woman resumes her monotonous slog, and I soon lose her behind the rubble.

Is this my future?

Unlike Roth, most state governors show their dedication in aiding towns like this, asserting their unwavering compassion for the millions of displaced Americans driven from their homes every year by erratic weather and perpetual superstorms. But what can the government really do? This woman's entire life has been annihilated. Major Disaster Declarations have become the norm, pressuring the government to choose which cities are worth saving with our dwindling resources. Whether people make the choice to move to a big metropolis or take on a nomadic lifestyle drifting through the fringes, one thing is for certain: they are on their own.

I hang the binoculars around my neck and shoulder my rucksack once more. Her own binoculars still pressed against her face, Ava takes two conservative sips of water before offering me the bottle with her free hand. I suddenly realize how dehydrated I am. How hot the day already feels only twenty minutes after sunrise. My hair damp with sweat, I slide off my beanie, freeing my head from the hellish oven.

We still have half a day's walk ahead of us to Amarillo. We need to rest. To figure out our plan.

Ava turns to me, pink indentions outlining her brows and cheek-bones like oversized glasses from the pressure of her binoculars.

Not here, her look tells me. I take two small sips, hand over the half-empty bottle, and we continue our silent march onward.

My adrenaline has drained away. I'm left raw and defenseless to answer for the neglect of my twisted ankle, now stiff and inflamed, the pain worse with every footfall. But my sister pushes me on. As does my fear.

A mile farther, the thick mesquite shrubs give way to asphalt and concrete. We walk along an old unused path until an abandoned mega-store comes into view. From the state of the crumbling structure and overgrown parking lot, I determine this place was forsaken long before the town.

All is quiet, with no sign of activity, but Ava keeps pressing forward, likely reasoning a large warehouse is a good place for unseen drifters to hide.

She points instead to a football stadium a few hundred yards ahead, somehow left untouched by the winds. I limp behind her, and we move through the gates, ascend the bleachers, and scan the landscape with our binoculars from atop our metal mountain.

Once I assure myself we're not being followed, I search the perim-eter for a safe place to shelter. I recognize the run-down exterior of a former bookstore and shove aside my immediate impulse to run inside, to witness all the empty shelves, to take in all those lost words hanging forgotten in the vacant air.

I shift my gaze right, and a field of massive oil wells fills my lenses. Behind their still and broken bodies, I spot the shell of a small factory set on fire by the rising orange light of the sun. I lift my hand and point. Ava trains her binoculars in the direction of my finger, examines the building for a long moment, then nods.

I scan the horizon one last time. There's no one here to hurt us, but there's no one here to help either. It's just Ava. It's just me.

As I look out on the long and endless journey I see so clearly before me, I'm thankful I'm not alone.

AVA

Mira stands at my back, searching left while I search right. We walk cautiously forward between a maze of perfectly aligned steel tables that are sealed into the ground. Sunlight streams through busted windows inside the old factory building, but I still use my cylinder work light to sweep the forgotten structure. Nature has reclaimed her right to this space, its walls and floor now covered in layers of dirt and thick weeds.

I note the absence of chairs—anything useful that isn't bolted down has all been looted. I raise my light and spot an overturned vending machine farther ahead, empty food containers littered around its shattered glass.

As I tilt my head up to the vast ceiling, I hear the elaborate song of a bird. I haven't seen a real bird in years. Intrigued, I narrow my eyes, looking for any movement above, but I see nothing except dust hanging in the air. The thin melodic song ends abruptly, and I refocus my attention on scanning the room.

Confident we are alone, I signal to Mira we should separate. I make it fifty paces into the room before a flutter of bird wings above my head causes me to trip over a wool rug embedded in the earthen floor. I'm launched forward, but I catch my fall on a crib that's pushed against the wall. Unable to hold my full weight, the structure caves in and sends me crashing to the ground.

Landing on my hands and knees, I find myself surrounded by dozens of used baby bottles. I sit back on my heels and come face-to-face with a stencil graffiti of a pregnant woman painted over the ruined crib. The deep-purple and black lines of her naked body are outlined with deliberate torment and desperation—it's in the curves of her back and in the bulge of her swollen stomach. Moving closer I see the woman shelters two small red hearts inside her pregnant belly, the paint faded but the meaning clear.

I realize with a pang that this place, long ago, must have been the refuge of a woman with a multiple pregnancy. Did she give birth here? How long did they last before they were detected and captured by the Guard? An image of my mother flashes into my mind, and I block myself from this line of questioning. I stand, dust myself off, and gather the bottles into a neat pile underneath the portrait.

"All clear," I say, turning my back on the pregnant woman.

"All clear," Mira says, emerging between a pair of tall supply racks. I notice her sharp intake of breath as she limps toward me. "Find anything useful?" she asks.

I shake my head. "You need to rest your ankle."

Mira leans her body against the nearest wall and slides down with a slight groan. I argue with myself about whether or not I should make her take the opioid pain medication packed away in my bag. We may need the medicine farther down the road.

Mira folds her pant leg up to her knee, and it hurts me to see how swollen and bruised her ankle has become. "You need the opioid," I conclude, sliding my rucksack around my waist.

"No, I'm fine. I don't want to risk becoming drowsy." She pulls out compression tape from a medical kit in her bag and gingerly slips off her boot. I bend down to help wrap her foot and ankle in tight layers of tape.

"Get out Father's box. I'll finish the wrap," Mira says, securing the tape at the top of her ankle.

I dig for the box at the bottom of my bag and unfasten the seal to discover an expected array of survival kit items. I flick quickly through the supplies—medicine, a compass, scent-eliminating spray—but my hands stop their search when I see the paper map. Mesmerized, I place the box on the ground.

My fingers cradle the paper delicately, like I'm handling a relic that requires my greatest caution. There's something rare and beautiful about the intimacy of the handwritten key in the corner of the map. I run my hand across my father's small, cramped letters: "Safe houses . . . Danger areas . . . Distance in miles."

Mira moves in close beside me, and with a light finger—we both can't resist touching the paper—she traces a thick highlighted route that leads from Dallas to Denver.

I point out the little flags our father drew along the way that symbolize safe houses. People's names are written below. The first flagged stop is way up in Amarillo: "Arlo Chapman." The second stop, "Kipling," is in Dalhart, near the northwest border of Texas.

I use the key to measure the distance with my fingers. "The first safe house is fifteen miles away," I say.

Mira half listens to me, circling the end of the route with her fingertip. She underlines the name written in bold below the final safe house in Denver: "Rayla."

"Who the hell are these people?" she asks.

I shake my head and study the map. Logistics flood my mind. Father is leading us out of Texas, through the Panhandle of Oklahoma, and into Colorado. It will take us nearly two weeks to walk there. We don't have enough supplies. I note the shaded red patches around state lines that Father marked as danger areas, but how are we supposed to elude the Border Guard?

"Ava, a journal," Mira says, nudging me with her elbow. She holds a thin leather-bound notebook that I must have missed and attempts to scan her fingerprint to unlock its cover. It won't open.

An infinity symbol is etched on the spine of the journal. Two oblong circles forming one knot, tied together forever.

"It takes two fingerprints to open," I say. Mira's and mine.

My heart starts pounding. I place my forefinger next to my sister's on the lock, and it opens. Mira quickly flips through the pages. All blank. Frustrated, she tries again, this time finding two pages caught together. She peels them apart, revealing a short poem that she reads aloud, her voice slow and captivating.

Resist much, obey little;

Once unquestioning obedience, once fully enslaved;

Once fully enslaved, no nation, state, city, of this earth, ever afterward resumes its liberty.

—Walt Whitman

Lost in thought, I take in my father's last instructions. My eyes glaze over, and I stare at nothing for so long the wall across from me turns into Governor Roth's face. His mouth splits open into a mocking smile before I can blink away his inescapable ghost.

I turn back to the survival box: a bag of makeup, scissors, a pair of silver bottles. A rush of adrenaline courses through my body. I pick up a bottle and squirt a thick, dark liquid into my palm. Hair dye.

Resist much, obey little.

MIRA

Ava moves behind me and raises the pair of scissors to my hair without ceremony.

We flipped a coin I'd found in a shelving unit by the back door. We had to use our work light to determine that the penny, discolored from decades of corrosion, had landed on the tarnished face of Lincoln.

I chose tails.

Seated on the toilet, I keep my back turned to the mirror above the sink. I don't bother saying good-bye to the image that has represented me for the last eighteen years. That person was gone the moment a handful of black-eyed Susans scattered across the floor of the greenhouse.

I hear a sharp snip and see a long strand of my red hair fall to the ground beside Ava's boot. Her pace quick, her hands sure, she repeats her methodical process until I am stripped bare, two pounds lighter, left with nothing to hide behind but my own grit.

"The back is rough, but the cut does its job," Ava says. She stretches vinyl gloves over her fingers, scoops up a wad of dye, and smothers my scalp with the rotting stench of chemicals.

"We let it sit for fifteen minutes." She peels off the gloves and pulls down the hood of her jacket.

As I rise, careful not to drip any dye on my freshly changed clothes, I catch Ava glimpse her reflection through the haze of the dusty, cracked mirror. *It's hard for her to let go.*

She pops the knuckle of her thumb, trying to hide her anxiety from me, and turns to take her place on the porcelain seat. I watch her closely as she sits, her back straight, chin high, and allow myself a final look at my sister. At my old reflection.

There was a fight for who got to keep more length. Who got to keep a closer semblance of our normal selves and the last traces of our mother's image. Ava won the coin toss, but now she looks up at me with uneasy green eyes as I hold a flame of her red hair between the two blades and snip. The thick strand falls to the ground, joining my own massive pile that surrounds us like the blaze of a hungry fire.

"It's all just dead weight," I tell her.

Soft sunlight pours through the window, creating a bright spot on a steel table in the corner. I lie in its warm glow, my right foot propped up on the bulk of my rucksack, and watch the dust above float aimlessly.

Damn these contacts. I try to blink away the stabbing pain that rips across my corneas, but this only causes tears to flood my eyes and spill down my cheeks like a busted faucet. The combination unbearable, I rub out the sting with my fists until the burn dulls to a mild discomfort and the overflow of tears slows to a drip. I test several quick blinks and open my eyes. I find my hands soaked with black paint and realize I smeared my new makeup. *Dammit.*

I tilt my gaze at the collapsed vending machine that lies beside the table and stare at the pixie blonde glaring back at me through the glass. With the collar of my fresh linen shirt, I wipe the dark stains from my face, grab the eyeliner from my vest pocket, and reapply the black wax along my lids in thick, chunky lines. This simple action is transformative, accentuating the color of my new contacts. Gunmetal blue.

I shift my gaze back to the hollow, seemingly endless ceiling and try to listen for the bird I heard singing earlier. I hear only the faint click of a lighter opening, the muted pops of rising flames, and the quiet work of Ava tossing all evidence of our makeover into her hobo fire.

The public doesn't know Roth is hunting twins. They will be on the lookout for only one Ava Goodwin, but how much intelligence did the governor disclose to the Guard or his agents? What is his strategy behind keeping my existence a secret? He knows the announcement would set off a bomb, and the shock wave would be felt all across the country. He knows he could stand behind a million screens and point to me as the terrorist who triggered the detonator. So why not set the mob on us and just end the game?

He has Father. And we're just two city girls stumbling across no-man's-land with high odds that at least one of us will starve or get killed before his soldiers even find us.

He thinks he's already won.

I hear a creak of wood, and out of the corner of my eye, I see Ava drop her rucksack to the floor. She slides onto the table and lowers herself down to lie in the circle of light beside me, bringing with her the strong smell of antidrone spray. Mesquite, to mask our scent in the desert. I wait for her to tell me everything is packed and we need to leave, but she remains still, staring up at the ceiling.

"How do you think they're treating him in prison?" I say, breaking the silence.

She takes her time to answer. "Father was—is—beloved in the city," she concludes. "He'll find his allies."

I don't know if I believe that. Or if Ava even does.

"Those ideas in the poem . . . They're words of treason." I whisper the last word, absurdly afraid the admission might somehow summon a drone or soldiers.

Ava doesn't respond, just lies stiffly beside me. I know she's repeating the words of Whitman in her head, speculating what they might mean. Obedience. Enslaved. *Resist.*

"Father hid a lot from us," I say, interrupting her private thoughts. She turns her eyes toward me, but I keep my own on the ceiling. "He would want us to focus on what's ahead," she says.

I release a long sigh through my nose and pull myself up to sit. Hugging my knees, I visualize the details of the map. The path, the houses, all so carefully planned. *He knew this would happen.*

With another sigh, I finally turn to face my sister. I jolt backward, genuinely startled by the stranger staring up at me. A blunt part splits her raven-colored hair that stops short just above her collarbone. Her bangs slicked to the side, she's unrecognizable beneath the paint of exaggerated thick brows and dark-red lips. She notices me scrutinizing her new disguise, but she holds her stare and I hold mine, and the more I look, the more I see Ava behind those russet-brown contacts.

She places her palms on the warm metal table and lifts herself to sit level with me. Her fingers lightly touch my shoulder. "Mira, we're both out of that basement."

I let her words sink in. They're so surreal, my head spins. But as their meaning makes its way down past my heart, landing deep in my gut, all I feel is the weight of guilt.

Our freedom for Father's imprisonment.

"My ankle is better," I lie, reaching for my rucksack. Ava's hand slips from my shoulder, and I slide off the table, the dust flying wildly around me. "We should get to the safe house before nightfall."

We walk side by side, two apparitions in a ghost town.

Beneath our umbrellas we pull our hoods low, but the sun always finds its way in, and Ava's nose and cheekbones are already turning pink.

I squint down at the wristwatch I found in Father's box. 7:04 p.m.

I need to forget the sting of my right foot. I need to forget the ache of no sleep. *We need to move faster.*

"If we lose the light, it will take us twice as long to find the house in the dark," Ava says, reading my mind.

She stops, and like a magnet I draw back, keeping close. She unfolds the map hidden in the waist of her pants, and even though I know she memorized the address before we left the factory, her lips read over the street name and number for the sixth time. "3505 Esmond Avenue."

I squat beside a fallen street sign buried in the ground. Ava grabs the other end of the aluminum sheet, and together we yank it from its grave. We brush aside the grass and dirt until we make out the letters *E* and *D*. Encouraged, I wipe the middle letters clean with the sleeve of my shirt.

"Emerald Street," I read aloud. I throw the sign back into the dirt, and we both stand, hiding our worry from one another.

Ava pulls out the map again and studies the key, expecting to discover some missing clue that will pinpoint exactly where Arlo Chapman is waiting for us. It's frustrating not being able to zoom in for a closer view of the city or to locate our exact position via satellite, especially having to rely on a paper map as our only navigation tool. But it can't be traced, and it's Father's guide, leading us to somewhere he thinks is safe. *And it's the only thing we have.*

We continue our search down the cracked pavement of the main road and turn left when we spot a neighborhood sign, intact and untouched a few yards ahead. Written in the granite rock: "Welcome to Westhaven Estates."

"The safe house has to be in there," Ava says, confident.

The steady winds push against us as we press forward, the fabric of our pants and hoods billowing out behind us like parachutes, making our pace slow and arduous. I bow my head against the force, and shoving my bangs off my face, I take in the scene around me with cautious eyes.

We pass street after street leading to nowhere, road after road lined with empty lots. Acres of infrastructure ready for a populace that will never come. *The death of the American suburbs.*

"It's hard to imagine people ever wanted to live out here," I say, unsure if Ava hears me or if the wind carries away my words. "It's so far from any major city."

Ava nods, but her concentration stays fixed on her search for another street sign.

As we move farther into the abandoned neighborhood, neat rows of concrete foundations eventually build up to the decaying framework of half-finished structures, and soon we're surrounded by entire blocks of run-down homes left to rot.

I don't know what I expected the safe house to be. But it wasn't this.

Six blocks in, a nagging feeling tells me to get out my knife. By the time we reach the end of the street, the feeling raises to an alarm and screams, *Don't go farther!*

One look from Ava and I know she hears it too. She pulls out her knife and flicks open the blade, pressing closer to me. We resume our advance, because there is only forward, Ava surveying the right while I sweep the left.

Bone fragments that look to be the size of small rodents lie scattered along the curb. We make it five more steps before Ava's clammy hand grips my wrist. I hear a deep, savage growl, and the sting of cold sweat shoots down my legs, freezing me to the pavement.

The danger of encountering feral animals never once crossed my mind.

Slowly, calmly, I turn my head and see a lone dog, ears plastered back, teeth yellow and sharp, crouched in the yard of a lopsided one-story house. I can count the ribs on his emaciated body, his brown fur patchy and matted.

Ava emits a gentle cooing sound, but there's little chance this undomesticated animal will back down. When food started to become more and more scarce, the majority of pets were either euthanized or turned out of their homes, forced to fend for themselves. Man's best friend reverted to the ways of their ancestors, and this wolf-like dog in front of me now looks at us as nothing more than food.

Do not make eye contact. Do not run.

I'm certain his pack is somewhere nearby, and we just walked straight into their den.

"Back away slowly," Ava whispers.

Three—or is it four?—more growls bounce off the walls from inside the decrepit house, confirming my fears.

Do not run.

Smooth and steady, Ava leads us backward even as the pack emerges from their den, tails wagging in cruel excitement, mouths snarling and foaming for a meal. I lock my gaze on the largest, her long snout disfigured with scars, as the pack spreads out to form a half circle.

They're backing us into a corner.

My mind battles with my body. Every muscle tells me to run, but reason tells me we clearly can't outrun them.

Don't. Run.

The canopy of Ava's umbrella begins to shake from her trembling right hand. She tries to hide the tremor from me like she did on the rail, but her efforts just make the handle shake even more.

My feet react before my mind can stop me, and I break into a sprint, pulling Ava beside me.

"Mira, no!" Ava screams, but it's too late. I made the first move, and now we must commit to a footrace.

As one, we charge across a gravel yard and shoot down a well-traced path between the houses, the male with the matted fur only a few paces behind. Every stride is a fight to keep ahead. I don't know how long I can keep this pace with my cursed ankle screaming at me. *Run or die!*

the rest of my body shrieks back, but my stamina is waning, the hot breath of the pack right on our heels. We're losing ground.

The dogs start barking. Ava starts shouting, "Drain spout! Look for a drain spout!"

We make it past another street and come to an alleyway.

"Left!" Ava yells.

The blinding glare of the setting sun draws my attention two houses down. A rainwater tank.

I drown out the violent hammering in my chest and the vicious cries of the pack, concentrating solely on that steel tank growing bigger with every step. The five yards it takes to get to safety feels unobtainable, but somehow we get there—Ava pushing me up the drain to the top of the barrel, me pulling her up with my last strength just as the dogs slam into the tank, jumping, clawing at Ava's dangling foot.

"Give them your umbrella!" I shout.

Ava releases her grip on the handle and throws our shield directly into the pack. Three of them take the bait and crush the umbrella with their bodies in their furious scramble to rip apart the canopy first.

I find a final surge of power and haul Ava over the side of the tank with a vulgar grunt. She lands on my stomach.

"The roof," she pants, breathing hard in my ear.

She shrugs her rucksack to the side and lifts herself to crouch on her heels. We lock arms and use each other's weight to stand, keeping our eyes on the dog with the mangled snout stalking the perimeter below. We climb onto the top level of the house beside the rainwater tank, look out from its edge, and confirm the mutts have no way of making the leap to reach us.

I drop my pack and my knife, and with my last ounce of energy, I collapse onto the flat metal roof, curl my body into a ball, and close my eyes.

AVA

There's a fire burning somewhere in the distance.

My nose is filled with the scent of smoke, but I can't see the flames. I want to find people gathered around a hot meal—or maybe it's just a brushfire—and ask them what to do. Find people and not be so alone, so frustratingly helpless.

I tear myself away from studying the route to Arlo Chapman and analyze the starving beasts still at their post below. They probably haven't eaten in days; I bet their bellies don't even know what it feels like to be full. They'll stay here for hours, days maybe, at the possibility of food.

"We should sleep in shifts. There's nothing to do but wait them out," I say, turning away from the roof's edge. A waiting game of who is more desperate: them or us.

Mira has already placed her long vest over the chipped metal solar shingles to act as a sheet. "We need to eat first," she says and holds out a piece of smoked meat.

I take a last look at the lifeless houses that surround us and join my sister on the makeshift bed. When we were children we used to love sleeping on pallets we made together underneath a castle of blankets. Sometimes we could even persuade Father to join us in our imaginary kingdom. There was something magical about sleeping on the floor as a child, away from your bed. But that magic is lost on us tonight.

"Give me your arm," Mira says.

I rest my head against her shoulder and let her drape my microchipless wrist across her knee. She removes my bandage and dabs a clear liquid to encourage the cells to regrow without stitches over the raw skin where I cut out my chip. I stare at her skilled, careful hands as they work. Hands trained to heal. I study my own hand on her knee, following the thin lines etched into my palm like interconnecting rivers on a map. But all the lines lead to nowhere.

Just like that, it hits me how I've been severed from every anchor I was tied to my entire life. My father is gone. I have no home. I don't even have a microchip—my identity. Everything I've ever known floats farther and farther away as I continue to drift unmoored into the vastness like a lifeboat lost at sea. *I'm going to drown.*

"We need to try and rest," Mira says, rescuing me from the water with a tight squeeze of her hand.

"I'll take the first watch," I say, but Mira stands before I can get my legs out from under me.

"I was able to sleep briefly on the rail. It's your turn to rest." She removes a knife from her pocket, no longer holding it like a healer but like someone ready to defend—to hurt—if necessary.

The purpose of her hands has changed.

"Wake me in two hours," I say.

I pull my sleeve down over my freshly bandaged wrist and settle onto the improvised bed. Scared and bloodshot, my eyes remain open. I tighten the grip on my own knife, and my heart jumps every time a noise breaks the silence.

Mira startles awake and is on her feet the moment the first crash of thunder explodes across the sky.

"It's just a storm. We're okay," I say, my eyes never leaving the dogs that stalk the yard beneath the house. A deep whine pulsates inside their throats, and their heads turn in agitated, aggressive movements.

Mira joins me at the roof's edge—now using her vest to block out the wind instead of as our bedsheet—and observes the thunderstorm in the distance. Dark clouds hang heavy with moisture, but because the air below them is so dry, most of the rain will likely evaporate before it can quench the parched landscape.

Another loud thunderclap sets the dogs into an onslaught of barking, and they snap at one another viciously. "They're terrified," Mira says.

A thunderous boom vibrates the ground, and the pack breaks into a frenzy of high-pitched yelps. Their conflicting urges to fight for food or fly to safety are driving them into a blind panic.

This is our moment.

"They're distracted. We can divert their attention," I say.

"Our food," Mira says, reaching for her rucksack.

I turn my back on the dogs and scan the roof. With the giant tree in the front yard dead and the roof littered with debris, it doesn't take long to spot the Y-shaped piece of wood I'm looking for.

"What can we use as tubing for a catapult?" I ask Mira.

She slides her hair tie off her wrist and tests its elasticity. "We can cut this in half and use a thick cloth as our barrel."

I carve a notch with my knife into each forked prong of our makeshift slingshot while Mira severs a corner of her shirt with a pair of scissors. Cutting a slit on each side of the cloth, I slide the pouch across the hairband and tie the ends into place, then walk to the edge of the roof.

"Aim high to get the distance," Mira tells me.

She loads a piece of leftover steak from the dinner party into the barrel, and I fire straight into the pack. An all-out brawl for the scrap of meat ensues.

Mira reloads and I launch two more shots, each one aimed farther away from the house. The dogs race for the food, clawing and biting each other's necks in their desperation.

"It's working," I say.

Mira and I quickly shoulder our packs and move toward the opposite end of the roof facing the backyard, but we discover the rainwater tank has been knocked to the ground. The dogs must have tipped it over in the night.

"Roll on your landing," Mira says.

I scan the lawn for a padded place and detect a thick patch of weeds a few yards away. I swing my body over the edge, hang for a moment by my fingertips, and let go. The ground comes up quick, and I tuck and roll to my side, away from the house.

I rise to my feet next to my umbrella, now completely shredded and useless. Good thing I packed an extra one, meant for Father. He's still helping us, even in small ways like this.

Mira falls in beside me. Jaw clenched in pain, she nods that she'll cope, and we take off down the street, lightning flashes guiding our path.

Half an hour later we haven't found a single street sign left in the entire neighborhood, and I'm about to give up hope locating the safe house before daybreak when Mira rushes ahead of me.

"Ava, look," she says, pointing.

I see nothing but shadows and the dark outline of houses until another bolt of lightning illuminates a slanting street sign with the name "Esmond Avenue" reflected in blocky white letters.

A renewed energy flows through my veins, encouraging my heavy legs to move faster down the street toward the man Father wants us to meet.

It takes another quarter hour of searching before we stop in front of a sad-looking two-story home with boarded-up windows. Nothing about the house distinguishes it from the countless rows of dull, mass-produced designs except the yellow color painted on the door.

The numbers 3505 hang crooked above the entryway.

Together Mira and I climb the stone steps to the porch before we separate, each moving to look through a different window.

"I can't see anything," she says.

I signal to her with a nod, and we loop around to the side of the house and use the collapsed fence to peer inside a group of bay windows. I see nothing but an overturned couch. No people. No signs of life. No Chapman.

"Should we knock?" Mira asks at the back door.

The idea of adhering to such a formality seems ridiculous, but I give a tentative knock anyway.

No answer.

I knock harder, and the door creaks open.

Mira and I glance at each other before we walk through the doorway, alert. We enter into a dark, still kitchen. The cabinet doors are all unlatched; several empty food cans are scattered across the countertops. Everything useful has been raided here just like at the factory.

"Hello?"

No response but the deep rumble of distant thunder.

We forage our way through each room on the lower level before we start up the stairs, every other step producing a loud creak.

"Mr. Chapman?"

Silence.

Upstairs we separate again—Mira goes left and I go right. After searching through two vacant rooms, I find my sister sitting on an old queen mattress that lies forgotten in the middle of the master bedroom. Brow furrowed, she breathes out a long, frustrated sigh.

"What if all the safe houses are empty like this?" she says.

I peer out the window. Looking to the east, I still don't see the morning light. Storm clouds cover the rising sun, forcing the sky to hold onto the night. I close the blinds before joining my sister on the bed.

"We don't know it's empty. Chapman might be out on an errand or gathering food supplies," I say. Our voices are hushed even though we know we are alone.

"Father might have made this map years ago. We have no idea how accurate the safe houses still are," Mira says.

"He wouldn't have given it to us if he didn't think the route would work."

"Or Chapman fled," she counters, rising from the mattress toward the bathroom, where she scavenges the shelves below the sink.

"He probably ran off after he heard the governor's threats. Who wants to risk their life for wanted criminals?" Mira continues, frustration plain in her voice. She finds a box of tampons and shoves it into her rucksack. All the previous scavengers must have been men.

I move into the small bathroom and sit on the edge of the stained acrylic tub, the corners of the map digging into my hips.

"We need to recharge. We'll stay here today, try to find supplies, and wait to see if Chapman shows up," I say.

Mira twists the knobs of the sink faucet but nothing comes out. She sighs and surges to her feet. What was she expecting? Mira forces the blonde hair plastered to her forehead out of her face. I miss the red already.

She looks at me with tired, bloodshot eyes. "If he doesn't return by sundown, we set off for the next safe house without him."

Reluctantly, I nod.

But he has to come back, I choose not to voice aloud. I don't know if we can make it through the Texas desert without him.

MIRA

Ava lowers her binoculars.

"If we keep our distance and make it quick, no one should notice our presence," she says.

We set out to resupply our water and are planning to make the trek back to the safe house to resume our wait for Arlo Chapman. Ava found an orphaned bicycle in the garage, the bike chain thick with accumulated rust, the brakes dubious and loose, but I had hopes this rickety vehicle could still make time shrink. We made it four miles with me on the handlebars before the front tire blew and the bike skidded, catapulting me and my misguided optimism to the ground.

One vile stray nail and now we must walk back to the house after our supply run, which will more than triple our travel time.

I look down at my wrist. 10:46 a.m. The more hours that go by, the less I believe this name on the map will show up to save us. The more I begin to understand that we must learn to adapt and rely on ourselves.

I raise my binoculars and follow the pitiful stream of brown water winding its way, listless and lethargic, alongside a massive slum a few miles out. Hundreds of poorly constructed shacks line the west bank, and piles of garbage and filth are crammed into narrow paths that snake through the maze with no clear direction. The shantytown stretches as far south as I can see, stopping short just outside the fringe city of Amarillo.

Despite the blatant poverty of the hovels, the soft blue light of hologram projections spills out hand-carved windows. I zoom in and shift my focus to a raucous group of children huddled around a pair of youths immersed inside a virtual game. Surrounded by the trees of a vast rainforest, the players battle masked, badgeless soldiers cloaked in all-black uniforms. I linger as they expertly draw back the advancing enemy, so realistically human, with holographic swords and axes. To the thrill of the unrestrained crowd, the star girl and boy mercilessly gut and behead every soldier that meets their path, their combined kill count 456 . . . 459 . . . 465 . . .

I stuff the binoculars back into my bag, and with my naked eye I mark each person scattered along the remains of the river. To our left small clusters of men and women gather the putrid water into buckets. Once full, they lift and balance what must weigh close to forty pounds on top of their heads and proceed back toward the slums, never once spilling a drop.

Three older women washing rags are the closest to us, about two hundred yards to our right. From where we stand I can hear the chaotic rhythm of their music echo across the bank.

By all rights this water source should be bone dry from the burden of supplying tens of thousands of locals, squatters, drifters. Fugitives.

They must be regulating the river. But regulated by whom? There is no Guard in Amarillo.

I pop the knuckle of my thumb, anxious. "The river could be monitored."

"We need the water," Ava counters, steadfast.

And so we take the risk.

We turn our backs on the crude dwellings and create our own pathway inside the narrow tree line following the river. The high grass sets loose a relentless swarm of biting insects, and the dense labyrinth of branches scrapes against my arms and thighs, making my skin itch and sting despite the protection of my clothes. I slap and scratch my way along the trail behind Ava, one eye on the grove, one eye on the riverbank.

We haven't seen anyone near the water for a good ten minutes. I start to suggest to Ava that we stop here when I see her fling aside a twisted knot of limbs, sneak through the opening, and release the mass behind her without a second thought. The sharp arm of the tree branch swings back and whips me right across my cheek. I suppress a cry and squeeze my palm against my cheek until the pain subsides, cursing under my breath.

"Sorry! Sorry!" Ava shouts, attempting to hurl herself back through the thicket. "Did it get your eye?"

I wave her away. "Just keep moving." I feel my agitation rising and tell myself to breathe.

She holds back the branch for me, and I walk through the gap, freeing my hand from my face to help push aside the brush.

"It didn't leave a mark," she says when I reach her.

Like that matters anymore. Our lives no longer depend on staying identical.

Ava turns toward the vacant riverbank. "This seems as good a spot as any," she says.

She gets out her water bottle and I get out mine.

"Keep your head down," Ava tells me.

"You keep yours down," I retort and move past her toward the river, pulling the hood of my vest low, just above my eyes.

At the edge of the tree line, I look left, right, and left again to make certain no drones or people might be watching. Finding the bank clear on either side, I step out into the dry, exposed land that used to hold the broad waters of the Canadian River. Judging from where I stand to the opposite tree line, this section of the river must have been a quarter-mile wide in the distant past. Now it's just a long, meandering puddle doomed to shrink and disappear within the next few years.

Water is a fickle bitch. Entire cities—Houston, Miami—flood and sink from too much, while others—Phoenix, Las Vegas—shrivel and diminish from too little. Millions die every year over the world's most precious resource, from wars waged over lake and river rights, contaminated and depleting aquifers, dwindling crop yields, and the ever-increasing demand of a bloated population that has reached well beyond our planet's carrying capacity.

Rainfall has doubled as we've learned to live in a warmer world—it just falls in the wrong places. Our land and people are thirsty. I am thirsty. And right below me is a filthy river that will give me life and a chance to keep moving. My knees crack as I bend down, unfasten the lid of my bottle, and fill it with the foul-smelling water like I'm scooping for gold.

Beside me Ava fills her own bottle and lifts the contents to her nose for closer inspection. "This water is disgusting," she says, pinching her nostrils as she crams the lid closed.

"It takes thirty seconds to purify," I say, holding my bottle up to the sun. Through the translucent plastic the water glows a nauseating brown, and I count three, maybe four, suspicious lumps floating below the filters.

I begin to have my doubts.

"Test it," Ava tells me.

I flip my bottle, only letting a small stream flow, and clear water pools in my hand. Still wary, I hesitate.

"I'll test it first," Ava says, stretching out her arm for the bottle.

"No, I'll do it," I say firmly. I'm being foolish. I'm acting spoiled. This is how the greater part of the populace drinks their water. *You're not in Trinity Heights anymore.*

I take a long gulp before pulling back, my lips twisted in revulsion.

"What? Does it taste bad?" Ava asks as I suppress a powerful urge to dry-heave.

"It tastes fine," I say, gathering my composure. "I just can't get past the mental image that I'm drinking people's shit."

A devilish grin plays across Ava's face. She grabs the bottle from my hand and shakes it, causing more mysterious chunks to appear.

"I mean, look at that! Is that shit?" I ask.

Ava nods, because yes, it probably is.

"Well, shit," I say evenly.

Ava's smile widens, and the moment we lock eyes, we both burst into laughter. A cheeks-hurting, eyes-watering, nose-snorting, ugly kind of laughter. My abs burn as I wipe the tears from my eyes. A wave of release passes through me, and for a second I feel weightless. Ava is still smiling. Big and unrestrained, the first since our escape.

"We should hydrate as much as we can while we're here," Ava says finally, offering me the next swig.

We empty the bottle after two more passes, and I squat down to refill it while Ava reviews the map. As I secure the lid, a surge of wind sweeps my bangs from my eyes and blows back my hood. My field of view opened, I catch movement to my right.

"Ava," I whisper before I even make out what it is. I jump to my feet, and we both turn, instinctively shouldering our packs, and discover a girl walking tentatively toward us from the edge of the stream.

"¡Buenas tardes!" she shouts over the howling wind, lifting her hands in a declaration of peace. "¿Hablan español?"

The girl wears a soiled scarf draped loose across her neck, but that's the only detail I discern before Ava and I pull up our hoods, pivot on our heels, and move calmly but quickly back to the protection of the tree line.

I hide my bottle in my rucksack, leaving my hands free in case I might need them. *Is she after our water?*

Don't think, just move.

Always, forever, move.

The girl continues to follow us, yelling out in Spanish. We do not engage or acknowledge her, and I try to drown out every word she screams.

"No les voy a hacer daño. ¡Solamente quiero hablar!"

We both pick up our speed, accelerating to a jog. Her shouts become louder, closer, and we move faster, never once looking back.

"¡No estoy tratando de robarles!"

The edge of the grove is a mere ten yards away. We sprint the last few feet, slip through the trees, and make for the trail without slowing, despite increasing evidence the girl has given up. The path behind us has grown quiet; the sounds of pursuit have ceased. The girl no longer shouts.

I shove my bangs from my eyes and rub a hand hard over my face. *We should have seen her sooner.* Just as Ava signals we can ease to a walk, a voice rips across the riverbank, desperate and final.

"Arlo Chapman!"

The name reverberates off the tree trunks around us, and instantly we both freeze.

We turn in unison and advance back toward the river, my head spinning, my mind racing. Ava moves her hand to her pocket, gripping her knife the moment we spot the girl leaning dejected against a tree along the perimeter of the small wood. She looks up as we approach, her expression raw and bone tired.

"¿Cómo sabe usted ese nombre?" I ask her. *How do you know that name?*

The girl's lip quivers in relief. "Porque yo estaba buscándolo también."

Because I was looking for him too.

AVA

"¿Por qué estabas buscando a Arlo Chapman?" I demand. *Why were you seeking Arlo Chapman?*

The bridge we shelter under towers high above our heads, as if we were standing inside an airy cathedral. Mira and I hug the shadows of a thick concrete column, a barricade between our latest threat and us.

I don't trust this girl.

"Lo encontré. Pero huyó," she says. *I found him. But he fled.*

I scrutinize her closer, calculating. She looks older than us—nineteen or twenty. Her long dark hair is tied low at the base of her neck, her lips dry and cracked. She carries nothing with her. No rucksack. No shield to block herself from cameras or the sun. No weapons that I can see. No food or water.

"¿Cuándo huyó?" Mira asks. *When did he flee?*

"Anoche. Algo lo asustó y abandonó su estación." *Last night. Something spooked him, and he abandoned his station.* She lowers her eyes. "Es un cobarde." *He is a coward.*

This could be a trick. She could be an informant for the Guard.

Don't let her draw you in, Father's training whispers to me.

We need to walk away now.

I grab Mira by the back of her shirt and steer her in the opposite direction of the stranger.

"Por favor . . . esperen," the girl says, a note of desperation creeping back into her voice. *Please . . . wait.* Her hands moving passionately, she gives a rapid, emotional speech in an unfamiliar, brassy accent that makes it difficult for me to translate.

Mira resists my grip on her shirt.

"No," I whisper firmly when she stops our retreat and turns to face the girl. I look to Mira for a translation, an explanation.

"She said she must get to the next safe house, or she will die." There is sympathy, clear and dangerous, in my sister's eyes.

"We don't know what this girl might do," I hiss to Mira.

Mira grabs her water bottle from her bag and tosses it over to the girl. She catches it one-handed and tears open the lid.

"Gracias," she says after two respectful sips.

Mira gestures to the shantytown down river. "Sé que hay personas aquí que pueden ayudarle." *I'm sure there are people here who will give you aid.*

The girl shakes her head, lifting her empty hand in a helpless gesture. "Solo ayudarán a su propia gente." *They will only help their own.*

Away from the bridge, the harsh noon sun beats down on the girl, illuminating what I didn't see before. The grime that lines her neck, the tattered clothes that hang loose on her body; the hollowed cheeks, the worn-out shoes and eyes that betray a grueling journey.

A sign of what's to come.

"¿Eres tú una Glut?" I ask point-blank. *Are you a Glut?*

"Soy de Ciudad de México," she answers evenly. *I am from Mexico City.*

A vehicle unexpectedly drives across the bridge, sending Mira and me flying to the ground. The girl just stands there unafraid as the deafening vibrations bounce off the concrete structure, and I search over my shoulder terrified, convinced a military brigade has found us at last.

When the reverberations die off, I realize it was only a lone civilian car. The girl studies us closely as Mira and I rise from the dirt. I pull my hood lower, covering my eyes from her scrutiny.

"¿Cómo llegaste aquí? Es imposible cruzar la frontera de los Estados Unidos," I say. *How did you get here? The United States border is impossible to get through.*

She hesitates, her sharp eyes focusing first on me, then on Mira. She's debating how much to reveal.

"Enséñame una pared de cien pies de altura y yo te enseñaré una escalera de ciento un pies," she answers simply. *Show me a hundred-foot wall, and I will show you a hundred-and-one-foot ladder.*

So she just slipped right past the Border Guard and the motion-detector lasers?

Mira lets go of the breath she's been holding, and I know she's hooked. She pulls me aside, freely speaking English, knowing the girl won't understand.

"We should take her with us."

"No." I shake my head, adamant.

Mira moves in closer to me, insistent. "We could at least give her the position of the next safe house," she argues.

From the corner of my eye, I see the girl's brow furrowed deep in concentration, trying hard to interpret what we are saying.

"We don't know what she will do with that information. She's not our problem—we have to worry about ourselves," I say.

She's worn out and weak—she will slow us down. She will use up our food and water supply. She will discover our secret.

"So we're just going to leave her here to die?" Mira throws at me, blasting through my justifications. I feel my defenses crumbling to the ground. I sigh, agreeing.

Mira turns to face the girl. "Puedes venir con nosotras a la siguiente casa segura," she says. *You can come with us to the next safe house.*

The girl bows her head, wrapping her fingers around a rosary she pulled from her pocket.

"Gracias," she says softly.

Mira and I shoulder our bags and open our umbrellas, preparing for departure.

"Me pueden llamar Lucía," the girl offers. *You can call me Lucía.*

I nod, not offering our names in return. The less she knows about us, the better.

Mira extends a smile, and we move out into the unforgiving desert. Lucía hesitates, uncertain.

"¿Salimos ahora? Es más fresco viajar en la noche. Con menos ojos," she says. *We are leaving now? It's cooler traveling at night, with fewer eyes.*

"Puedes venir con nosotras ahora o quedarte," I answer. *You either come with us now or stay.*

She's right, but we have no time to waste.

The big Texas sky is without mercy.

The sun assaults the brushy, rough terrain we walk on, beating through our umbrellas, drenching us in a sticky sweat.

We travel in a tight line. I lead, with Mira in the middle and Lucía bringing up the rear. In every direction we turn, there is only scorched, flat land. I've never seen a skyline without soaring skyscrapers dominating the horizon. I take in the unobstructed view, refusing to blink until my eyes fill with water. I breathe the open air deep into my lungs. Surrounded by so much danger, I've never felt more free.

No one speaks. We all simply walk, one step in front of the other, focused on our own thoughts to help melt away the hours.

It takes about twenty minutes to cover one mile. I calculate we have sixty miles until the next safe house. If I keep track of the time and we keep up the pace, we face roughly twenty hours of trekking through the arid, seemingly endless desert. We will have to strictly monitor our ration intake—it will be a miracle if our water supply doesn't run out before we reach Dalhart and the next name on Father's map: Kipling.

This safe house can't be empty.

I'm worried about Lucía's stamina. I'm not sure her body can make it to the end of this desert journey. She's only taken a few sips of water and refused any of Mira's offers to take a break. I peer over my shoulder to gauge her condition.

Body slightly hunched, she marches along with no umbrella to shield her from the sun. She's been completely exposed to the elements for who knows how long, and it shows.

I can't help but wonder where her final destination leads. It's hard for me to believe it's in the United States. While the US is better off than her home country of Mexico, the allure of the country that once famously proclaimed "Give me your tired, your poor, your huddled masses yearning to breathe free" has faded. Canada is now where the masses flock in droves. Not to breathe free, but to survive. One of the few countries to come out on top when the climate crisis shook up the global power structure, the Canadian superpower possesses the lucky trinity: a moderate climate, an enormous supply of freshwater reserves, and a robust food resource thanks to a melted Arctic Ocean. The International Boundary Wall that protects the border between Canada and the United States is the longest and tallest wall in the world. Lucía may have done the impossible and somehow successfully made it through our southern border, but there's no chance in hell she will ever make it through theirs.

She feels my gaze on her now and quickly pulls her shoulders up, high and proud. "Puedo seguir," she says. *I can keep going.*

Yes, but for how long? We have another ten miles before we stop to rest.

I lower my umbrella and pass it back to Mira, who in turn offers it to Lucía. With a small nod the girl takes the handle, and I slow my pace to walk in step with my sister, sharing her shade.

And the three of us continue onward.

The vast landscape seems to swallow us whole as we make our way between a maze of rock formations that look like massive tabletops.

While my feet continue to take me north, I keep my head turned to the west, unable to tear myself away from the setting sun. I stare at the breathtaking yellows, purples, pinks, and oranges of the bright, unhurried ball that sinks lower and lower into the ground. Not a glass or concrete building in sight.

Mira stops abruptly. "We should camp here," she says. "These rocks will give us protection."

I nod. "We will rest in shifts, then head out again at midnight," I say.

Interpreting the plan, Lucía moves to set up camp against an indentation in a large rock face. Mira remains still beside me. She is as transfixed by the setting sun as I am.

I look up just in time to see the top of the majestic star disappear into the horizon, and I smile to myself, knowing I will watch it rise free and clear on the horizon tomorrow. I give Mira's hand a quick squeeze, and I can actually feel my heart inside my chest.

There is hope, and I can see it.

MIRA

I lie beneath our umbrella shelter, wide awake. I stare unblinking out into the dark expanse where Lucía disappeared, ticking off her absence in my head.

It's been twenty-four minutes since she left camp. *What is the girl doing out there?* She seems genuine, but in the cold midnight hours, my sympathy shifts to doubt.

I really should be sleeping. There's only one more hour until it's my turn to take over watch. Two more until the forty-mile hike to the next safe house. The sore muscles of my quads and upper back tingle, and I know at least my body is recharging. But my brain just won't shut off.

It's all this quiet. It's deafening.

I look up to see my sister gazing down at me from her seat against the rocks, her binoculars still raised and pointed toward the placid darkness that borders our meager camp. I notice Father's journal rests in her lap, pages opened to the clean, short lines of the poem.

"Have you slept at all?" Ava whispers, voice rough with fatigue.

For the first half hour, I tried to drift asleep to the soft mutterings of her recitation, visualizing her mouth forming each new word, repetitive and devout like the memorization of a prayer. But as my mind wandered in and out of consciousness, the nightmares were right there

waiting for me. I was falling, the hands were everywhere, and this time my mother did not sing. Instead, I heard my father screaming.

"Mira, there's two of us so we can do two things at once. You sleep, I guard. You guard, I sleep," she says reasonably.

She turns back to the eyepiece, her elbows on her knees, and combs the desert with her night vision. The filters on the lenses make the eyes of her binoculars glow an emerald green, reminding me of our old eye color.

"Two against one is better odds if Lucía decides to attack us," I reply.

"I thought you trusted her?"

Then everything happens in one synchronous moment. Lucía materializes from the shadows just as the first vibration of an aircraft thunders across the night sky, and I shout "Hide!" as Ava throws her hands over her head and nosedives into the umbrella shelter.

I cushion her landing with my arms and help her onto her knees. We huddle close, listening blind as the low buzz of the aircraft builds to a deep roar, surrounding and encompassing us. Swallowing us.

"Did you see it?" I whisper, her ear smashed against my cheek. "Is it a drone?"

"I couldn't see anything above the clouds."

"It has to just be an airliner. Even Roth couldn't afford to send out a surveillance aircraft to search for us." Ava nods, but the tension in her jaw tells me she's not convinced.

Whatever is up there passes overhead, and I duck and cover beneath the hood of my vest, despite fully knowing that if it *is* indeed a surveillance drone, then the infrared cameras would have already detected our presence. *But they won't know it's us,* I persuade myself.

The oppressive rumble of the aircraft wanes as it speeds over our position, heading south—away from us and somewhere toward the heart of Texas.

One threat gone, I turn my attention to Lucía. I find her curled underneath a rock beside our shelter, scanning the starless sky.

"¿Dónde estabas?" Ava asks. *Where were you?*

Ava rises from beneath the canopy and tries to keep her voice calm, but her words sting with suspicion.

Lucía shifts her eyes to Ava and crawls out from the refuge of the cliff. She struggles to her feet against the strong Panhandle winds, the loose strands from her ponytail floating above her head as if from electric charges in the atmosphere. I notice her fingers are caked in dirt as she reaches for something in her pocket. Simultaneously, Ava and I reach for our knives. She fastens her eyes on Ava, then me, but we keep our weapons drawn. Slowly, she lifts her hand from inside her jacket, revealing a fistful of what looks like the small green pads of a cactus.

"Nopales," she says. She holds out her open palm, offering us the pile. "Para darnos fuerza." *To give us strength.*

There's such frank sincerity in her countenance, it shames me into lowering my blade.

"También podemos usarlos como medicina," I say, accepting the nopales with a respectful nod. *We can also use them for medicine.*

"Agarren más. Tengo muchos." *Take more, I have many.*

Ava lifts her hand, palm red and blistered from the steady grip of traveling beneath her umbrella, and accepts several nopales from Lucía's generous stockpile.

"Gracias," Ava says and turns back to the fort to resume her watch.

Lucía nods, and with one last look at the pitch-black sky, she sinks down into the dirt. Molding her body into a shallow indentation along the cliff, she hugs her knees for warmth and closes her eyes.

I squeeze in next to Ava at her lookout and tuck my head into her shoulder. I drape my vest over our legs to shield us from the chilly air. As Ava scrapes away the spikes from the cactus pads with her knife, I replay the terrorizing sound of the aircraft in my mind. I dissect every layer of vibration, scrutinize every note, every tremor. Finally I conclude

the engine sounded more like the vacuum noise of a passenger plane than the characteristic hum of a drone.

"Dron," Lucía repeats as if she were listening in on my thoughts. "Era un dron." *It was a drone.*

"Roth," I exhale in a long, flat sigh. I clutch my sister's hand, our cold fingers intertwining, uniting. *Courage,* Ava tells me with the pressure of her grip.

Lucía's hair blocks her profile, but the wind picks up and blows her dark veil away from her face, revealing her worried, red-rimmed eyes. No need to ask how she knows this with certainty. Drones swarm the entire US-Mexico border, supplying 24/7 surveillance. She must have memorized their sound before she crossed, knowing they meant capture. Knowing they meant death.

She watches Ava and me closely, her eyes flicking back and forth between us before landing on me. Even with the dark as my protector, I shrink from her inspection. I lift my head from my sister's shoulder and use the end of my vest to deflect her gaze.

"Está bien," she says quietly. *It's okay.*

There's something in her tone that draws my eyes to hers.

"Ellos dicen que no soy bienvenida aquí tampoco." *They say I don't belong here either.*

I do not hide, recoil, or even blink. We stare at one another with an intense understanding before she finally turns away to nestle against the rigid rock face. Ava's muscles harden, and she begins to rise.

"It's okay," I say, both to her and myself. "She doesn't seem to know who we are. Just what we are."

The tightness in her muscles softens slightly, but she releases her grip on my hand and moves her fingers to her knife.

"Three more hours of rest, then we move."

I nod and close my eyes, the deafening silence from earlier replaced by the sound of my beating heart. In spite of the incredible danger, there is liberation, and profound relief, in having another person know

I'm alive. In having this knowledge accepted with no outrage or indignation. No hostility or condemnation.

As I drift into oblivion, my last conscious thoughts are of Roth. The eye in the sky might have been him, but there are thousands of transients wandering around the open spaces still left in this country. Millions of acres left for us to drop off the map. We just have to keep him guessing.

Same game, different scenery.

Except now I exist.

AVA

The night feels close and heavy around us. It's almost as if we're wrapped inside a dark blanket with holes poked into it to let in the stars, except without the benefits of a blanket's warmth and protection. But I don't mind being cold and exposed—it keeps me alert and moving.

We walk in line once more—Lucía at the end, Mira in the middle, and me at the front leading our quiet progress north. Twenty-seven miles until we reach Kipling. Our bodies rested and sufficiently nourished, we should make it to the second safe house in ten hours with minimal breaks. We just have to keep pushing.

Suddenly the wind brings a faint cry from ahead.

"¿Escucharon eso?" *Did you hear that?*

Uneasy, I raise a fist to stop the line. I close my eyes and stand perfectly still, listening for anything hiding in the dark.

Nothing at first, but then a series of thin wails. A flash of red flickers across the back of my eyelids. *Danger.*

"It sounds like an injured animal," Mira says, moving beside me with her binoculars.

I slide my hand into my pocket and remove my knife.

"We should fall back and loop around downwind," I breathe just above a whisper. I signal to withdraw, and as we're pulling back, a shape slowly emerges.

"I think it's a child," Mira says, amazed.

I realize it really is a child—a small boy—all bones and filth, stumbling closer to us in the moonlight. His tiny frame barely clothed in rags, he shivers uncontrollably. He's so malnourished it's difficult to say how old he is by appearance alone.

"Help me," he moans before bursting into sobs.

To my right, Lucía searches the night, wary.

"No debemos parar aquí." *We shouldn't stop here.*

Tears fall down the boy's dirt-stained cheeks, and he attempts to wrap his twig-like arms around his waist for warmth.

I hesitate, unsure what to do. Mira holds her water bottle out for the boy. He stops his pitiful howling and rubs a hand over his snotty nose, but he doesn't take the bottle. He just stares up at Mira with big innocent eyes.

"Are you out here alone?" Mira asks the boy.

The child's gaze suddenly shifts from my sister's face to the darkness over her shoulder. A smirk crosses his lips.

There's someone behind us.

The Guard.

Before I can even think to move, a hand violently covers my mouth. I taste blood slipping down my throat—something hard sliced open my lower lip—and I have to fight to breathe. I jerk my head to the side, sucking enough air into my lungs to let out a muffled scream.

"Shh . . . there's no need for that," a raspy voice breathes into my ear.

Not soldiers. Bandits.

Struggling to grip the knife in my hand, I attempt a hasty jab to his stomach, but I'm thwarted immediately. This isn't the man's first time. His rough hands twist my wrist until I scream again, my palm opening easily for him. He takes the blade and presses it to my throat with a threatening growl.

"I told you not to scream."

My rucksack ripped from my shoulders, I feel his heavy body replace it, pressing tight against my back. The man is three times my size, his hairy arms locked around me like unbreakable shackles. I can't move an inch.

Panic takes over. My vision flickers in and out of focus as I struggle to grasp hold of a plan—any plan at all—to get us out of this. Two men drag my sister and Lucía at knifepoint in front of me, and my vision narrows.

Mira!

Our eyes lock for a single agonizing moment. I watch—immobile, useless—as my sister fights against the arms that bind her. She pushes and pulls with all the strength she possesses. But it's not enough. The brutish man who holds her just smiles, his dark eyes crinkling with amusement.

"You don't have to put on a show, pretty," he mocks. "You've already got my attention."

He drags his lips across her cheek, and a powerful rage ignites inside my chest. The decoy child resumes his pathetic crying somewhere outside the circle.

"Shut that kid up," my assailant demands. His relaxed, even voice expects to be obeyed. He must be the ringleader.

Holding Mira's rucksack, a teenager with a shaved head approaches the child. Taking a large gulp of our water, he briefly pats the boy's shoulder and drops a handful of our nopales to the ground. The boy quiets his howling and greedily dives for them.

Lucía doesn't struggle against her captor. The older boy—who looks like a starving blonde bull with a silver ring through his septum—rips through her pockets without resistance. She just stands there, eyes closed, lips mumbling incoherent words under her breath.

"He's not listening, mamí—whoever you're praying to." Her captor laughs loudly and sucks on one of the nopales he took from her pocket, the juice trickling down his chin.

My assailant ignores him and runs his hands down my body in his own search, his fingers lingering under the waistline of my pants. He finds the map—*shit*—and pockets it.

"What else do you have hidden down there?" he asks me, caressing the top of my underwear.

I jerk forward angrily and see my sister's captor slip his filthy hands underneath the collar of her shirt to grope her breasts.

"What's wrong? You don't like the way he's touching her?" my captor taunts, cupping my cheek gently. He blows his sour breath against my neck and slides his calloused hands along the curves of my body, stopping between my legs.

"Is this how you like it?" he whispers in my ear.

Every part of my body—my entire being—recoils against his touch. I snap my head away from his mouth and see Mira's captor kissing her neck while she struggles to escape. But all she can do is close her eyes.

Fire burns hot in my belly, spreading into my limbs, making me feel dangerous and powerful. He needs to take his hands off my sister now. If he doesn't, I won't be able to stop my heel from plowing into my captor's groin, freeing myself to tear the smile from his face with my bare hands. Screw not having a weapon. My rage is my weapon.

That will do nothing for her. He'll cut your throat first.

The brute comes up for air. "Hey, Carlos, this girl kinda looks like that bitch the Guard is after."

Mira attempts to keep her head low, but his dirty fingers grab her chin, forcing her to expose her full face.

No . . . no . . . no . . . no . . . no . . .

My protest bubbles hopelessly into my throat—*it's me, not her!*—when I'm shoved roughly to the teenage boy. The back of my head collides painfully with the binoculars he has raised to his face, stolen from Mira's bag. He doesn't hesitate to wrap his arms around me, but his grip lacks the eagerness shared by his cohorts.

Carlos scrutinizes Mira's grimy, sunburnt face. Her lips tremble uncontrollably above the blade at her throat as the man carefully takes in the black eyeliner smudged across her cheeks, the cropped blonde hair, and the wrong-colored eyes.

"I'm not that girl," Mira says, her voice soft but firm.

With alarming speed, Carlos serves a brutal punch to her stomach. "I didn't say you could speak," he growls.

Mira bowls over, painfully gasping for air.

"It's not her," he says, certain. "Let's go." He turns away, dismissing Mira.

"Can we still keep her?" Mira's captor asks. "I think mine likes me."

"No!" Mira and I scream in unison. I battle hard against the teenager's arms.

Mira's captor turns to the teenager with a sadistic grin, taking joy in our cries. The boy hangs his head, refusing to join in. I drive my head up, forcing the teen to meet my eyes. *Help us,* they plead, but I can see in one glance he's just as helpless as I was in the city square watching that woman get tasered over bottled water. He won't save us.

"You can have her. But don't expect me to feed her," Carlos says, placing my rucksack on his shoulders. "We're done here. Leave the others."

The brute grabs hold of Mira and turns to follow his ringleader, ripping my sister away from me.

"Mira!"

Unleashing a deep, savage roar, Mira fights, thrashing and kicking, to get back to me. We're dragged farther and farther apart, our screams becoming violent cries as we continue to wildly claw out for each other. But she's slipping away from me. My heart breaks free from its ribbed cage inside my chest and flees to her side, where it belongs.

I'll find you again. I'm sorry, I'm sorry, I'm sorry, I'm sorry.

Without warning the sharp blast of a gunshot cuts through the air, and everything goes still.

Then the wailing of the child and the ringing echo of the bullet overwhelm me, and I clasp my hands to my ears, disoriented. From the corner of my eye, I see Carlos drop hard to the ground, the moment prolonged and distant. He clutches his upper back, dark crimson coating his frenzied hands, trying to stop the bleeding, his throat producing horrifying noises in his great effort to breathe.

Oh God, he's going to die.

Lost in a haze of shock, I look from his hemorrhaging body to the gun still raised in Lucía's steady hands.

She turns her concentration to the leaderless gang of bandits and aims her cocked pistol at each of them, daring them to move. Fear spreads clear and contagious across their faces. Her assailant backs slowly away in disbelief, both hands clutching his bleeding nose. The teenager loosens his grasp on me, and I rip his arms from my body. But the brute doesn't let go of Mira.

He glares at Lucía, calculating if he should charge. She points the gun at his head, the tip of her index finger tightening on the trigger. The man backs down, reluctantly releasing his grip on Mira. She bursts free of him, stumbling to the ground.

I rush to my sister, falling into the dirt by her side, lost in a whirlwind of dust and emotion. I lock my arms around her, tight enough to bruise. My mind frantic, I grab her hand and she grabs mine. We lift each other up and scramble behind Lucía, behind the power of the gun.

"No nos sigan," Lucía warns, backing away from the men. *Do not follow.*

Together the three of us disappear into the night.

MIRA

My feet are a hundred pounds each. I watch them as they rise and fall, one after the other, two leaden boots dragging me across the dead grasslands of their own volition. I wonder idly what keeps them going.

My mind is full of air. The strong Panhandle winds have finally made their way inside me, and I am hollow. Numb. I no longer feel the stab of pain from my poorly healed ankle, no longer feel the fiery sear from the cold-hearted sun.

But those hands.

I can still feel those hands.

And the gun.

I will always feel the echo of the gunshot that saved me from the void.

Twenty-one miles. Ava keeps shouting out the new distance every few hours, trying to give me something to walk toward. Trying to make me believe she still knows where we're going.

Lost in fear, we were too shaken to remember our rucksacks. By the time we realized our error, it was too late to go back. Too dangerous. Now we have no map. No compass. Only the highways and farm roads to orient us and lend us any clues we're headed in the right vicinity. Ava studied the map every night, her tireless eyes poring over every small town, neighborhood, and scrap of terrain. I wonder if she's recreated the map in her mind. If she sees our precise position and imagines we're tracking the exact inked line Father drew for us to follow all the way up to the edge of Texas in Dalhart. Or did she just look up at the night sky, turn her body northwest, and hope all roads really do lead to Rome?

Ava walks a good fifty yards ahead of me, Lucía by her side. It started off as ten yards, but mile after mile I've let the distance grow, wanting to be alone, wanting to be free of someone listening for my every breath, watching my every move. Ava turns her head to check on me again.

Yes, I'm still here. I stop and wipe the dirt from my eyes and let another yard extend between us. I don't know why this protective gesture annoys me so much—she almost lost me, and I almost lost everything. But it does.

Ava's gaze shifts to the bulge now unmistakably visible beneath Lucía's linen jacket. She pulls down the soaked cloth she cut from the ends of her shirt to protect her face from the grass and sand and addresses Lucía. The howling wind carries her words to me.

"Nunca he visto a un civil con una pistola." *I've never seen a civilian with a gun.*

Her voice is weak. I hear the strain. See the exhaustion in her hunched body. In her short and heavy steps.

"De donde vine yo, no se puede sobrevivir sin ella," Lucía responds. *You don't survive where I'm from without one.* She drapes her soiled scarf over her shoulders, maneuvering the frayed ends to blanket her secret weapon.

"¿Usaste tu última bala?" *Did you use your last bullet?*

124

The wind brings me nothing more except its own violent shrieks. *Yes*, the wind screams for her, *she used her last one.*

I hug my body and take five sizable steps forward, narrowing the distance. Ava turns her head, checking on me once more.

Still here.

I can feel the sun now.

My numbness has thawed. Sweat leaks from my every pore, my insides seeping dry. The thirst is so bad, I keep reaching for the water bottle that I know isn't there, like a ghost limb. My head aches. The relentless wind twists and whirls and spins my brain. I squint my eyes and my lips crack. I see a thousand windmills far on the horizon. Or is it an army of soldiers come to watch us melt away in this immeasurable wasteland?

"Nine more miles!" a voice shouts back to me.

I shake my head and focus my parched eyes. Two figures walk before me, miles and miles between us.

My sister. She's so far away. She's an extension of me. Half of me. And she's so far away.

I reach out my arm for her and become distracted by the dancing numbers on my wristwatch. The watch's hands twirl and swivel, disorienting me, and I stretch out my fingers to catch the maddening arrows when suddenly they stop, revealing the time.

1:35 p.m.

A rush of clarity. The hottest time of day is still ahead.

I stumble on.

It's better than what's behind.

I'm running on autopilot.

I blink and somehow find myself walking beside Ava, Lucía on my other side. Our ragged breaths and the steady tread of our mechanical slog are the only sounds left on this earth.

We stop in unison when we see it—a stone ranch house, small in the distance. I blink again, ensuring it's not a mirage.

"This has to be it," Ava rasps. She puts her hands on her knees and tries to clear her throat. "West of Route 385, north of Ranch Road 767. We passed both," she barely manages to finish.

"You should sit . . ." I wheeze into my sister's ear, placing my hand on her shoulder.

She jerks from my touch like fire licked her skin and looks up at me, instantly forcing images of last night's torment to reflect in both our eyes. Lucía steps forward, saving us from having to talk. To acknowledge what happened.

"¿Crees que es la casa segura?" *You believe this is the safe house?*

I turn my gaze back to the stone homestead. Still there. It shimmers in the scorching air.

It could disappear at any moment.

Ava rises, her nod of assurance nearly imperceptible. I watch her scan the large property guarded ominously by high barbed-wire fencing and warning signs. Leery, Lucía surveys the land with a hunter's eyes, searching for a target. *You don't have any more bullets. We're the prey,* I want to remind her. But if I talk, I will fall.

She seems to hear me.

"¿Cómo podemos estar seguras?" she asks. How *can we be certain?*

Her body teeters dangerously, and I know her fixation on this assumed refuge is the only thing keeping her upright. Ava gives Lucía a look before setting off to meet what might merely be an illusion on the horizon.

"Nunca podemos estar seguras," I interpret Ava's expression aloud. *Nothing ever is.*

As we walk closer, I discern a row of crumbling limestone buildings neighboring the main residence. Fractured deer antlers are mounted above several doors that appear sealed shut from sand and time. This must have been a hunters' lodge in the ranch's past life.

There's no one in sight.

Ava keeps her eyes right, Lucía fixes hers dead center, and I watch the left. A few yards beyond the fence, I spot a water-pumping windmill working hard above a well. The multiple blades catch the strong wind just like the sails on a boat, sending the wheel into a dizzying eternal spin. There's a meter near the base of the well that monitors ground-water withdrawals. Surely no water pushes through these pumps. The source of this well, undoubtedly the Ogallala Aquifer, has been sucked dry for years. But I'm tempted to see. Tempted to unscrew that well cap and dive headfirst into its concrete tube. To dig and scratch until I unearth the treasured aquifer itself.

It's the smell that stops me. A pungent, musky odor blended with the sharp scent of dung, blown to us from the house by the sudden shift of wind.

Animals.

Massive holding pens line the gravel path leading up to the main residence. Cattle? Sheep? Horses? I can't tell from this distance, but all three seem unlikely to survive in these hellish conditions, out in the center of nowhere.

We keep our line and inch deeper onto the grounds. We move slowly, but I feel my heart racing. There are a hundred yards of gravel road before us. I hold my eyes open and slap my sunburnt cheeks, willing myself to concentrate and fully awaken from my muddled haze.

As we draw closer to the pens, a distinctive curry-like smell hits my nostrils, overwhelming my senses. When I peer through the metal bars, I think the sun must be deceiving me again. I swear I see a mob of furry creatures hopping languidly on two legs. Or is it three legs?

Kangaroos.

The acre-wide fencing that borders either side of our pathway houses at least fifty or sixty of the massive brown and gray creatures. Most rest in shallow holes dug alongside the shadowed edges. The two nearest me lick their front paws and rub the moisture onto their pale chests in what I can only guess is some sort of cooling technique.

The rocks crush and grind beneath our feet, openly announcing our arrival. The kangaroos are taking increasing notice of our presence, several disgruntled ears twitching at the sound of our intrusive approach. I turn my gaze to the house but find all doors and windows closed and empty. Cold sweat slides down my body. I know eyes are on me somewhere close by.

"A man," Ava whispers.

I snap my head right and spot a lone figure standing among the kangaroos. Stained denim covers his six-foot frame from wrist to ankle, disrupted only by an oversized silver buckle dividing his thickset waist. His feet sport worn leather boots with rounded tips, and his head is crowned with a spotless western hat as white as the clouds that never seem to form above this roasted piece of land.

A living, breathing cowboy.

He tilts back his wide brim, revealing his weathered eyes. Yards stretch between us, but his message still reaches me. So loud and clear I can almost hear his thoughts shout above the shrieking wind: *Get out.*

I hesitate, but Lucía pulls me forward. "No tenemos miedo." *We show no fear.*

The cowboy walks relaxed and unhurried to a gate near the end of the holding pen, his gaze never leaving our pathetic party. Filthy and possessionless, we must look like nothing more than beggars. Ava lifts a feeble hand to the man, a greeting the cowboy does not return. Instead he pushes down his hat, blocking his face, and shuts the gate behind him with a deliberate bang. Several kangaroos slam against the fence, causing the three of us to jump. A male who's been stalking our path punches and kicks the metal barrier, a number of his lethal jabs making it through the bars, nearly striking my head.

No fear.

We huddle close and continue our laborious quest forward as the man moves onto the gravel road. He stops a few feet from his front porch, turns, and holds out a commanding hand: we've come close enough. His massive palm is calloused and red, and I note how easily it could wrap around my throat.

"Those signs said this here is private property," he growls, his voice every bit as threatening as his appearance.

Barely able to raise her head, Ava clears her throat and pushes out a plea just above a whisper. "We were sent here . . . We were told this is a safe house . . ." Her voice trails off and I wonder if he heard the last few important words.

I lock eyes with the man and conjure up my last fighting vigor. "Safe house!" is all I manage to shout before my voice vanishes with my strength. My body sways and my vision blurs.

The cowboy tips back his hat, and I see a dark warning in his glare as his eyes study each of us in turn. He locks his thumbs around his buckle, emphasizing a giant knife sheathed at his waist.

"You three better leave this property. Now."

My knees give, my will breaks, and I drop to the ground with a resounding thud. The grit and sand fly up around me, and I hear the shrill scraping of the kangaroo's talons ripping at his cage to my left.

I, too, will be inside a cage soon. Death or capture. The only two things that await us. I'll be trapped inside a box either way.

Lucía looks back at the endless inferno. "No puedo volver. No puedo . . ." *I can't go back. I can't . . .*

Ava turns to me, and her eyes find mine through the dust and despair. A light of conviction still burns in her eyes. It's dim and fading, but the flicker is there. She straightens her weakened frame and takes a step toward the man, who moves to unsheathe his knife. Ava continues to advance, nothing left to lose.

"Resist much, obey little. Once unquestioning obedience, once fully enslaved. Once fully enslaved, no nation, state, city, of this earth, ever afterward resumes its liberty."

The man stares at Ava in uncomprehending silence. Lucía stops breathing beside me, and even the kangaroo ceases his incessant rattling.

The wind shifts, and suddenly the cowboy smiles. He lets loose a deep belly laugh that transforms his entire demeanor into a genial host greeting long-awaited guests.

"Well, I'll be damned."

"Stay below ground," Kipling tells us from the top of the steel ladder.

The rusty hinges squeal as he lowers the ceiling door and seals us inside an unlit passageway. Immediately I'm thrown back into our own hidden tunnel in Dallas. The memory pierces my heart as the lights abruptly flick on and I see a gloomy concrete path that once led me to my home.

"If the lights start flashin' red, don't even breathe. The Guard sniffs 'round here every coupla months." Kipling's voice echoes above me, pulling me from the past.

I descend the final four rungs and fall in line behind Ava. Her faraway gaze on the passageway's smooth walls tells me she sees the phantoms too.

"I think my stinkers throw 'em off," he says as he reaches the ground and turns from the fixed ladder. He points up to the muted thumping of kangaroos hopping above our underground roof. "My male western 'roos."

He chuckles amiably and squeezes past me to get to the head of the line. "Sorry about that sour welcome, thought ya'll mighta been spies. Can't be too careful nowadays."

Lucía presses tight against the wall as he moves in front of her, shielding her eyes from him with her ragged scarf. Kipling readjusts his hat, and the clicks of his boots guide our travel-weary train down the narrow tunnel. Lucía has not spoken a word to him, guarding who she is with silence. She holds her rosary firmly by her side, pushing forward bead after bead with quick fingers, counting her prayers with blistering speed.

I peer up at my sister's face protected beneath her hoodie. I wonder if Kipling knows who we are. Maybe cowboys don't frequent the Internet or stay current with news from the outside world. If he does know, he's being coy. He's given no indication he's put two and two together and has added up what Ava and I are. Twins. A life sentence in a prison farm.

A few steps ahead, a wall sconce illuminates an oval door painted in the same bright yellow as the safe house in Amarillo. Kipling pulls out a set of identical gold keys from his jeans pocket and expertly selects one. He turns the key inside the lock and shoulders open the heavy door with a forceful shove.

There are shadowy figures everywhere. Huddled around wooden tables eating jerky, resting on metal cots with no mattresses, crowded in every corner dealing cards or swapping hushed stories. The vast room is poorly lit, relying on a single bulb that hangs precariously from the high ceiling, obscuring their faces from me. But I can feel their collective energy as Kipling leads us farther into the room.

Fear and uncertainty smother the very air of this space, making it difficult for me to breathe. But as I stumble on, my eyes adjusting to the blackness of the poorly lit room, I catch a glimpse of the faces packed against the wall. There's a restrained hopefulness, a quiet determination, set on every feature of every individual we pass. An unmistakable courage that mirrors Lucía's and tells me as plain as day who these people are.

Gluts. Those from beyond our unwelcoming shores and beyond our unconquerable borders. Maybe even hidden multiples.

At first I hear only faintly accented English and the familiar Spanish, but as we move deeper into the claustrophobic room, I hear fragments of French, Mandarin, Russian or a similar Slavic language, and another guttural dialect I cannot begin to identify. The whole world is in this room. Or as much of the world as I'm ever going to see.

My old self would yearn to find a friendly face, my curiosity barely containable, and ask them to share everything there is to know about their culture and the land they left behind. But as our guide stops near a table beside a row of cabinets, I keep my eyes low to respect their privacy, and lower my hood to respect mine.

My gaze lands on the feet of the table's occupants beside us. Their shoes are caked with dirt, ripped and tattered, soles worn down so thin they might as well be barefoot. I imagine how far these people must have come. How much they must have *over*come.

Kipling's keys rattle as he twists the lock of a dented steel cabinet. He grabs a generous handful of jerky and hands it to Ava.

"Folks really can't tell the difference from a cow and a kangaroo. Not with the way I make 'em."

My mouth waters from the smell of the salt, and my empty stomach clenches with hunger. Ava passes me ten pieces of the dried meat, and I struggle not to immediately shove every crumb into my mouth. I pocket all but one. We must preserve our food. It needs to last us until Denver, a journey that could take weeks in our weakened condition. Kipling offered us water from his own rations before we came underground and offers us more now. Two bottles of water each.

"Thank you, sir," I say, humbled by such straightforward compassion.

"Sir nothin'," the cowboy says as he closes the cabinet and turns the lock. "The name's Kipling."

He claps Ava amiably on the shoulder. She shrinks from his touch but hides the involuntary reflex with a smile that doesn't quite reach her eyes.

"Get some rest. I'll come back in the evenin'." His mouth stretches into a wide, beaming grin, shining into the gloom. "Got somethin' to show ya'll."

With a tip of his hat, he nods farewell. I turn to hand Lucía her water when I realize that she's gone.

"She's over there," Ava says, pointing to the orderly cluster of cots and mattresses near the far wall. I start to follow her, but Ava holds out a hand to stop me. "Wait."

My temper flares. "No one will see my face. It's fine," I whisper hotly, pushing aside her hand.

As I make my way through the room, dropping my head to avoid all the eyes, Lucía approaches a sturdy woman leaning against the wall beside an open cot, her strong arms wrapped protectively around the swell of her belly. I wonder how this woman came to be in this basement. Did she make it over our Big Fence after fleeing an ill-fated land, or is she here to hide an illegal pregnancy with twins or even triplets? I wonder how long she'll last.

Not long, I suspect. No one ever does.

My focus returns to Lucía as she murmurs something to the woman. The woman shakes her head, and Lucía stumbles forward to a man on the next cot, repeating her two-word appeal. He looks upon Lucía with pity, bowing his head in silence.

"Rocío? Nicolás?" I hear her high-pitched plea as she drags herself from person to person. "Rocío? Nicolás?" she shouts over and over.

For every face she scans and passes, her body seems to bend and sink under the heaviness of her mounting anguish.

"Rocío! Nicolás!"

She meets a steady wave of shaking heads. Her legs buckle. She stoops so low that I fear the weight of her despair will sink her deeper and deeper beneath the ground until her voice grows hoarse and there's no one left to listen.

She reaches the end of the line and staggers backward, crashing into Kipling. He catches her, and she looks up at the cowboy with a faith that keeps her trembling body vertical.

"Por favor. Busco a mi madre Rocío y a mi hermano Nicolás." *Please. I'm looking for my mother, Rocío, and my brother, Nicolás.*

Kipling holds a thick notebook that must contain the names of every individual who has sought shelter within these walls.

"Deben estar aquí. Tienen que estar aquí," Lucía says. *They should be here. They must be here.*

Kipling flips through his records, scrutinizing every line until he comes to the last page. "Lo siento," he says. *I'm sorry.* He removes his hat and places it over his heart.

"Puedes quedarte aquí y esperarlos todo el tiempo que necesites." *You can stay here and wait for them as long as you need. We'll get you fixed up in the meantime.* With a tip of his hat, he takes his leave, knowing he can do nothing more.

Ava and I watch from the center of the room as Lucía's rosary slides from her wrist onto the floor. She falls with it, collapsing to the ground, and I run to her, scared she'll slip through the concrete.

Lucía looks up at me with tearless eyes. *She's already been drained dry.* I stand immobilized, shamed at my inability to provide any aid or comfort to the friend who has given so much to me. My shame heightens to guilt as I feel Ava's presence move beside me. I still have her. She still has me.

"Encontraras a tu familia," Ava tells Lucía softly. *You will find your family.* Her words are empty solace, but her conviction makes them sound like a promise.

I hold out my hand, Ava holds out hers, and with our remaining strength, we help Lucía to her feet. The three of us stand there, unsteady and unsure where to go inside this crowded basement. A few shadowy strangers break away from the darkened corners to lead us to a row of vacant mattresses on the floor. They offer us their blankets, their smiles, their warmth.

Roth calls these people parasites. If they are parasites, then Lucía is a parasite. Then I'm a parasite.

Roth is the bloodsucker. Not us.

My watch tells me it's 4:30 p.m. It feels like midnight down here. I close my eyes again, hoping to trick my body into thinking it's on a normal sleep cycle, when the oval door shrieks open.

In walks Kipling, two stuffed rucksacks swinging from each hand. He stops in front of Ava and me and offers us each a bag.

"We have nothing to give you for these supplies," Ava says, covering the fresh bandage that hides her microchipless wrist. Our old way of payment, gone.

"Already paid for," Kipling answers simply.

Ava and I lock eyes. *Father.* He must have foreseen we'd find trouble along the way.

I unzip the front pocket and find a small bag of cosmetics—*good*—and a sharp pocketknife, the handle wrapped in the steel rings of a knuckle duster. *Even better.*

"If ya'll wanna say yer good-byes and prepare for departure . . ." Kipling says with a tip of his hat. He circles the small room, checking on travelers, and returns to the open door, where a short line has formed. The shaded outlines of men and women shoulder their packs, concealing weapons and maps beneath worn-out clothes. Kipling shakes their hands and issues soft wishes of smooth travels on the road to their next safe house. *Where? Oklahoma City? Kansas? Denver?*

I turn to Lucía. She pores over a map of Texas beside Ava, who grips her own, their fingers tracing routes and cities where Lucía's family could be waiting. Wichita Falls, Abilene, Lubbock.

Finally, they each fold their paper guides and put them safely away. We hover with awkward gestures, not sure how to say good-bye. We wish each other luck. I pull Lucía in and hug her. An ordinary human act I've never done with anyone outside my family. I could never get too close.

"Come with us," I hear myself asking her. She shakes her head. Of course not. She has her own journey.

"Recuerda. No tenemos miedo," Lucía says to me. *Remember. We show no fear.*

AVA

When I first laid eyes on Dorothy, Kipling's ill-favored baby-blue pickup truck, I couldn't help but feel a pang of admiration. The rusty old thing looks like it's been blessed with the luck of a cat clinging to its nine lives. Various pieces—the solar-paneled roof, doors, truck bed, everything—clearly originate from different sources. The truck's been torn apart by God knows what and welded back together so many times, yet somehow she still continues to purr as she carries us valiantly across the Texas desert.

I wish I could put myself back together so easily.

A hot rush of panic suddenly threatens to take over my body. Wedged tight in the single cab seat between Mira and Kipling, I squeeze my knees together and count the insects that hurtle to their death against the windshield. Five . . . eight . . . ten . . .

I remember the symptoms of an oncoming panic attack from my studies at school. Sweating, chest pain, heart palpitations, nausea, and shortness of breath can all mimic a heart attack. I try to take deep calming breaths, but I can't. It's like those hostile hands are trapped inside my lungs, suffocating me. I'm overwhelmed with the fear I'll never be able to breathe without the touch of those calloused hands again.

A dead man's hands.

Sixteen . . . twenty . . .

I turn my focus away from the suicidal bugs when Kipling begins to softly sing aloud. His voice is full of heartache and twang and works as a balm against my secret red-hot wounds.

> *Look at our photograph of 'en,*
>
> *the one from the night we firs' became lovers.*
>
> *Keep it in the pocket 'gainst yer chest,*
>
> *so it can seep into yer wounded heart.*
>
> *Lemme dance there from time t' time,*
>
> *'cause I still remember how nothin' mattered*
>
> *when you had yer arms wrapped round me.*
>
> *I promise t' make it a slow one.*

Underneath his worn ten-gallon hat and rugged exterior, a playful smile tugs at Kipling's eyes, like he can see something in the distance that is hidden from me.

"Where exactly are you taking us?" I ask.

Mira shifts her gaze from the barren desert floor that races past the window to the maverick cowboy at the wheel. I note how much only three days on the road have hardened her. All the innate softness in her nature is now buried somewhere deep inside or gone forever.

Kipling lifts his right shoulder in a shrug, and his smile spreads from his eyes to his lips.

"Well, it ain't exactly on a map."

Mira and I exchange a sidelong glance just as the shabby truck veers wildly off road and into the open desert, our bodies slamming hard into the passenger window.

"That's why you wear your seat belts," Kipling says, chuckling to himself.

I wish I shared his humor.

All at once the flat land drops into a massive canyon, and my mouth falls open in wonder.

Wind, water, and time have painted perfect layers of red, white, and soft pinks into the ancient rock. The sheer canyon walls plummet hundreds of feet to the valley floor, dazzling me with nature's vitality. There's green in every hue imaginable: forest green in the scale-like leaves of the juniper trees, patches of kelly-green grass, pure jade in some species of subshrub, and the surprisingly bright emerald green of the familiar prickly pear cactus.

I'm drawn away from the picturesque view when Kipling stops the truck. He steps out and invites Mira and me to follow him.

"It's a bit of a hike, but somethin' tells me ya'll are used to walkin'."

We trek for a mile before I spot a curious rock formation ahead. A tall, thin rock shaped like a steeple juts out from the ground with a larger, heavier rock balanced on top.

"Fascinating, ain't it? They're called hoodoos," Kipling explains. He turns to point out the toadstool-shaped arrangement to Mira.

She nods but doesn't engage in conversation. She just keeps walking and I walk with her, never letting her get too far away from me. But Kipling isn't following, and I turn to see him standing in front of the dark mouth of a cave.

The hoodoo is a marker.

I didn't see it before, a trick of the eye with shadows or angles, but now that it's been revealed to me, the elusive entrance is clear and unmistakable.

Kipling beckons to us before disappearing into the veil of darkness. Mira and I cautiously follow, inching our way into the opening.

Four steps in, pitch black fills my vision. The sun—only minutes ago a nuisance—cannot reach its light this far into the cliffside chamber. I sense open space surrounding me and detect the scents of sweat and musty, damp earth.

And *rubber*?

Work lamps turn on in unison throughout the cave, revealing the mystery: automobiles.

Mira and I each release a small, breathy noise of astonishment. Half a dozen different makes and models, some of which appear to be barely more than scrap metal, but others look like highly valuable vintage cars. It's as if we've stumbled into a version of King Tut's tomb.

"Where did all of these come from?" I murmur, keeping my voice low in fear I'll unleash the mummy's curse.

"I build 'em. With no horses, a cowboy has to have somethin' to ride." He winks good-naturedly and leads us to the back of the cave.

I spare a glance at the rocks that hang like sharp brown icicles from the ceiling and motion Mira ahead of me, lost in speculation. How does a man in the middle of the desert have all these cars? Especially the foreign models. Even if he did build them himself, where was he able to acquire such rare overseas parts? I carefully eye the cowboy walking in front of me, his stride sure and cheerful.

Kipling must be a dealer on the black market. Maybe the names on Father's map are all part of some interconnected underground network, and they sell illegal goods to fund their interests, interests that I'd bet include more than just smuggling people across the States. Was Father somehow involved with this group, or did he simply know this network could lead us to safety?

Whatever the answers, Mira and I are a part of it now—whatever *it* is.

Kipling pauses next to an object draped in white linen and motions us closer. He dramatically pulls back the sheet to reveal a perfectly restored Triumph motorcycle, the name emblazoned with pride underneath the silver handlebars. My eyes rake over the bike's sleek black frame in appreciation. He's converted the gas engine into an electric motor, there's a sturdy headlamp attached to the front, and the seat looks like it's been extended to perfectly fit two small bodies.

Mira's and mine.

"I've been waitin' for ya'll," Kipling says. "My momma waited too. Had it down in my station notes for years that two girls might be comin' my way." His hand glides through the air like he's performing a verse of poetry. "They will speak the words of Whitman."

He settles his hand on his ornate belt buckle and stares at us for a long moment before he speaks again.

"I never thought ya'll would ever come."

From the corner of my eye, I see Mira turn away, avoiding his stare. "The bike's been paid for too?" she asks.

Kipling nods and moves to wheel the bike forward, excited to show it off. "Ya'll must be somethin' special. This beauty cost a pretty penny."

"We're just trying to make our way through like everyone else," Mira responds promptly.

"It ain't none of my business," Kipling says. He lifts the kickstand shaped like a bird's wing with his foot. "It *is* my business now to teach ya'll how to ride."

Mira's arms wrapped around my waist, I curl my hands tight around the motorcycle's grips, my fingertips pushing against the steel throttle, increasing our speed.

It's a thrill to race completely exposed through the elements, to feel the power of the wind tearing at my body, the earth rushing past me in a terrific blur. I feel like a bird flying through the endless, open sky.

"What are ya'll gonna name her?" Kipling asked after our riding lessons on the canyon floor. He told us it's tradition for every vehicle to have a name and that it has to mean something.

"Lucía," Mira said immediately.

I smile at the memory and at the idea that Lucía is helping us speed across the desert toward the last stop on a map that exists safely inside my mind.

The hostile hands loosen their grasp on my lungs, allowing me to breathe a little easier.

Somewhere outside Boise City, Oklahoma, dusk settles around the vast, untouched countryside.

I turn on the bike's headlamp, our beacon of light as we rip across a desolate back road. We haven't seen another soul in over fifty miles, and I wonder when's the last time a human eye has actually looked on these remote lands outside the view of a drone's camera.

This leg of our journey—from the cave where we said good-bye to Kipling to Denver—will take less than six hours. It took us an exhausting three days and two sleepless nights to make it from our home in Dallas to Dalhart. It's maddening how much simpler travel is with a vehicle. I think Mira actually *was* going mad from our foot odyssey through the desert.

My sister's muffled shouts penetrate my helmet, stopping my musings. "The trees have changed! We must be in Colorado."

She points to the forest of pine trees whipping past us on our left. Turning my head, I realize how stiff my shoulders and lower back have become. *Make sure to take breaks and stretch. If you push too hard, fatigue will just slow ya'll down,* Kipling warned in his old-fashioned twang.

I carefully steer the bike off road, and Mira and I switch places. It's her turn for the driver's seat—I've driven double Kipling's recommended time. Clasping my hands together, I reach into the sky to stretch the muscles between my shoulder blades before I saddle up behind her.

"Remember to lean in to the corners," I remind her, receiving an irritated scowl in response.

An hour later a full moon shines bright above. Its bluish light allows me to scan the night for any new dangers, but I find only the trees taking note of our passage.

Mira steers in a zigzag, avoiding potholes on the unkempt pavement. My stomach clenches with the twisting motions, and I focus on the back of Mira's neck to calm the nettlesome motion sickness, keeping my head still.

"The charge is running low," Mira shouts into the wind.

Even in the dark, I can make out the Rocky Mountains miles ahead on the horizon. We'll be in Denver soon—the charge will last.

Somewhere close to the metropolis, we see another pair of transients walking down the middle of the road, tired shoulders hunched. With their entire lives strapped to their backs, their pace is slow and arduous. As Mira zooms past the couple, careful to keep a wide berth to avoid a collision, the man drops his left arm at a low angle, two fingers extended toward the pavement. A greeting, a passing connection, between fellow travelers. I extend my own arm in acknowledgment and catch a glimpse of the road-weary wanderers in the rearview mirror.

That is not our fate, I tell myself. We are not racing aimlessly down a road with no final destination. Father is leading us to Denver for a reason. The last safe house on the map will be our answer. Our discovery. We will not always have to keep running. And hiding.

And hurting.

Denver will be the end, and maybe the final name on Father's map will help make it all stop.

MIRA

Beep. Beep! Beep! The motorcycle lags, then altogether dies.

"Battery's dead," I shout behind me. The bike keels over, and Ava and I catch its weight with our legs.

"Let's drag it from the road," Ava says, pulling off her helmet.

The headlight shuts off, and the world around us goes black. I'm surprised how unsettled I feel. Surprised by how the steady beam of light made me feel safe. To have it taken from me is unexpectedly jarring. It shakes my confidence, enticing me to keep my helmet on until we find another light.

Ava slides off the back of the bike, but I remain seated, twisting my hands on the sticky black grips of the handlebars.

"We'll come back for it," Ava says, sensing my hesitancy. Kipling didn't have an extra battery for the motorcycle, and we thought this one would last. And it would be too risky to enter a charging station, even if we both did have microchips.

I remove my helmet with a quick jerk before I can use it as my crutch, swing my leg over the leather seat, and together we push the bike toward a dense grove of aspen trees. Their white wood soars above us like nature's own skyscrapers, guiding Ava and me through their ancient colony until we find ourselves knee-deep in foliage and a quarter mile from the road.

We rest the motorcycle under a bed of leaves and overgrown weeds and use fallen branches to conceal a handlebar and mirror that poke out from the woodland floor. Ava buries our helmets inside the lush vegetation beside a ghostly aspen, its chalky bark riddled with the scars that come from living in the wild.

Bending down, I let my fingers be my eyes as I search the ground for something sharp. My hand finally wraps around a small branch with a sharpened tip, and I move back toward the white tree that guards our hard-earned valuables. I choose a spot above a blackened stub from a missing limb and mark the letter X. I wonder if we will ever find this place again.

Ava nods at our quick work and hands me a bottled water, then turns back for the road. I linger a few moments longer beside the Triumph, my eyes acclimating to the darkness.

We keep leaving things behind.

As I sit on a lopsided tree stump stretching out my right ankle, I watch Ava paint her brows with a coffee-colored powder. The lights of Denver extend for miles behind her, outshining even the brightest of stars.

"The last stop on Father's map," Ava says, turning toward the skyline.

I think of the millions of people, the thousands of cameras, and the hundreds of soldiers that wait for us inside that concrete maze. I wonder if Ava and I will be able to locate one specific woman before all those enemies are able to locate us.

Ava turns back to me, her crimson lips raised in an encouraging smile. She tosses me the small bag, and her russet eyes pop with intensity beneath her strong defined brows. There's fearlessness there. A single-minded purpose toward this one last push, one last stop on this purgatory road until we reach our terminus. And then we can rest and breathe and maybe even live.

I hold the palm-sized mirror up to my face and outline my eyes with a charcoal powder until they are rimmed and shadowed and mask me with my own intensity, like one who is ready to face battle. *War paint,* I think.

"Are you ready?" Ava asks.

I rise, throw up my hood, and narrow my eyes on the broad cityscape that dazzles the night sky as far as I can see.

"I have to be."

We blend in easily with the huddled masses that march along the congested path headed north.

Just like in Dallas, the people of Denver walk the nighttime streets cloaked beneath hats, glasses, and the ever-popular umbrellas. But unlike in the urban sprawl of my home metroplex, a constant cloud of smog does not veil this city. The clean air offers me a clear view of every skyrise for several blocks, and I see with my own eyes what I've only witnessed in videos: the first great American attempt at sustainable urbanism.

Soaring thousand-foot skyscrapers boast foliage on every terrace, like giant trunks of steel wrapped in vibrant green moss. I peer out from my umbrella canopy as we pass a block of food towers, buildings dedicated solely to feeding the citizens of Denver. Hints of massive vegetable gardens line their roofs, and the tips of immense glass terraces, stacked one hundred stories high, house acres' worth of organic crops and free-range livestock.

The familiar uproar of a bustling city pulls my focus back to the ground as the infinite flow of bicyclists and autonomous buses zip past in a blur. The crowd pushes Ava and me down the street and pulls us to a stop beside the zebra-striped lines of a crosswalk. The solar traffic light turns red, and the commanding orange hand signals all northbound pedestrians to wait. I scan the other side of the avenue and immediately spot our first objective.

"Two o'clock," I whisper in Ava's ear.

A light-rail station. I glimpse the blue-and-yellow glow of a hologram between the crush of arms, torsos, and parasol canopies. A map of downtown. A guide through the city's wilderness.

The pedestrians press tight around us, elbows sharp and business-like, jostling against Ava and me for a closer space beside the street. Ava's fingers grip the bottom of my shirt, anchoring me to her side within this swell of a hundred strangers. A few rogue walkers slip through the horde in front of me and sprint across the crosswalk just as the first wave of oncoming bicycles and autos gain speed.

I blink as a camera flashes overhead, and when I open my eyes, I see a double-decker bus nearly clip one man's legs before he reaches the safety of the sidewalk. The man seems certain his identity was protected beneath his large mirrored sunglasses, but he only makes it halfway down the pathway before a Colorado State Guard is on him, scanning his wrist.

Ava cracks the knuckle of her thumb, and I reach for my pocket, needing the reassuring touch of the warm blade.

We must remain invisible. A million eyes are on us.

Burying my nose into the high collar of my vest, I turn my focus ahead, toward the countdown of our traffic signal. Another seventy seconds.

I quell my instinct to move by keeping my eyes active. I count the surveillance cameras nearby. One camera atop each traffic light, two just behind us suspended from the first floor of an apartment tower. I glimpse at the glass windows of the building directly across from us and spy a camera stealthily placed inside the eye of an Ava Goodwin "Wanted" hologram three stories tall.

Ava's face did end up on a skyrise after all.

I squeeze my fingers around my knuckle duster and inspect the crowd once more, confident no one will look too long at my face, because no one has looked at *anyone* since we've been waiting for the light. The people surrounding us gaze only at the screens in their hands, and I fix my gaze on the rail station that is now fifteen seconds away.

But it only takes one pair of eyes to recognize us, and it takes all I have not to look back up at Ava's dark holographic eyes watching from above. I tune out the barrage of noise bouncing off the towers, keeping my ears open to just one sound. Over the blast of horns from angry vehicles, the chatter, and the screech of tires, as the eastbound light finally turns red, I hear Ava's warning whisper.

"Six o'clock. Another Guard."

I don't need to look behind me. I can feel his presence in the shift of energy. From the corner of my vision, I see him approach the pedestrian crossing to my left. The umbrellas dutifully part, providing him a pathway as he steps out into the street, ignoring the orange hand commanding him to stop.

Every ridesharing auto and bicyclist waits patiently for the Guard to complete his leisurely crossing and blatant display of authority. A few people even smile and wave as he strolls past. A man beside me spits on the ground, the thick wad of saliva landing on the toe of my boot. He mutters a curse at the Guard below his breath, so low that no one could swear they heard what he said.

Before the Guard makes it beyond the bike lane, our light turns green, and Ava and I are carried away once again by the hurried force of the herd. I tuck my chin low as we reach the walkway, and Ava turns our route east. She drives us forward, still clasping the bottom of my shirt, until we stand before the digital map of Denver.

We hang near the back of the station, mixing with those awaiting the next light-rail that's speeding toward us on the nearby tracks.

Our sharp eyes find our target quickly: Clearmoor Street.

"Twelve blocks away," Ava calculates.

My eyes linger on a Family Planning ad projected above the transit map. "One Child, One Nation" flashes below a steady rush of famous couples and their prized only child. The luxe, joyful images reach a final crescendo, closing on the president and finally the governor of Texas and his wife. Roth's claw-like fingers clutch the shoulder of his own progeny, Halton, uniformed and grand. Both parade such pomp-ous airs, my stomach turns.

The wide, glossy streets in front of me, the curve of Ava's hood beside me, the people, the cars, the buildings—everything vanishes into an unfocused haze, and all I see is Roth's face: sharp, distinct, defined, and staring straight at me.

Somewhere in the distance the warm timbre of his mechanical voice spews words like *united, future, Gala, celebration.* But his thin lips form a message meant for me alone: *It won't be long now. The game will be over soon, and you will be mine.*

I close my eyes, but his face is burned onto the back of my lids in red and gold.

Just like your father is mine. Just like the country is mine.

Ava pulls me away from the hologram, awakening me from my hypnosis.

"We're almost there," she assures me as we join the teeming pedes-trian lane heading for the center of downtown. She must have read the traces of unease still written across my face.

I relax my features into an unreadable mask, erasing all feeling and thought that does not aid in the task of getting us inside the last safe house that belongs to Rayla Cadwell.

We're almost there, I repeat to myself. This can all be over soon.

Twenty stories of modest balcony gardens and small windows sealed with metal bars rise above the tip of my sun-bleached umbrella.

"Room 8008," Ava tells me, remembering it from Father's map.

I lower my head and skim the sidewalk overrun with improvised tents and shelters made of primitive scrap materials that provide a temporary home for the swollen population of Denver's homeless. A Guard patrols the corner, one hand gripping the holster of her taser gun.

"Now," Ava says.

Casually, with a timing calculated to attract little notice, we separate ourselves from the cardboard refuge that lines the bike lane and follow a balding man in a tailored gray suit.

For nearly an hour, Ava and I have staked out Rayla's apartment building, waiting invisibly on the edge of the hodgepodge tent city for the right person to pass. Forty-nine people crossed our gaze and failed our scrutiny, but Ava has pegged this man to be a resident of the unit and the one who could finally be our way in.

We are rewarded for our patience. The man turns left into the covered entrance, swipes his wrist to unlock the building, and glides his way through the revolving glass doors. Ava and I sneak inside behind him, and before the rotation locks again, requiring another microchip scan, we push forward, slide out from the enclosure, and step into the bright and sterile lobby.

A broken security camera dangles in the low-ceilinged corner, the only disruption in the white-walled space. Vandalized surveillance. I send Ava a look of caution, but she just nods, signaling for us to close our umbrellas and keep moving.

As we trail the man to the elevator, I clench the aluminum handle of my umbrella like the hilt of a sword. I count six seconds before there's a lackluster ding and the dull single-panel door of the elevator opens.

A rowdy group of four, all twenty-somethings and drunk, spill out of the compact carriage, plowing through Ava and me before we have a chance to move aside. They race through the lobby, their laughter loud and abrasive, their youthful spirits announcing to this stale room and the world outside: *I'm untouchable. Infallible. And this joy will be everlasting.*

If only that were true.

I turn and file into the elevator, hoping a second microchip scan is not required to gain access to each individual floor. Ava and I judged an apartment tower in this area would unlikely supply such high-priced security, and a cursory glance at the mirrored walls of the carriage tells me we were once again correct.

Ava stands to the side of the man with the shiny pink scalp, our lone fellow passenger. The door closes, and the man pinches his nostrils as I wedge myself into a corner.

"Level two," he says aloud before lifting a cotton surgical mask over his nose and mouth.

"Level four," Ava says, disguising her voice beneath a flat tone.

The elevator door opens, dumps out the man, and we are alone inside the claustrophobic box, crowded with our reflections.

"Cancel level four," I tell the elevator, choosing a sonorous voice for myself. "Level eight."

There's no sensation of upward motion, but the coarse elevator chime indicates we've arrived. The door slides open to the empty eighth floor, and we move forward, shoulder to shoulder, treading lightly down the carpeted hallway.

We stop when we reach Apartment 8008. I concentrate on my slow breaths, damming the flood of doubts and expectations that threaten to overwhelm my courage. Adjusting our hoods, we step closer to the door, placing our grungy boots on the worn-out mat smeared with the fresh stains from someone else's shoes. *Someone is here.*

Ava raps firmly, twice, on the door, but there is no response. She tries again, the knuckles of her fingers striking the door seven more times, each blow louder and stronger, exposing her impatience.

Between the intervals of hammering, I hear the faint sounds of shuffling feet beyond the steel barrier. Ava hears it too.

"Hello?" Ava says, dropping her hand but keeping her fingers clenched into a fist.

"We're looking for Rayla Cadwell," I add when no one answers.

Pressing my ear against the door, I close my eyes and listen for signs of life. I hear only the strangled throbs of music vibrating the walls from the floor below and the blaring alarm rising inside me, urging us to leave.

"I know someone's in there," Ava says, her impatience heightening to intense frustration. She raises her hand to resume her knocking, but I catch her arm before her fist hits the hollow steel.

The padded footsteps have returned.

"Please, will you speak with us?" I ask whoever is on the other side.

"We were sent to this address," Ava continues. "We were told Rayla Cadwell would be here."

Ava brushes my shoulder, and I peer over in time to see a shadow cross the oval peephole. We both stand there, straining to see through the tiny fisheye lens, waiting for something to happen—the handle to turn, the door to open, a voice to answer our questions. But nothing does.

The music's rhythm somewhere underneath our feet quickens, antagonizing us to act. The flush of anger on Ava's cheeks nearly matches the stain on her crimson lips as she shoves her mouth into the thin gap that divides the door from the wall, using the last card we have to make this damn door open.

"Resist much, obey little—"

I jump when the door cracks ajar, revealing a single green eye.

"Hush!" the green eye growls.

A slender hand flecked with liver spots reaches out, seizes Ava by her sleeve, and pulls her into the apartment. I issue an unintelligible cry and jam my right boot into the entrance before the door can close.

The heavy steel smashes against my foot once, twice, three times, but on the fourth strike, my healing ankle can take no more.

Before I can stop it, my foot ignores my commands and yanks free from the torturous pressure. I'm thrown backward onto the ratty mat, and all I can do is outstretch my hands uselessly as the door slams shut in my face.

Ava

Clutter and long silver hair.

That's all I register before I'm thrown roughly into a corner and my vision blurs. I shake my head clear and find a woman—the silver hair belongs to her—securing one of the deadbolts on the door.

Bam. The door shudders. *Bam. Bam.* Mira's using her body as a battering ram to get through. I pounce on the woman and twist the lever to open the lock. Mira bursts into the room.

Without missing a beat, the woman drives the door closed and fastens two deadbolts with a grunt. She turns and zeros in on me.

"Who are you?" the woman demands as she uses her body to block Mira from me.

"Are you Rayla Cadwell?" I ask in return.

Somewhere in her sixties, with a robust, wiry frame, the hostile woman regards me with a crazed look in her eyes. I raise my empty hands, showing that I bear no weapons. We did not come to fight.

The woman lunges and yanks off the hood of my jacket, taking a handful of my hair with it. White-hot pain rips across my scalp, and her hand smothers my explosive scream.

"Who told you to say those words?" the woman shouts. "Who sent you?"

"Get off her!" Mira cries, diverting the woman's attention from me. The woman dives for my sister and pins her hard against the wall.

"Is your name Rayla Cadwell?" Mira asks. "Is this a safe house?"

"Are you wearing a recorder? Where is it?" She claws frantically at Mira's body in a mad, desperate search. "How did they find this address? Are there more of you outside? Who sent you?" she demands.

Her rough frisk uncovering nothing except more frustration, she grabs hold of Mira's shoulders and slams her into the wall.

"We're not spies!" Mira shouts.

I surge forward in an attempt to pull Mira free, but I'm thwarted immediately, the older woman knocking me back with startling strength.

"Who sent you? Who sent you? Who sent you!" Again and again Mira's back collides violently with the stained wallpaper.

I was wrong. This woman has no answers. We will find no help here.

My eyes quickly sweep the apartment for a weapon, and I dive for a half-empty bourbon decanter I locate on a littered end table.

She's here alone. Two against one. Strike a blow straight down the back of her head and she'll fall.

"Who sent you!" the crazed woman screams into Mira's face, slapping her across the cheek.

I raise my weapon, ready to strike—to make it all stop—but find myself shouting instead.

"Darren Goodwin!"

The woman goes limp as if I had actually struck her across the head. She hesitates, her long fingers hovering gently over my sister's red cheek. Peering close into Mira's eyes, the now-docile woman sees through my sister's disguise, and all the exhaustion, dirt, and grime.

"Ava?" she asks softly.

Mira shakes her head, water pooling in her eyes.

"I've played Ava my entire life . . . but my name is Mira," she reveals, pulling the heavy secret from deep inside her and throwing it into the open for the first time. Her body slides down the wall as if suddenly relieved of a great burden, and she doesn't yet know how to stand without its weight.

I feel the same weightlessness Mira feels. The same manic energy that comes from admitting an eighteen-year-old secret that could kill us both.

For the first time outside of our basement, my sister is truly known. She is Mira.

She is Ava no longer.

The woman turns her wide eyes from my sister to me.

"And you're—"

"We were instructed to come here. Why?" I demand, emphasizing my weapon still held firmly in the air.

The woman doesn't answer right away—she takes her time to ana- lyze each of our faces. *Let her see. We have nothing left to hide.* Tears begin to flow freely down her cheeks, but she doesn't move to wipe them. She just stands there, marveling at us.

"You were sent here because I am your grandmother," the woman finally says.

Mira's mouth drops open in disbelief. I slowly lower the decanter— everything happening in slow motion as if I'm outside of myself—and I see the glass slip loose from my fingers, spilling bourbon all over the white carpet.

"Lynn. You're both my daughter Lynn's?" she asks, still not able to believe it fully.

Overwhelmed, it's all I can do to nod.

"Twins. Of course you are. Of course you are," Rayla says, reaching out her arms. She pulls Mira and me into a powerful embrace, and we collapse into our grandmother's arms.

Rayla's living room is the perfect example of a well-ordered mess. Every square inch, save a narrow path that leads to the kitchen and bedroom, has something useful occupying its space. A coat hanger tree stands beside the door, its metal branches holding a dozen hats and coats that look like they each belong to an entirely different person. Clear plastic boxes, all labeled, full of every possible supply—food, blankets, tents, flashlights—line the walls, as if our grandmother is preparing for the end of the world. Thick blackout curtains prevent any streetlight from invading the apartment, but several vintage lamps give the room a warm orange glow that illuminates no hint of the modern world.

I peer around the room and find not a single trace of technology. No computer. No tablet. No holographic displays. No advancement in household appliances that a normal home boasts to make life simpler. There's an old stovetop burner and refrigerator in the kitchen and old-school light switches on the wall. I'm able to detect only archaic ways of communicating and storing information: cumbersome filing cabinets, endless amounts of journals, pens scattered atop tables, loose sheets of paper scribbled with cryptic messages. Tower upon tower of dense books soar almost level with the ceiling, color-coded bookmarkers hanging out of their pages.

In fascination, Mira runs her fingers across the cover of a weathered hardbound volume. Her fingers twitch, and it makes me glad that she must be itching to grab hold of one. A hint of the old Mira has returned. But she lets her hand drop, and with a pang I see her turn away from the books and their unexplored stories.

I browse the paper photographs fixed inside simple frames scattered throughout the room. My eyes lock on a picture of my mother displayed above the fireplace across from me, and a chill runs down my spine. Everywhere dust hangs in the air like secrets, and it's as if I've stepped inside a living museum, frozen in another time.

A teakettle goes off with an angry hiss.

I move to the edge of my seat on the worn polyester couch as Rayla emerges from the kitchen, balancing several plates and cups. She sets down the modest spread beside an open notebook, not bothering to cover the cramped, closely written pages, knowing its contents are all safely coded.

"You attempted to track Ava?" Mira asks, joining me on the couch.

She motions to our left—the entire wall is swallowed in investigative work. A large paper map of Texas dominates the center with tiny, pinned flags marking a handful of cities fanning out from Dallas, most leading south to the Island of Houston. Rope strings attached to each marker connect to a section on the wall labeled "Possible Sightings." Various printed articles chronicle the nationwide manhunt for Darren Goodwin's criminal daughter in a detailed, careful sequence. There are reports from major metropolises—Anchorage, Portland, Minneapolis, Salt Lake City, Detroit—all promoting my wanted photo, making my head spin. It's a shock to see my own name plastered across national news.

I scrutinize Rayla's meticulous web, hoping to find an update on my father's fate, but my heart sinks when I find nothing but tabloid journalism and fodder for gossipmongers.

"I've been searching for you since the moment Darren was arrested," Rayla says, turning away from her obsessive research to offer us two chipped, clean glasses filled with a mysterious blend of what seems to be herbal tea. "I never dreamed he would actually send you to me."

She motions toward the tea in an encouraging, yet commanding way. "Drink it. You both look like you haven't slept in days. I'm sure you haven't, or you would never have made it this far."

I give a small nod and raise the cup to my nose, expecting to breathe in the soothing notes of chamomile or the powerful stench of valerian root. Instead I'm met with an earthy, bitter scent that I can't identify. Taking a cautious sip, I'm suddenly aware how utterly exhausted I am.

I close my eyes, enjoying the hot liquid dance inside of me. Its tranquility moves from my throat down to my chest, settles for a time in my stomach, then spreads throughout my whole body before finally taking root in my toes. My aching shoulders sink into the lumpy cushions, but I'm jolted painfully back to attention with Mira's blunt words.

"Our father said you were dead," she says, refusing Rayla's tea.

I place my cup back onto the table. Mira stares at the woman like a wary interrogator as Rayla sits in an armless upholstered chair across from us.

"Your father was right. I am dead," she says. "Well, Rayla Cadwell is."

Lifting her hand to her rectangular face, she strokes her straight-edged nose, high cheekbones, and square jawline.

"A new face," Rayla says. "New prints." She holds up her open palm and glides her thumb along each of her fingertips.

I watch, bewildered, as my grandmother rolls up the sleeve of her shirt to reveal an elaborate snake tattoo coiled around her right wrist. Its diamond-patterned body slithers up her arm and disappears beneath her dark shirtsleeve, every other scale a faded yellow.

The old man on the rail also had a tattoo.

"A new microchip," Rayla says, drawing attention to the soft skin of her inner wrist. "Rayla Cadwell is untraceable. I'm dead to the system, reborn as Jane Wilson."

"I don't understand. How is that possible? The government—" I begin.

"The government may always be watching, but they do not always see," Rayla declares.

"Counterfeit microchips don't exist," Mira says, shaking her head in disbelief.

"Just like twins don't exist?" Rayla says.

Mira shuts her mouth, momentarily bereft of a response. Fascinated that Rayla, too, has found a way to outplay the government, I can't help but lean forward in my seat.

"Why did you go into hiding?" I ask.

"Retirement protocol for all former leaders."

Mira and I exchange perplexed glances.

Rayla tightens her lips in obvious disapproval. "Darren really kept both of you ignorant, didn't he?" she says, a sharpness edging into her voice. "Resist much, obey little. You were speaking the words of the Common."

Mira shifts in her seat next to me, her brow furrowed either in confusion at Rayla's revelations or in anger at another one of our father's secrets. I can't tell which without meeting her eyes.

"The Common? How come we've never heard the name before?" I say, choosing confusion for myself.

"The NSA, the news media, the military, the president . . . every powerful agency and official participated in the cover-up of the people's rebellion. I was only six years old, but I knew what was happening. My parent's generation watched helplessly as one constitutional right after another was taken from them—replaced with microchips, surveillance, and oppression."

"But how could the government get away with it? The people must have fought back," I say.

"Fear," Rayla answers.

Mira shifts in her seat, uneasy.

"The government used fear as its weapon—exploiting the fallout from the climate crisis to take control from its citizens," Rayla continues. "The Common rose up to overthrow the regime that was quickly turning America into a brutal militarized state—a far cry from our leader's declaration that we still remained an elected ruling body *of* the people, *by* the people."

Rayla lets out a scornful sigh and pops her knuckles to calm her impatience. The familiar gesture jars me as much as the shocking statements she's claiming. *It runs in the family,* I think with a strange thrill.

"And what happened to the Common? Where is it now?" Mira asks.

"Underground," Rayla says. "The government was successful in their unwavering determination to bury the very idea of its existence. The Common was censored across the country—news reports, the Internet, the arts. Its name has been completely wiped clean from history. People became afraid to even whisper the name aloud in their own homes, terrified of being overheard by hidden surveillance and branded outright as a traitor."

My grandmother speaks with a passionate, quiet voice, forcing me to move in closer to make sure I don't miss a single word.

"The Common remains alive only where the government could never hope to censor," she says, placing her hand over her chest. "Inside of those who still resist."

She holds no apprehension of speaking the name—I feel a sort of bold energy emanating from her every time she says the words aloud.

"Were our parents members of the Common?" I ask, drawing from her courage.

It seems outrageous that our father would involve himself with such a dangerous cause. He is—was—an important member of Governor Roth's staff and the protector of our momentous secret. The carefulness of his character would never allow it, the People's Champion or not. *But the dinner party. The journal.*

Mira and I know practically nothing about our mother, though, except for the idealistic picture our father painted. I could never bear to see the pain in his eyes when we goaded him for stories of what our mother was like outside of the happy holograms he showed to us. We eventually learned to stop asking. In grief all the little flaws of those we loved are colored over.

But I never stopped wondering about the entire portrait—the sharp edges and hidden cracks. How did she react when someone angered her?

What did she look like when she cried? When she screamed? Did she let others see her weaknesses, or did she build a wall as high as mine?

I can't see any trace of her in the face sitting across from me now, but I know Rayla must keep her daughter somewhere safe inside her heart, melded alongside her fervor for rebellion. *Share her with me.* Let me see my mother as she once was, before that fatal egg split into two.

"Your mother was on the path of becoming a valued leader. She was eager from a young age, just like I was when I joined at fifteen," Rayla says, a smile tugging at her lips for the first time.

The pulsating music from below suddenly cuts off, leaving the room in silence but for the quiet hum of the old-fashioned refrigerator in the kitchen.

"Lynn was brilliant. Unrivaled. By the time she was barely older than you are now, she was a growing influence within the Denver community, with her great sense of compassion and charm. I was convinced the cause would burn once more in the hearts of the public when it was her turn to take the helm of the movement. I knew she could give the people knowledge and courage, and under our leadership the rebellion would emerge from the shadows once more," Rayla says, a vivid pride lighting up her eyes.

Then a shadow darkens her face. "But before she was able to reach her potential, she met Darren and her focus became clouded," she says.

Rayla looks down at her hands, breaking off her speech. I'm anxious for her to continue the untold backstory of my parents, but I wait respectfully during this interlude, knowing she must be wading through heavy memories.

"And our father? What happened then?" Mira asks, pulling our grandmother back to us.

"Darren was already working on Roth's staff by then, which I of course did not approve of," Rayla continues, rolling down the sleeve of her shirt to cover her brazen tattoo. "He didn't approve of me either, to put it mildly."

She sharply sucks in a lungful of air and breathes out the rest of the story in a hurry, as if each word is a stab to her tongue that she can only withstand in one painful burst.

"They knew I would never give my consent to their union—it would never last with Darren belonging to a man like Roth. So one day, she just vanished. Out of the blue, gone. I tracked her down in Texas, found out she was with Darren in Dallas. Pregnant. I showed up at their home in Trinity Heights unannounced. But it was Darren who answered the door."

She pauses, lost in thought.

"And then what happened?" I press.

"Your father demanded I permanently cut off all communication with his new family. He said he was going to protect Lynn and their child. I thought he brainwashed her."

Rayla stares at Mira and me from across the table, and a long-sought clarity crosses into her eyes.

"All these years I could never answer the question why. But now . . . here it is." She gestures toward Mira and me. Her illegal twin granddaughters.

She closes her eyes, letting this new knowledge sink in.

Suddenly Rayla rises from her chair and stalks to the far wall, where she stops face-to-face with a photograph of my father.

"Darren must have joined the Common after the death of your mother."

"He played for both sides . . ." I say, realizing how big the game actually is.

Father smiles in his impressive ceremonial uniform—his Family Planning Division badge fastened over his right breast—enclosed in a gaudy golden frame, completely incongruous with the rest of the apartment.

"You hypocritical son of a bitch," Rayla says an inch from his face, her voice seething. "You still did Roth's bidding!"

All at once she pounces. Her anger and hurt, which must have lain dormant for years, manifests in a single punch, and Father crashes onto the carpeted floor in a spray of glass and vengeance.

Mira springs to her feet.

"Our father sacrificed himself for us!" she shouts passionately in his defense.

Rayla turns away from Father, the knuckles of her right hand cut and bleeding onto the leg of her pants.

"As he should have. As your mother did," she says evenly.

I rise from the couch, disoriented from the twists and turns of our family history, to stand next to my sister. I open my mouth, a hundred burning questions begging to be asked, but Rayla holds up her hand, stopping me. She takes a breath, gathering back into herself all that spilled emotion, and by the time she breathes out again, she has sealed herself shut.

She signals to the bedroom behind us.

"You can both sleep in my bed tonight, and there's enough water for a shower. You both stink."

She walks toward the front door.

"Where are you going?" Mira demands.

"Do not leave this apartment, and answer the door to no one."

Without another word, our grandmother slips through the front door and secures the twin locks behind her, leaving Mira and me staring blankly at the yellow door glaring back at us.

MIRA

"I know what you're thinking," Ava tells me from the other side of the steamy glass door.

"You took all the water," I say. The dented screen below the showerhead, the only piece of modern technology I've seen in this ancient apartment, reads ".25 Gallons Remaining."

"She might not be the nicest person, but nice won't keep us alive," Ava says.

The water pressure is weak and comes out in fitful spurts, but it's hot and does its job of rinsing me clean of the filth I've acquired from the long journey getting here. I watch it all spill down my shins, slide over my toes, and sink through the drain to be purified, stored, and recycled for tomorrow's shower.

If we're still here tomorrow.

"But I feel good about her, Mira," Ava continues, "and she's blood."

I don't want to talk. I just want to stand still and soak in the warm, comforting water that drizzles over my head, massaging my tired muscles and my tired mind.

In Dallas, the night before it was my turn to go up, I would bathe in our tub for what seemed like hours, allowing the transformative powers of soap and water to cleanse me until I was pink and raw, a clear canvas, restored and reenergized to confront another day in a dangerous world I had no right to be in.

I don't want to think either, I decide.

Before I can staunch my unwanted thoughts and absorb any sense of peace, the shower turns off without warning.

"Dammit!" I shout, punching the screen that flashes "Empty" in my face. The heated moisture hangs heavily in the air, concentrating above my arms and chest as if the steam were rising from my fuming temper.

"I'll see if the recycling tank's been purified yet," Ava says coolly, a formless blue blob in the cloudy vapor.

"Don't bother," I say a little too harshly, the shampoo dripping down my forehead, stinging my eyes.

I hate how vulnerable I feel standing naked inside this flimsy shower. Blindly, I reach for the towel draped over the glass enclosure and wrap the scratchy cotton tight around my frame. Tepid droplets trickle down my ears and neck from the soapy ends of my short hair, but I don't bother to mop them dry. I throw open the shower door and encounter my sister, her body cocooned in an oversized navy robe, blocking my path.

"I know you're angry with Father," she says, her damp hair the color of midnight.

Ava thinks she knows everything.

"I'm angry, too, that he kept so much from us," she continues, her hand on my bare shoulder. "But he's showing us now."

"By handing us over to some woman he never even trusted?" I shrug off her hold on me and plow through her barricade, stomping toward the sink. The mist is already lifting, evaporating slowly on the square mirror in front of me. Impatient, I swipe my palm across the glass, speeding up the process.

Ava looms over me as I unscrew the cap of a small case, pluck out one disinfected contact lens, and pull down my bottom eyelid. After several maddening attempts, I finally swivel the lens into place before Ava can ask if I need her help.

I repeat with my left eye and linger near the mirror, analyzing the effect. My eyes water and burn, but I hold them open and glare at my reflection, owning my anger, striving and failing to focus it all on me.

"We really were ignorant, weren't we?" I say.

"Stop fighting this," Ava snaps at me, moving closer to my side. "We made it. We're safe."

My gunmetal-blue eyes find hers in the foggy glass.

"We didn't make it," I say bitterly, accepting the cruel truth. "And we're never going to be safe anywhere."

The rapid convulsions of the mattress wake me with a start. The covers are ripped from my body as Ava rolls to the far end of the queen bed, monopolizing the blanket and any chance of continued sleep.

Beneath the weight of my head, my left arm tingles with pins and needles. Gradually, I slide my hand out from under the flimsy pillow and gently hang my stinging limb over the platform bedframe. I peer down at my wristwatch. 4:14 a.m. I lie motionless in the predawn quiet, gazing cross-eyed at the pockmarked ceiling until my arm awakens.

I don't remember falling asleep, but the residual potency of a forgotten nightmare tells me my slumber was restless. My jaw aches—I must have been clenching my teeth all night—and my ankle throbs from its brief time as a violently mistreated doorstop.

My composure gone, I outstretch my left arm, the blood flow returned, grab a fistful of my side of the covers, and jerk the blanket back over the exhausted lump of my body, where it belongs. I turn my back on my sister and scoot myself parallel to the edge, taking most of the covers with me.

Ava jolts awake. After an extended silence, no doubt searching the room in a panicked alarm, she discovers the disturbance was only me, and plops her head back down on her pillow with an annoyed sigh. *Good.*

The door suddenly flies open, and I squint at the harsh intrusion of light.

"Get dressed," Rayla's silhouette tells us from the doorway. "We're leaving."

She tosses a plastic box on the floor near the foot of the bed. New clothes for a new journey, I assume.

Obediently, Ava rises to her elbows and sits up against the mahogany headboard.

"Where are we going?" I ask, remaining exactly where I lie.

"I have tea waiting for you in the living room," Rayla says. She turns and disappears, leaving the door open behind her.

Lamps from the adjacent room highlight the container. Secondhand shirts and pants spill out its sides, every piece of clothing colored white, beige, or gray. The mattress dips as Ava pushes off the bed and switches on the overhead light. Squatting, she rummages through the pile and digs up a clean pair of khaki pants, shapeless and forgettable.

Where is this woman taking us? This city, this apartment, this room is as promising a hideout as any other likely sanctuary. And staying in this queen bed is a hell of a lot more agreeable than the prospect of returning to life out on the perilous road, with its high probability of once again traversing innumerable miles by the waning power of our own two feet.

I stir from these thoughts and notice Ava is fully dressed and glowering at me beside the door. My reluctance transparent, I hurl the sheets to the ground and move irritably to the box of clothes.

She hovers over me as I crouch to the floor and throw the first shirt I see over my head. I feel her scrutinizing me, judging every choice I make. I pluck a pair of ripped jeans that I know she will hate and try to block her from my sight, flattening my scraggly bangs over my brows, the ends dusting the tips of my lashes. But I still see her through the strands. Kneeling beside me, she reaches out a tentative hand and brushes back my blonde bangs for a clear view of my eyes.

"When I looked at you, I used to see me." Her voice sounds wistful and homesick. "My reflection."

She pauses, as if expecting me to look up. I don't. I can't. She needs to let go. We both do.

"Now I don't know what I see," she whispers.

I lift my eyes and spare Ava a glance. My former mirror image.

"Isn't that a good thing?" I tell her, and turn back to my futile quest for a decent jacket.

Ava bows her head and stands, smoothing out the wrinkles in her lightweight duster.

"Yes, of course it is," she mutters, shouldering her rucksack. She detaches herself from my side and moves for the door. "I'll be in the living room if you need me," she announces, and I'm left alone, receiving my first solitary moment since the catastrophic night in Trinity Heights that feels like a hundred years ago.

A separate life, lived by someone else.

Ava stands with Rayla behind the rounded glass coffee table. They speak with hushed voices, heads together and bowed over Rayla's cupped palm.

I swing my rucksack loaded with extra scent-eliminating clothing over my back and weave my way through Rayla's organized clutter. The wool carpet mutes my approach, and I make it to the ring of furniture encircling the couch before either lifts their gaze to me.

"Mira," Ava says breathlessly, pointing to the contents in Rayla's hand. "I can't believe it."

I lean over the back of a wing chair and follow Rayla's open palm. Using a pair of microtweezers, she pinches two tiny objects the size of my fingernail, their metal gleaming in the lamplight, and rests them casually on the glass table, side by side.

Logic, common sense, and a lifetime of conditioning and deception tell me I'm seeing things. Seeing what I want to see, what I've lacked and dreamed of my entire nonexistence. But right before me, within my reach, are two counterfeit microchips. One for Ava. One for me.

Impossible.

But then again, so are we.

"How did you acquire these overnight?" I ask, moving closer, the chips' allure undeniable. "From who?"

Rayla places the tweezers on top of an instrument bag and rolls five latex finger cots over the fingertips of her left hand. Noting her left-handedness, I remember how I also favored my left hand as a child. This problem was promptly remedied, as I was made to adapt to my right and conform to Ava's development.

"We must hurry," Rayla says, beckoning to Ava. "You first."

She removes a gun-like instrument from a clear bowl filled with rubbing alcohol, then loads the sterilized microchip and seizes Ava's arm. The needle pierces the tender flesh of Ava's wrist—she barely flinches when Rayla pulls the trigger—implanting the microchip deep under Ava's skin. After disposing of the needle, Rayla turns to her instrument bag for the final touch.

Her gloved fingers reveal a portable 3D bioprinter, a clunky model I've never seen used in our university labs. Holding the printer over my sister's arm, Rayla scans a slice of Ava's healthy skin for duplication, then locks the printer onto Ava's wrist. My sister winces as a laser reopens the scar tissue from the half-healed incision she gave herself the night of our escape, and we both watch engrossed as the bioink begins to print layers of fabricated tissues over the incision, repairing Ava's damaged skin like magic and concealing any evidence of tampering or wrongdoing.

"This chip is really activated?" Ava asks, inspecting Rayla's work.

"Both microchips are in the system, linked to thousands of fake metadata records that establish you both as average students from Colorado. The NSA has no reason to monitor these chips," Rayla says firmly. "And we will give them no cause for suspicion."

She slips Ava a notecard with handwritten scribbles. "Memorize your new identification."

From the far side of the table, I make out the first four slanted, nearly illegible lines.

Name: Aeron Rowe

Age: 20

Address: 151 Euclid Avenue, Boulder, CO 80302

"Your wrist," Rayla demands of me.

"Where are you taking us?" I ask, offering her nothing until she answers.

"North," Rayla says tersely.

Half of me thinks, *That's too vague. She's keeping us ignorant.* The other half thinks, *Who cares. Take the chip.*

"Take your freedom," Rayla tells me, her eyes earnest and clear.

I notice the liver spots on Rayla's hand have multiplied and spread to her arm, just below the corkscrewed tail of her snake tattoo hidden beneath her jacket. She must paint the blemishes on as a disguise. Or use them as a subliminal message to the Guard, or anyone, that she is fragile and unthreatening. She is clearly neither.

"Will we get new features too?" I ask, unsure how I want her to answer. I touch my nose and cheeks. *Ava's nose and cheeks.*

"You'll hide from surveillance the old-fashioned way," she answers, nodding to the umbrellas.

I pull up my sleeve and present my right wrist without looking at Ava. I want this moment for myself.

With little observance to the enormity of what is happening, Rayla pricks the needle into my skin. I grit my teeth when she pulls the trigger and the microchip shoots into my wrist, embedding itself inside of me. Covering my imitation.

"Memorize your new identification," Rayla repeats and hands me my own paper notecard.

Name: Marley Townsend

Age: 19

I stop reading, focused only on the piece of metal that is now fixed beneath my skin. No one could tell by looking at my inner wrist that anything is different or special. The room is the same. The air is the same, and I'm sure the outside world is the same. But I press my thumb over the implant, and I know that it is real.

I have changed and that is everything.

AVA

We wait patiently in a short orderly line to board a massive autonomous bus, its destination sign helpfully announcing "Denver, CO to Casper, WY." Shivering in the morning light, I stand and listen to a middle-aged couple in front of me chatter excitedly to each other. They are traveling on vacation to some exclusive river lodge—their fishing poles and wildly overdone adventure outfits on full display.

I step forward after a narrow-shouldered youth scans his wrist with a loud *ping* and enters the double-decker bus. An umbrella shield safely protecting my now-infamous features, I turn my head to check on Mira three strangers behind me, tightly gripping her own surveillance screen. She looks away, feigning an interest in a nondescript building across the street.

A seed of resentment sown the previous night suddenly shoots up and flourishes inside me, heating the back of my neck and stopping my shivering. I spot Rayla furtively surveying the station at the tail end of the line before turning to face the bus. I willfully contain my emotions while the couple ahead of me scans their wrists. A double *ping* of approval indicates they may board, then it's my turn to step up to the scanning device.

Instructed by Rayla to be the first to enter, I swipe the counterfeit microchip freshly embedded in my right wrist. My face and body convey full confidence, refusing to betray my internal hesitancy. Does this foreign metal capsule inside me signify I've died and become someone new just like Rayla?

Ping. Approved.

As Aeron Rowe from Boulder, Colorado, I enter the crowded bus and quickly discover there are no open seats left on the lower level. Standing by the door, I press up against a woman's bare knees in the first row, waiting for my sister to board. A display panel on the wall across from me reveals our exact location and route, as well as seat availability. Only two rows are filled on the upper level; when Mira joins me we'll move to the top together.

A stout man squeezes past me, mumbling a terse complaint at my loitering in the narrow aisle. I shouldn't be risking attention of any kind, but I won't allow Mira out of sight even for a moment.

Rayla says we must change our clothing every day to remain inconspicuous. Enveloped in her new taupe scarf, Mira reaches the front of the line and exposes her right wrist to the scanner. My mind fires off possible scenarios that could go wrong: *the new microchip is a fake after all . . . the imitation chip she's worn in her wrist for over eighteen years somehow affected the—*

Ping. Approved.

A single twitch of excitement flicks across Mira's face before she moves into the bus, exuding complete self-confidence in utilizing public transit. She saunters past me like a stranger, headed directly for the winding staircase.

I follow my sister up the stairs and find her seated in the back row by the window. When I take the open space beside her, she places her rucksack between us and turns her body toward the tinted glass, still affecting a keen interest in the structures surrounding the downtown station.

"First stop Cheyenne, Wyoming," an automated voice rings pleasantly from the speakers. "Please sit back and enjoy your travels."

Rayla emerges from the staircase and walks down the aisle, covertly examining the passengers one by one. Satisfied the compartment is secure, she takes the seat to my left. The three of us sit together as companions—the strategy being that nothing stands out more than a young girl traveling alone.

With a tranquil *beep*, the bus rolls silently forward. Mira throws her legs onto the seat back in front of her, exhaling heavily through her nose. She leans her head against the window, her eyes focused on her feet. She pops her knuckle.

"From this distance the mountains look like one enormous tear in the atmosphere," I say, pointing to the jagged place where the Rocky Mountains appear as a rip across the clear blue sky, fooling the eye. I speak lower than a whisper, ensuring Rayla does not overhear our twinspeak.

"Maybe we're headed up to live at the peak of the tallest mountain," I say, and for all I know, we might be. We're still ignorant of Rayla's plans, the bus's destination our only clue.

"A small cabin in the Teton Range. Near Yellowstone," Mira continues the fantasy with a slight grin. *Finally.*

A hologram newscast abruptly materializes at the front of the aisle, forcing me to abandon my daydream. I jerk my head around and see my father, garbed in a prisoner's uniform, dragged out of the Dallas courthouse surrounded by a mob of frenzied journalists.

Reality makes a mockery of all our dreams.

"Dr. Darren Goodwin has been found guilty of treason," a newscaster recounts, unable to mask his exhilaration at this gripping development in Father's scandal. "Will he receive a presidential pardon or face a firing squad? You'll hear it first on United Network."

Roth's going to kill him.

The screen changes to Governor Roth standing live behind a podium in his mansion's palatial gardens. I want to close my eyes, to shield myself from the triumph etched across his smug countenance, but I keep them firmly open and watch.

"The highest court in Texas has spoken, and soon justice will be served. Until that time, we will not let the treasonous acts of one man deny our great country the right to memorialize seventy-five years of hard-earned prosperity," Roth's strong voice declares. "The Anniversary Gala will proceed as scheduled."

From the front row a man in a dark baseball cap hurls an umbrella through Roth's digital head, and it hits the wall with a loud thump.

"Enough!" the man shouts.

Immediately a surveillance camera zooms in on the protester's face, but the brim of his hat protects his features from being scanned. The elderly woman seated next to him rises, lifts her oversized purse to block her face, and heads for a new seat as far away from the marked man as she can manage.

Was the umbrella thrown in support of my father or out of pure hate for Roth? Whatever the reason, I want to stand up and lend my angry voice to his, but Rayla's grip on my leg prevents me. The man jumps from his seat and flies down the stairs two at a time.

A strangled cry followed by a loud commotion from the downstairs compartment drowns out the rest of Governor Roth's speech. Mira tenses beside me, and all my weight moves to the balls of my feet in case I need to rise quickly. Will a single man's protest attract the Guard? What if they're waiting for him at the upcoming stop?

I turn to Rayla, anxious to know our next move. She sits motionless and perfectly calm—furtively demanding we do the same.

"He's fleeing," Rayla says, lips barely moving.

Mira places her hand on the glass behind us, her fingers tracking the man's baseball cap lying in the middle of the road. He's nowhere in sight—he must have pried open the doors and fled into the trees.

A successful escape, for now. But the Guard already has irrefutable evidence of his presence on the bus—his microchip scan made sure of that. They will identify him and track him for the rest of his life. No matter where he runs.

A United Network exposé entitled "The Double Life of Darren Goodwin" replaces Governor Roth's public address. Strategically edited sequences of the disgraced Goodwin family—digitally altered events that include scantily clad women hanging on my father's arms and me indulging in a carefree drug binge—redirect the passengers' attention as the bus continues its steady progression north.

I look away from the slanderous program, tired of seeing my face, and instead see a vision of my father lined up before a firing squad, a blindfold over his eyes.

In an isolated town outside Casper, Wyoming, I exit the bus behind Mira and step into a sleepy downtown composed of a handful of outdated stone buildings lined in a neat, lonely row.

A few structures are scattered against the slope of a small mountain range, the only indication of the mining that once made this town prosper. The old mineshaft was sealed over long ago, and shiny plaques declare the site a national historic landmark.

Rayla led us to a ghost town populated by phantoms. *And to someone with sympathies for the rebellion.* Why else would we be here?

The empty bus pulls silently away, and Rayla signals for us to reopen our umbrellas.

"Keep close," she says, surprising me by turning away from the town.

She heads east toward a vast shortgrass prairie, shepherding us into what must be the edge of the Great Plains. Using her jacket to pad the sharpened steel of a barbed wire fence, Rayla beckons for Mira and me to follow.

"Father was found guilty," Mira says openly now that we're once more in remote land. "Why are we out in the middle of nowhere walking around when we should be trying to save him?"

She pushes back her bangs and takes a deep breath, trying to calm herself. I walk beside her, Rayla just ahead, forcing a quick pace.

"Are you even trying to help him?" Mira asks.

"It's important not to distract yourselves with things you cannot control," Rayla says without slowing down. "You both must focus on the task at hand."

"And what *is* the task at hand?" Mira snarls.

"Making it across this prairie," Rayla answers.

Mira bites her tongue. I feel like I should act as a moderator between the two, but I don't know how, so I remain silent, following our grandmother. I have to trust that she's leading us somewhere Father would want us to go.

Each step produces a loud crunch beneath my feet. I take in the sweeping grassland surrounding me, all yellow and withered, finding it hard to believe this land used to be a part of America's bountiful Great Plains, once boasting over thirty million acres of life-sustaining farmland.

The moment the first person planted a seed in the earth thousands of years ago—ending the hunter-gatherer way of life—the world changed forever. No one nation is to blame for the climate crisis. This outcome was inevitable.

The former Secretary of State Emma Alvarez used that poignant statement to defend the United States against the East's vehement and widely supported accusation that America was responsible for the starvation of our planet.

I glance at Mira, fists balled up tight, walking beside me.

"Are we going to another safe house?" I ask, loud enough for Rayla to hear in front of me, aiming to initiate conversation on neutral ground.

"We are," Rayla answers, unhelpfully short and to the point.

"You said you retired from the Common," Mira says.

"I did." Her brisk stride is unrelenting despite having walked for hours.

"Did you abandon the movement when our mother died?" Mira probes further.

Rayla tilts her head to the sky and looks directly at the bright sun as if to gauge the time. She continues moving, ignoring Mira's question.

Mira suddenly stops marching. I whip my head around as she closes her umbrella and leans on the hilt for support. *Is she staging a protest?*

"Keep walking, Mira," Rayla says, not glancing back, accustomed to being obeyed.

I pause four steps ahead of my sister, hovering between the two. The look on Mira's face tells me she's searching deeply for something inside herself and that she won't back down until she roots it out.

"Father would never confirm what happens to people like us . . . to multiples," she says, raising her voice to make certain she's heard. "Or what would have happened to our mother if she were caught."

Rayla's body goes rigid and she stops.

"Will you tell me?" Mira asks, looking past me straight at Rayla.

In the half second it takes for our grandmother to turn and face Mira's question, I brace myself for whatever truths she may reveal.

"Less than one percent. There's a less than one percent chance a woman's only pregnancy will result in multiples," Rayla says, lowering the full-sized umbrella that doubles as her walking stick. "Twins. The Achilles heel of the Rule of One."

Mira presses forward, drawn in by Rayla's hushed words.

"If a woman is in that unlucky percentile, she will be quickly taken away by the Family Planning Division, by men and women like your father," Rayla continues. "After she has given birth, she is denied the right to see both her newborns. The doctors swiftly and brutally tell the mother to choose."

I close the distance between my sister and me, wanting, needing, to be next to her as we finally learn the harrowing fate we were both spared.

"The mother always chooses her firstborn. They encourage this," Rayla says, a dark shadow crossing her face.

"And the second-born?" Mira demands. She locks eyes with Rayla, unflinching.

My stomach lurches and my palms break into a sweat. I turn away, focusing on the faint mountains in the distance, afraid to know the answer.

"The official lie of the Family Planning Division is that the illegal multiple goes up for adoption to infertile couples willing to spend the money . . . and not ask questions," Rayla recites the rumor Father would never authenticate. "A bullshit fantasy most Americans choose to believe because they were told to."

Rayla drives the point of her umbrella into the ground, her usually even tone now barely containing her rage.

"But those few still willing to stare the truth straight in the face know that the second-born is not given life. They become a piece of property. Owned by the government, brainwashed, raised in coastal work camps never knowing who they are. What they are. Many are sent south across the border if the mother can't pay the fine. An indisputable death sentence."

Mira's breath quickens. Her face is a hardened mask.

"All live a short, brutal existence, knowing only duty and loss," Rayla continues. "Half a person. Half-alive."

Slowly, I grab Mira's slack hand.

"How do you know all this?" I manage to ask.

"Because I was forced to choose."

I stagger, blown away by the revelation. I tighten my fingers around Mira's hand.

"Our mother . . ." My words falter.

"Was the firstborn."

"Did she know?" Mira asks.

"Yes. I told Lynn her truth in the end," our grandmother says. "To make her stay." *But it was the reason she left me,* her unspoken words linger audibly in the air.

Mira frees her hand from my grasp. She stares down at the dead grass, drifting away from me. Untethered from my sister, I watch Rayla inhale heavily and throw her umbrella back over her head.

"The task at hand," she repeats decisively and recommences our march through the grassland.

Concealed within a dried-up wheat field, Rayla and I cautiously survey a quaint, sturdy farmhouse situated fifty yards ahead. While Mira continues to study the ground, lost within her own mind, I note the small sustainable garden that hugs a shed with a yellow door, and an electric vehicle charging on a gravel driveway nearby. *Did we come for the car?*

The lace curtain in the front window stirs.

"I won't be long," Rayla says. "Stay in the field."

With a final look over her shoulder, she advances into the open lawn, leaving us under the protection of the dead wheat stalks. Body taut with unease, I watch Rayla approach the house without her weapon drawn. The screen door opens, and a middle-aged man emerges. Powerfully built and wary, he holds a sleek black baton in his hand.

My fingers curl around my new knife—Rayla told me the curved rosewood handle belonged to my mother—and I take an involuntary step forward. *We should make our presence known. Let this man realize that the woman standing on his doorstep is not alone.*

I draw back when Rayla removes her hat and displays her face to the man.

"You don't recognize an old friend?" she inquires warmly.

He moves closer, hand shielded over his eyes against the sun, but conveys no sign of recognition.

"It's been a long time, Xavier."

"Rayla?" he says, astonished, his body relaxing at once.

My grandmother nods, and suddenly she's in Xavier's arms, lifted off her feet in an affectionate embrace.

"I was hoping you would come," he says, the corners of his eyes crinkling with his brilliant smile.

I let out a breath I didn't realize I was holding and turn to see what Mira thinks about Rayla's "old friend."

But she isn't there.

Wandering through the hardened stalks, I track the top of Mira's head as it bobs through the sea of wheat. She makes a series of quick turns and disappears from my view again.

I find her squatting over the cracked dirt.

"We shouldn't separate," I tell her. "It's safer when we're together."

"I'm peeing . . . or did I need to get your permission first?"

I swallow my retort. It tastes hot and bitter and doesn't go down easy, but I refuse to let this develop into a fight. We need each other too much to be divided.

Remaining a short distance away, I pick at a tall blade of grass, and turn toward the quiet farmhouse.

"Do you want to talk about what Rayla said?" I ask.

"Nope."

But I do. My mind races. *Our grandmother was caught with twins . . . Our own mother was a twin . . . The chances of two generations in a row having identical twins are so small, so incredibly rare.*

"What can Rayla possibly be doing in there for so long?" Mira suddenly asks. She pulls up her pants in one quick motion and rises.

"We wouldn't be here if it wasn't important—"

"She's hiding information from us, like everyone always does," she answers, cutting me off. She shoulders past me.

"Mira, no! Rayla told us to wait—"

But she just charges forward.

"We want answers, so let's go and get them."

MIRA

I prowl the two-story farmhouse. I pass three sides of its cedar exterior, testing every door and window. Bolted levers and opaque glass seal its insides from me—taunting me, goading my obsession to see.

What secrets are you keeping locked within these walls? What truths are you obscuring?

Tiptoeing, jogging, possessed with the need to know, I round the final corner of the safeguarded building, past more tinted windows and unyielding cedar walls.

"Mira, there's no way in!" Ava whispers behind me.

But there, above the dark-red branches of a dogwood shrub, I spy my opening. I plunge into the leaves and press myself against a clear glass pane, searching for Rayla, the man with the baton, and my answers.

"Mira, get back here!" Ava orders, keeping her voice low. "You'll be seen!"

At first I see only the three reflections of my knife through the triple-glazed windows. Then my eyes adapt, and I realize I'm staring into an unoccupied bedroom. I spot a telescope. An unmade bed. An open door.

Ava sneaks into the foliage and stands to my right, her breathing quick and forceful like a seething wild boar that has been outrun. And overruled. Silenced, she leans her forehead against the glass and holds her hands over her brows, blocking out the glare.

"Find anything?" she finally mutters.

Through the bedroom door I make out the profiles of three figures huddled inside the living room: Rayla, the man named Xavier, and a teenager who must be his son. The glow of a hologram flickers between their heads. I piece together from the slivers of images—the steel chair legs, two ankles bound in fetters, one-way glass walls—that this footage is surveillance from a prison. An interrogation room.

Shut up, shut up! my mind tells my shaking hands. My sinking heart. My burning blood. It's not him. It can't be.

Rayla shifts her weight and rakes her fingers through her tousled hair, exposing the high-angled image of a frail man slumped over a table in the center of the barren room. His hands are lacerated and cuffed, his head bruised and shaved. His chin stoops over his chest so I can't see his face.

Look up. Look up. Look up. I have to see. I have to know.

Xavier barks out an order that I can't hear through the thick layers of glass, but I see his son raise a steady hand and use his fingers to zoom into a close-up of the prisoner. I see Rayla mouth two words over and over: "Look up. Look up. Look up."

"Look up, dammit!" Ava cries out.

The man lifts his head as if he hears her call.

His skin is pasty and sweaty. Chin patchy with a rough beard and dried vomit. Cheeks hollowed. Lips chapped and busted.

But it's my father's eyes that tell me of his torture. The way they stare blankly before him, focusing on nothing. Empty, like no one is behind them.

Father, Father. Oh God.

Bile rises up my throat, and I swallow it. Swallow the truth and what I've done.

Suddenly his sunken, bloodshot eyes snap to the surveillance camera. They begin to blink a code. The rapid fluttering of his lids lasts for six more seconds before two Texas State Guards charge into the room, stuff a bag over his thrashing head, and the footage cuts to black.

"Don't touch him!" I scream.

I smash my fist against the window over and over, trying to break the glass, oblivious to the noise I make. I will break everything to get to him.

The smart glass instantly darkens, shutting me out. Leaving me to stare only at the vague outline of my reflection next to Ava's.

"They saw us," Ava says.

Neither of us moves. We stand crippled by the reality we've tried so hard to censor.

"Mira," Ava says beside me.

I can't look at her. I can't look at me. I need to *un*know. I need to *un*see.

The smart window switches to clear again, and Xavier gapes down at us, his breath fogging the glass. His head swings like a pendulum as he looks from Ava to me. Ava to me. Ava to me. His son, golden eyes fixed on mine, walks slowly toward the window, as if approaching mythical animals. Unicorns. Bigfoot. Twins.

"Impossible," he mouths.

Once you see you can't unsee.

Rayla lingers in the background. She wants them to get a good look at us. Like we're creatures in a zoo.

I resent this. I resent her.

"Xavier, we need your car," I hear her command.

I lose feeling in my fingers. I begin to suffocate, choking on my guilt. I cover my face with my trembling palms and turn away from all the eyes.

"Don't follow me," I say to Ava, my voice shrill and distant.

I need to *un*know. I need to *un*see.

Dry heaving, I feel spit dripping down my chin as I trip my way toward the dying field, away from the house, away from the eyes, with Ava following behind.

It should be me in there, Father.

It should have been me.

"Are they going to kill him?" I ask from the backseat of the car.

"We don't know," Rayla says, her knuckles white on the steering wheel.

Ava moves restlessly in the passenger seat as if walls were closing in around her. And I sit still. Very, very still. The monotonous *pa-plunk, pa-plunk* of the four tires hurtling over potholes masks the silence. Aggravates my brooding thoughts of what's happening back in Dallas.

We're going the wrong way.

"Why can't the Common save him?" Ava asks. She pops her left thumb. Her right. "You obviously have people on the inside. They can help him escape . . ."

"Listen to me," Rayla says, her eyes never leaving the road that takes us north. "Darren is out of our reach now."

She says this like it's final. Like it's not my father. Like I'm not the reason.

We're going the wrong way.

"He's *not* out of reach!" I snap. "He's still alive!"

In one explosive motion I reach for the door and flick up the lock. Before I can pull the handle, I hear a *click*. Locked.

"Let me out of the goddamn car!" I shout, my words trembling, my head splitting, my stomach queasy from going the wrong way.

Rayla's fingers hover above the lock controls, ready for any sudden movements. "To do what? Turn yourself in? Get yourself caught? That will do nothing for him," Rayla says, her eyes still on the cavity-plagued pavement leading north.

"We're going the wrong way!" I scream with a force that tears at my vocal chords, making my eyes water. I ram my shoulder into the glass window. I will break everything to get to him.

"Mira, calm down!" Ava yells at me from the front seat.

"Calm down? Our father is going to die because of us!"

The car keeps moving, and I want to cry, howl, and scream until my voice gives out and someone finally listens, but Rayla cuts me off.

"Do you think freedom comes without a price?"

She shifts her gaze to the rearview mirror. I keep mine on the lock.

"Darren sent you both to me for a reason. The prison surveillance footage only confirmed this."

Ava stops her fidgeting. "Was our father sending us a message?" She slides off the baseball cap she's been wearing since we boarded the bus and leans over the center console, entreating Rayla to answer.

"He sent us all a message."

Rayla twists her head from the passenger seat to me, before turning back to the road.

"Revive the rebellion."

Ava whispers the three words aloud to herself—considering them, absorbing them, accepting them. She looks at me, but I refuse to digest this insanity.

"To join the Common is a death sentence for our father," I tell her. "We might as well be the ones pulling the trigger."

For a microsecond I think I'm calm. Then my body launches forward, my right shoulder shoves my sister aside, and my hands rip Rayla's arm from the wheel. The car swerves.

"What are you doing?" Ava cries as the car's lane-keeping system jolts us back onto the pitted asphalt.

I slip through the hands that fight to prevent me from doing whatever the hell it is I'm doing, flip up the lock on my door, and pry open the handle before Rayla can bolt me in again. A tornado of wind bursts into the car, and I'm hit with a chaotic blend of stinging dirt, whipping hair, and horrified shouts that seem to come from far away and all directions.

"Shut the door!"

"Stop the car!"

Master of the wheel once more, Rayla accelerates the vehicle to eighty, eighty-five, ninety miles per hour, the potholes zipping past at light speed.

"She's going to fall out!" Ava yells over the gale-force winds. She reaches out for me, her fingertips nipping at my collar and sleeves, straining to pull me from the open door and the road that can lead me south. *The only direction that connects me to my father.*

"We're going the wrong way!" I repeat, the winds drawing me closer to the blur of black pavement.

"Get back in your seat, now!" Rayla orders. "You're not leaving this car!"

I do not comply. Rayla increases our speed.

Ninety-five. One hundred.

I can't jump. But I can't abandon him.

"Stop the car!" Ava cries, her left hand clamped around my forearm, her right madly frisking the center console for the buttons that control the transmission.

"We can't just let him die!" I rasp into the violent air, battling to breathe.

Rayla stabs her finger at the dashboard, and the car lurches to a sudden stop. The tires shriek as Rayla jerks the wheel and cuts a hard right, tossing me like a ragdoll against the opposite door.

Everything falls silent and goes still. The dirt and dust settle—on my shoes, the headrests, on the umbrellas scattered across my stomach—and I'm stunned into inaction. I look out the open door, the car positioned smack in the center of the road.

Rayla twists her body and turns her eyes on me. "The cause is greater than you. It's greater than your father."

I gaze dully at the southern horizon, counting the strips of clouds stained by the setting sun.

"The United States was once the most idolized superpower in the world. Our power lay in our equality, our liberty, and our democracy of the common people," Rayla says, her quiet words emanating strength, drawing Ava even closer. "And look what we've become."

She pauses, triggering a wave of images behind my eyes. The first person I see is the homeless man from the train, then Lucía, then my mother. Or is that my mother's twin? I try to blink them away—I do not want to see any more—but then my father's ruined face appears. Blinking out his message.

"We've allowed our country to deteriorate into a military state. We've allowed ourselves to be monitored, controlled, ruled unchecked by the corrupt elite—subservient to leaders like Roth and his State Guard."

The only way of life I've ever known. Or ever will know.

"They will always have the power," Ava says. "They have the guns."

"But we have the both of you."

My father vanishes from my sight, and Rayla stares me dead in the eyes.

"Your very existence as twins is a living rebellion. Together your faces can symbolize a revolution."

Ava breathes heavily—her chest moving up and down, up and down—taking it all in.

"The US is dried up and dying. All it needs is that one spark, and change can spread like wildfire."

Rayla's face softens as she touches Ava's hand. And mine. She looks at me now not as a former rebellion leader, but as my grandmother. Or as close to that role as she can manage.

"Your father wants a better future for you both. He is a brave man."

I turn back to the road that points south—the potholes, the painted lines, the horizon all disappearing into the dusk. I feel the spotlight on me as they wait for my response.

Shoving the rucksacks and umbrellas to the floor, I crawl across the seat, and pull the door shut with an unsatisfying bang.

I hear a final sharp *click*.

Locking me in.

Ava

I can only see three feet in front of me.

Thick clouds cloak this isolated back road in darkness, shrouding what lies ahead, the harsh yellow headlights revealing the last of our journey in quick, shallow increments.

Leaning against the headrest, I angle my neck to watch Mira through the rearview mirror. She lies across the backseat, unmoving, her eyes closed, shutting me out. I pay close attention to her hands. They rest folded over her chest, laced tightly together, but at any moment I fear her fingers will twitch, restless to pull up the lock again.

A piercing light cuts through the dark, and I see a warning sign zoom past my window: "Checkpoint 1/2 Mile. Prepare to Stop."

"A checkpoint?" I cry out, horrified.

"What?" Mira shoots forward. "You said these rural roads don't have a Border Guard!" she shouts at Rayla.

Metal road barriers make it impossible for a U-turn escape. Rayla has no choice but to pull in behind a short line of cars.

"Dammit," she curses angrily under her breath.

Massive floodlights ahead illuminate a makeshift military station— dozens of Guards, a pack of canines, and surveillance cameras in every direction. *You will be caught, and you will pay for your crimes,* Roth's cold promise echoes in my mind, turning my thoughts to ice.

This trap was set for us.

Throwing my arms over my head, I duck down in the cramped space underneath the dashboard. *Oh God, it's over.* We're caught. And they're going to take Mira away from me.

"Get in the trunk."

Rayla's fiery order jolts me into action. I desperately lunge for the back of the car, but Mira doesn't move. She sits frozen as I fold down the middle seat to expose an entryway into the compact trunk. *Is she thinking of giving herself up?*

"Get in, Mira!" I plead, throwing our bags in first.

The car inches forward in line, every second bringing us closer and closer to detection by the soldiers, the cameras, or the dogs. *The canines must know my scent.*

Rayla turns to Mira, a dark look of warning in her hard eyes, and I grab hold of Mira's wrist, imploring her to move. A decision flicks across her face, and she plunges into the opening. I dive in after her and seal ourselves into claustrophobic darkness with fumbling, shaky hands.

Mira and I huddle close together in a ball, limbs overlapping, foreheads pressed together. For a moment all I hear are our fast, terrified breaths and the pounding of my sister's heart.

Then the car advances once more before it glides to a stop.

I'm able to catch the muted sounds of a soldier's heavy footsteps followed by the hum of a window rolling down.

"Why hello there, soldier!" I hear Rayla say in a cheerful voice. "I'm surprised to meet you all the way out here."

"Present your wrist," the Guard states robotically.

"Of course, of course," Rayla responds, upbeat and casual.

"Clear your face for the cameras."

"My apologies, soldier! An old woman's forgetfulness." I hear my grandmother release a pleasant chuckle. "At my age, it's amazing the things that simply vanish from your head. Poof! Gone."

An actress in her past life. *A rebellion member,* I think with sudden pride. I visualize Rayla removing her wide-brimmed fedora, a broad smile on her face, while the Guard bends his knees to peer into the empty backseat. Searching. Calculating.

Rayla continues her mindless banter, assaulting the soldier's patience, hoping he will surrender out of sheer annoyance.

"Is that a German shepherd? Oh, I just love dogs! My mother would tell me stories of how her family used to own one as a *pet.* Can you imagine that? Some absurd name like Marshmallow . . . or was it Smooches?"

A warning that a dog is approaching the car.

Tens of thousands of our dead skin cells are floating around the backseat—an invisible trail just waiting to be sniffed out. The dog is so close; the antidrone spray can't mask our scent. If he was given anything of ours to smell—the bedsheets Mira slept on or a uniform I wore—it's too late to cover our tracks now.

Mira's knee finds my stomach, and I bite the inside of my cheek to stifle a groan.

"What is the purpose of your visit to Montana?"

Get us out of here, Rayla.

"Well, it's an unfortunate one, I'm afraid," Rayla begins. "A dear friend of mine passed away. We knew each other since primary school— oh my, where does the time go? But Penny, God rest her soul, lived a good, honest life—"

"Move along," the Guard cuts Rayla off with brusque impatience.

Relief washes over me when I hear the window roll up and feel the car shift into drive.

But then a terrifying rattle of a dog leash causes me to seize hold of Mira's hand. Steeling myself, I squeeze hard, making her knuckles crack. A well-trained nose greedily inhales the exterior of the car, sniffing the tires, door handles, and bumper. A high-pitched whine signals a discovery to his master: *She's here! She's in the trunk!*

No . . . no . . . no . . . This is not *the end.*

"Turn off your engine and step out of the vehicle, immediately!" a second Guard demands aggressively.

"Is that really necessary, soldier? The heat tonight is unbear—"

An eruption of barking and shouting cuts through Rayla's words—cuts through everything—and suddenly the car rocks with furious paws scratching to get inside. After two heart-crushing blows, the trunk flies open—and the facial recognition cameras instantly recognize Ava Goodwin's wanted face. Twofold.

Sirens blast, and I struggle to see beyond the blinding spotlights. Snapping canines come into focus. Shouting Guards and a gun pointed at my sister's forehead.

Through the dense fog of shock and panic, I hear a single hostile command.

"Ava, put your hands up! Put your hands up, *now!*"

But I will never put my hands up. I will never let go of my sister's hand.

More Guards rush out of the station to surround the car.

"The system says they're both Ava Goodwin!" a confused voice shouts.

Everything and everyone combine into one babel of noise screaming in my ears: "Under arrest . . . There are two of them . . . Traitor . . . *Put your hands up!*"

Rayla presses her foot down hard on the gas. The car surges forward, and Mira's head collides painfully against mine as we are thrown toward the front of the trunk.

My vision spins, and it takes three cracking *pops* for me to recognize the soldiers have opened fire. A rain of bullets shatters the rear window in an explosion of glass.

"Get out of the trunk!" Mira yells, dragging me by my shirt collar.

There's a crashing thud as the car drives straight through the metal barrier. I cover my head and crawl behind Mira on my hands and knees—glass shards stabbing my elbows and thighs—into the backseat.

I pull the compartment entrance closed, blood dripping onto the fabric, the wailing sirens of pursuit preventing me from feeling my wounds.

"How many patrols?" Rayla shouts.

My eyes scour Mira's face, body, fingers, and feet. She's not hurt—she's okay. We both whip around and peer out the broken window. The lid of the trunk bounces out of control with each bump in the road, making it difficult to count the flashing blue lights that chase us in the distance.

Nine? Two? An entire military unit?

"Brace yourselves!" Rayla calls out in warning.

Mira and I cling to the backseat headrests, holding on for dear life, Kipling's voice chuckling absurdly in my ears, *I told you to wear your seat belts.*

With a sharp squeal from the tires, the car makes a perilous left turn, and the trunk slams shut, giving me a clear view of the pursuit.

"Five patrols!" I cry, spinning around to make certain she hears. I lean into the empty space between the two front seats, trying to rein in my rapid, frightened breaths. "What are we going to do?" I ask, unable to keep my voice from shaking.

Rayla simply tightens her fingers around the steering wheel, and I follow her stare to a cluster of lights a few miles ahead.

A small town. A possible place to hide.

"They're catching up!" Mira shouts with alarm.

She presses in beside me, anxiously searching through the windshield for drones. Our arms brush against one another, and I feel fear in her tense muscles and in the shivering of her skin. But I don't sense the curious vibrating sensation I used to feel between us—our shared field of energy. It's disappeared.

"Listen to me carefully!" Rayla says. "You both must get to Canada. There is a way through the border in Glacier County. These are the coordinates."

She gropes around in her pocket and hands me a yellowed piece of paper with a set of numbers scratched on it.

"Memorize them, then burn it."

I stare dumbstruck at the coordinates. A simple longitude and latitude that promises a way into Canada. To freedom.

She stuffs a handful of Canadian banknotes into my hands. *Paper money?* I shake my head in disbelief.

"The wall is impenetrable! There's no way through!" Mira's voice rises to hysteria, and I catch hold of her panic.

"Even if there were a way through, the border's surrounded by ground sensors. We'd be detected and shot before we could even—"

Without warning Rayla tears off the road and into a field of tall grass. She cuts off the headlights, plunging us into darkness.

"Propaganda," she says firmly. "The Canadian border is over five thousand miles long. Every fortress has its weak points and on that piece of paper is one of them."

I snap my eyes to the rearview mirror—blazing blue lights illuminate the inky black sky. The hell-bent patrols are gaining ground. Once they spot us in the grass, they'll overtake us within minutes.

"Rayla—"

"When I stop, run for the closest building," Rayla cuts in. "Hide until you know that you're safe . . . then get to Calgary. There's a brick building with a yellow door. 968 Paramount Point. You will find friends there."

"But we can't—" Mira begins.

"There's no time for arguing! Repeat the address to me."

"968 Paramount Point," I repeat, breathless.

The car shoots out of the field and skids to a stop on the outskirts of town. No obvious surveillance. No sign of people. A perfect refuge.

"Get out, now!"

Mira grabs our bags and throws open the door. I hold back, hesitating.

"Will we see you again?" I ask, my voice catching in my throat.

I don't want to let her go. Her fervent green eyes—my eyes, Mira's eyes, our mother's eyes—tell me, *You are not alone.* I instantly feel courage rush into my veins.

"Do not wait for me. Run!"

I spring from the car, slam the door shut, and join my sister in a dead sprint—the light of my family burning inside me—toward a crumbling parking garage twenty yards ahead.

We dive behind a pillar just as the car charges back into the pitch-black field. Our grandmother means to face the hunting patrols, Roth, the government—anyone and everything that stands in our way—head-on. She means to openly resist. To rebel.

And so the revival begins.

MIRA

White wind turbines sprout from the grass all around me like giant pale flowers, their three long blades spinning slow and dream-like in the hot air. They must grow for over one hundred thousand acres. I wonder if I can pry off the petals and play my own version of the old French game, "He loves me, he loves me not."

"Father's dead, he is not dead."

"Rayla's dead, she is not dead."

"We are dead, we are not dead."

There are three petals and two phrases. Every game ends the same way it starts.

"Less than four hundred miles to the coordinates," Ava says in front of me, her eyes on her paper map.

And we're just going to walk all that way?

I stare unblinking at my right wrist, visualizing the chip fixed inside me, lying dormant.

"Did you memorize them?" Ava says.

I open my fist and find the crinkled piece of paper inside. I take out a lighter from my rucksack and raise the flame to the coordinates. They disappear into ashes.

"How's your ankle?" Ava says. "Can you keep up without a break?"

My focus returns to the spinning blades, sluggish and apathetic to their purpose outside this peaceful metal garden.

"Why are you so quiet?" Ava says, spoiling the solitude.

"Why do you keep asking the wrong questions?" I stop short, loose rocks sliding underneath my worn soles.

Ava must feel the pause in our small procession north, but she continues to charge forward. She eventually pauses, folds the map into a tiny thick square, places the paper on top of her head, and covers it with her washed-out, patched-over cap.

"After everything Rayla's told us," Ava says, turning to me, "how can you still be so against this?" She flaps her arms as she speaks every grating word. "How can you still be doubting?"

She looks like a miniscule wind turbine. Trying to energize the world. Trying to pick up my slack.

"I'm not going to Canada" is all I say. It's all I need to say.

Ava drops her hands to her hips and slowly scans the land and sky, forming the best way to coerce me into following her. Her eyes finally make their way to me, convinced that she's right.

"What do you think is left for you here? There are no more safe houses. No more maps telling us where to go." She lifts her baseball cap and grabs the map, wielding it like a weapon as she takes a step closer. "Except this one, guiding us to our only option."

I look back down at my microchip, seeing past the faint crisscrossed lines of my sunburnt skin, past my veins, bulging and blue.

"Enlighten me. What is the logic in running around and hiding out like cowards until we get ourselves caught? How will that help Father? Or us?" The wind picks up, slapping Ava's hair against her cheek. She throws it back impatiently.

"You're not going to hand yourself over to Roth, or you would have done it at the checkpoint. So tell me, what's your plan?" She takes another step closer, her hands again emphasizing every word. "Do you even have one? Or are you just acting impulsively? Just being stubborn and stupid?"

I take a step forward. My turn.

"I know I'm not going to get myself shot or blown up by trying to cross an impassable border. And I know I'm not going to chase after some hopeless rebellion that died decades ago."

Ava opens her mouth to counter, but I cut her off before she can utter a syllable. "Our mother died to keep us hidden. To keep *me* alive. And I'm not going to throw my life away by being a poster child for a half-assed revival that will only put a bigger target on our faces. And a blood-red bull's-eye on our father's."

I take another belligerent step toward her, but Ava stands her ground, shaking her head and squeezing her map so hard I can hear the paper crack in protest beneath her fingers.

"Do you really think the public will rally behind a former Family Planning Director and his twin daughters?" I press, arms outspread. "They'll crucify him. There will be riots for his execution. And the mob will come for us next."

I lower my arms. They feel so tired. "We're running no matter what, Ava. Doesn't matter if it's here or in Canada. But if we keep quiet and stay hidden, Father has a chance."

"A chance for what? Life in prison?" Ava advances another step. "You saw what Roth's already done to him. Crossing the border is the only chance to save him. There's hope on the other side."

She stares at me for a long moment, her face knotted with angry conviction. I notice freckles that weren't there yesterday above her flared nostrils, below her earnest eyes.

"Reviving the cause will change the future for millions of families. Not just our own. Don't you see?"

She throws her arms north, begging me to see.

"I see a girl who wants to follow yet another person's idea of what our lives should be," I answer. "You're spewing out words that were fed to you. You're caught up in your own self-importance, actually believing that anything you do matters."

"It matters that I try," Ava says. "Even if we fail, at least we'll go down showing the people they can defy the government because we ourselves have done it! With no guns, no army—just by the two of us living and existing—our family has proven that we can win."

"This is winning? Look around you." I point to the hundreds of metal flowers waiting to be picked. All waiting to tell me another person is dead. "This is victory?"

"Mother guided us here. She led us to Rayla and the Common. She planned all of this with Father. She must have. They both want this," Ava insists, raising her voice as if I'm just having trouble hearing and will soon reflect her fervor. "I don't understand! You of all people should want this."

"Why? Because I'm the second-born? The throwaway?" I fling aside my bangs and toss back the hood of my jacket, suffocating beneath all the layers. "I don't want any of it!" I hurl my rucksack to the ground, freeing myself from any and all burdens.

"Your guilt is blinding you."

"My guilt?"

"For getting us caught."

My eyes turn to slits. "Excuse me?"

She charges toward me, a single step dividing us. "You're acting like a selfish bitch, considering you're the one who got us caught!"

Her words detonate inside of me, and I explode toward her, releasing everything I've held back and locked away until now. Ava shuffle-steps backward, feeling the force of my pent-up rage.

"Are you serious? You're the one who broke routine and made me go up for dinner! I would have never been in that greenhouse with Halton if you didn't always push to get your way."

Ava tries to speak, but I smother her words.

"You were always the self-anointed tyrant, lording over me, superior about being the firstborn. *Ava Goodwin*, bearer of our name, owner of our identity and the life-enabling microchip. You made the decision that night in the basement. It was *you*. You're the reason we got caught!"

"You're the one who drew attention to yourself!" Ava regains her ground, her voice loud enough for every four-hundred-foot wind turbine to catch and broadcast my mistake throughout the vacant, foreign land. "You kept touching your stupid wrist! You weren't good enough—"

"You mean I wasn't good enough being *you*!"

"Stop acting like the victim! We both had to play the same game, and you lost it for us."

She pushes two steps closer, brandishing her finger in my face.

"Do you think I wanted to spend my days watching over you, making sure you were happy? Making sure I kept you alive? I knew you were our weakest player, so I indulged you and catered to you and carried you for eighteen years! I knew you'd be the one to mess it all up. So did Father."

My rage emanates from deep within—thrums across my skin, animates my fingers, balls them into fists.

Ava presses on. "You're the reason we're standing here. You're the reason Father's imprisoned, and you're the reason he's going to die!"

With one violent surge I close the gap between us and thrust Ava backward, sending her flying across the ground. She lands hard, her elbows and hands taking the fall. She lifts her palms and studies the bloody scrapes and shallow gashes of her broken skin. Our broken bond.

I feel no guilt. Only the sky's spotlight and my smoldering fury.

"Go lead yourself into an unwinnable crusade," I spit. "I'm not following."

Ava glares up at me from the dirt like she's finally seeing my full evolution and hates what I've become.

Something other than her.

"The Guard knows we're in Montana. They're going to catch you," she threatens as she rises.

I grab my rucksack. Chuck the strap over my shoulder. "I have just as good a chance to outrun them as you."

Ava wipes her bloodstained palms against her pants. "You won't survive without me."

"I can. I don't need you anymore to have a life. I have my own microchip now."

"You're a coward!" she screams at me.

"And you're a fucking fool."

I turn away from Ava and stomp toward the field's boundary, overgrown with its clairvoyant flowers.

"You will not die; you will die."

I will not die.

I don't look back.

PART III
THE ADMISSION

AVA

In Greek mythology, humans were originally created with four arms, four legs, and a head with two faces. One soul in two bodies.

These beings had great strength in this form, and the gods, fearing their power, sent Zeus to divide them into two separate parts, splitting apart the soul. Weakened and consumed with yearning, humans were condemned to spend their lives in search of their other halves in order to feel complete.

I was born with my soulmate. One soul in two bodies. I didn't have to search the whole world over. But now mine is gone. Mine turned and walked away from me.

In that moment, I learned you could hear a heart break.

Disguised in a dark hooded jacket—the Guard will be looking for a baseball cap now—I stop walking and survey the golden hills that roll across the land as far as I can see. My anger has driven me ten miles from my sister by now. A heavy feeling of loneliness stabs at me, piercing its blade into an already-severed soul.

I never thought I could tire of open land. I dreamt of it all my life in the suffocating urban sprawl of Dallas, and I naïvely used to think that if I could just find enough of it, I could keep Mira there, safe.

You're a fucking fool.

The cuts on my palms suddenly burn as if submerged in hot coals, and then I'm back at the wind farm again, Mira's hands on my chest, pushing me to the ground.

Rage rips through my loneliness, and with Mira's words still ablaze inside my mind, I tear the rucksack from my shoulders and launch it through the quiet, empty air, its contents escaping into the grass.

"You're the fool, Mira!" I recklessly scream.

Stop it, I chide myself, biting down hard on the inside of my lips, forcing my mouth shut. *You're going to get yourself caught.*

Standing alone in this vast field, shaking with a desperate need to do more violence, I'm overwhelmed with the notion that I'm suddenly surrounded by too much space.

I kneel to slowly gather up my spilled supplies and place them carefully back into my bag, one by one, centering my mind.

"Focus on the task at hand," I say aloud for the sixteenth time.

This has become my battle cry.

A highway looms ahead. I glance down at the map and locate a farm road that will connect with Interstate 90 farther north.

It's too much of a risk to travel three hundred and seventy-five miles on foot through exposed land now that Roth knows where his fugitives are hiding. The more days I'm on the run, the greater the danger. One surveillance drone flyover and the game is done. I have to find a vehicle to get me to the border. And if there's a highway, there will be a charging station somewhere nearby.

A glare from something on the road temporarily blinds me. I blink away yellow bursts of light to see a pair of armored military vehicles hurtling south in my direction.

I fall to the ground and crawl, dirt stinging my cut elbows, behind the nearest hill. Tucking my body into a narrow indentation, I sit as still as the air and wait for the cover of darkness.

My anger is my armor, and I am made of steel.

The sun fades to twilight. Fireflies flicker like tiny bolts of lightning, dancing in the soft semidarkness. The temperature drops and the wind disappears. Crickets sing their soft, elegant song, and still I wait.

Night hits, wrapping the world in black.

Only then do I step from my hideout in the earth and point my feet north by the light of the moon.

I chew the last bite of my last kangaroo jerky, my tired, heavy eyes locked on a service road next to I-90. Four vehicle charging stations line a dimly lit rest stop in front of me. All have been empty the hour and a half I've been here.

Just outside the surveillance camera's range—I counted four, one in each corner—I wait unmoving, sandwiched between two benches. I kneel uncomfortably, a sharp corner digging into my lower back, to stay awake.

My stomach growls at me to pay more attention to the 3D food printer I saw posted outside the restrooms. I still have my microchip and my umbrella—the government doesn't know to track Aeron Rowe yet—so I could grab a few supplies for the rest of my journey. Mira has the megaprotein kits from Rayla's survival food supply in her bag. But I have all the water—and I can survive up to three weeks without food. Mira will need water within three days.

Despite this biological fact, my belly emits a loud grumble at the thought of the freeze-dried chicken and black beans in Mira's possession. The label promised the food would taste just as great today as it will in twenty-five years. *Be quiet,* I scold my stomach. If the cameras detect a lone, skulking figure at a vehicle rest stop, the military might descend upon the area with a drone or an entire company of soldiers.

Suddenly the benches on either side of me begin to vibrate. A harsh, low rumbling of what seems a thousand thunderous engines seeps into my bones, overtaking my eardrums.

Motorcycles. A gang of them.

Lights off, cloaked in blackness, the souped-up bikes storm the station, and I press my body tight against the pavement, attempting to make myself invisible. I turn my head and dare a shadowy peek from between the bench's legs: half a dozen bodies fly off terror-inducing metal monsters, all wielding handcrafted weapons designed to inflict property damage or bodily harm.

What the hell is going on?

I squint my eyes to zero in on their faces. Shockingly, every single one has the same bland features, tanned skin, and an identical five o'clock shadow. John Doe masks. The gang members all illegally share an identical 3D-printed prosthetic face, essentially becoming one man. I've never seen anyone wear a John Doe before. They're forbidden by law, seen as impersonating a false identity. Merely owning the mask is cause for arrest. This defiance is a stinging slap in the face to the government's multibillion-dollar surveillance system.

A slap that leaders like Roth would never allow.

Screaming like madmen, the anonymous bodies disperse, each one running full bore at a predetermined target. Chilling yells ring through the air, and I hear the naked defiance in their voices. I watch, a shiver creeping down my spine, as they swing their clubs over and over, smashing the cameras like piñatas.

I'm not afraid—of the recalcitrant gang, of the Guard showing up any second, of the weighty task I was entrusted to carry out—even though I know I should be. The John Does' angry cries only harden my certainty.

The government can be wounded. Blinded.

Four of its eyes were just plucked out right in front of me.

The gang returns to their motorcycles and charges back into the night, leaving me alone once more on the cold, rough pavement.

Barely clinging to consciousness, I wait in the quiet stillness for something to happen. Either the Guard will come sweep the station, or another vehicle will eventually pull into the rest stop.

I go over my plan again, fighting to remain alert. First, I must find a driver headed west on I-90, then abandon the vehicle to locate another headed north on I-15 toward Helena, then possibly Route 287 . . . Sleep stubbornly pulls at my mind, closing my heavy eyes, relaxing my clenched fingers that grip the rucksack resting against my chest.

A loud squeak of brakes and my eyes fly open, my senses at once sharp and wary. Scouring the area, I quickly find the source—a water-tanker truck pulling into the wireless charging station farthest from me. A sleepy uniformed Water Guard emerges from the cab, yawning and stretching. She must have fallen asleep on duty, leaving the autonomous system to haul the precious resource across the dark highways of Montana. She scans her wrist with a high-pitched *ping*, and the red light above her station turns green, authorizing the power transfer to begin.

I shift into a crouch as the woman turns to evaluate each broken surveillance camera. *She's going to report the vandalism.*

The Guard reaches for something in her inside pocket—a communication device? a gun?—but I'm unable to tell what it is until I hear the soft click of a lighter followed by a whirling puff of smoke. The woman exhales with a deep, satisfied sigh, relaxing her wide shoulders against the truck's door.

This is my chance. The monitors inside the cabin will be unattended for the next few minutes while she freely enjoys her illegal cigarette. Tobacco is strictly prohibited; the US doesn't even grow such a planet-destroying product anymore.

Trusting the Guard will take her time, I exploit the shadows, quickly making my way toward the far side of the truck unseen.

A soft *ding*—charge complete—right as I reach the top rung of the ladder. I rush to flatten myself against the smooth cylinder tank. I push forward on my stomach, taking pains to produce no noise, before plunging into a depression outside the passenger cabin.

Through a small gap to my left, I see the Guard suck in a final, hefty inhale, then toss the cigarette to the ground. With a slight groan, she crushes it with the toe of her boot and places the butt inside her pocket, hiding any evidence of her infraction.

I duck when she turns to climb back into the truck. Pulling my hood low, I tuck my body into a ball and tightly grasp a protruding metal bar.

The door slams shut, and the engine starts up quietly.

Racing west at ninety-five miles per hour, the hours inch by painfully slow.

And lonesome.

Not even the moon glistens above, my only companion shielded by clouds.

Before, I could sense Mira somewhere in the back of my mind. Distant, but still unmistakably by my side.

When I reach out for her now, she's no longer there.

I can't feel her at all.

MIRA

I am Marley Townsend.
I am Mira.
I am more than just part of Ava.

It's 9:00 p.m.
The seconds could be hours, years. Time doesn't matter.
I peel off my analog watch—glass cracked, leather scratched—and shove the timepiece into a flap inside my rucksack. I would just as soon trash the timepiece among the willowy gray needles of the western wheatgrass that pad my hideaway, but I can't leave any breadcrumbs for my capture.
My stomach growls.
The disquieting hum of a low-flying drone was stalking the land just to my right. But it died away long before sunset without passing over the gnarled gray branches of my ceiling. *A bald eagle hunting for weakened lambs.* I imagine the governor behind the eyes of the camera, reveling in his God's-eye view.
My limbs crave sleep, but my dry mouth and pounding head tell me to move. I must find water.

I emerge from the shelter of a lone tree and turn left. West, east, south. It doesn't matter.

With slow, labored steps I climb the hills. In the daylight it must look like I'm walking atop golden waves across a rolling sea that leads to the end of the world. *I've never seen the ocean before.* Maybe I will if I just keep walking.

I reach the summit of a particularly unfriendly knoll, its incline steep and packed with loose rocks, and allow myself a moment to catch my breath. Sweat drips down my sides, pooling in my belly button, clinging my shirt to my skin, and I curse myself and this hill for wasting such essential water to the greed of evaporative cooling.

My quads are on fire but I stand, pivoting in a tight circle, searching for lights or a hint of the moon's reflection bouncing off a lake or a stream. I have roughly three days to survive without water. *Two and a half,* I think, mopping the beads of sweat from my upper lip.

I complete my circle and end where I began. No lights. No reflections. Adjusting my rucksack, I descend the hill to begin another.

The darkness is total. Clouds cover the moon, and I can barely see my feet as I walk. Or am I climbing?

I stumble when the ground flattens out beneath me. I've reached another hilltop. Hilltop number eight. A batch of lights appears in the remoteness, disrupting the night's reign. From up here the buildings of what must be a community farm look only a stone's throw away. But I know it will take miles and hours of sweat-inducing toil before I make it to the luminous haven with its promise of water.

I trip my way down the invisible slope and plunge once again into the pitch-black void. Deep within the nothingness, thoughts of my mother's twin come to light.

Are you here inside this vacuum? Or did you make it out? Are you alive somewhere out beyond this empty space I find myself in?

She doesn't respond. No one can hear you here.

A ring of wind-powered streetlamps illuminates a square-shaped cluster of sustainable homes, with a small garden flourishing in the center. Ten yards beside a leafy row of bush beans and newly ripe parsnips is the rainwater tank I've traveled and gambled for. I linger on the outskirts behind a wooden fence, evaluating the risks.

Solar shingles glimmer from every rooftop, exposing corner after corner of defaced surveillance—six cameras all dangling from the gutters, swinging like dead men from their wire ropes. These are just the local farmers' cameras, used for their own crop security. Why would they be . . .

I shake my head and refocus. I don't care why the cameras were damaged, or how. Only that it blinds my sprint to the rainwater tank. A fiberglass container that is guaranteed to be locked or require an authorized chip scan.

It matters that I try.

My feet stutter. Ava spoke those words to me. Today, or was it in another life?

Time doesn't matter; none of that matters anymore. All that matters is water.

I crouch, scurry, and creep the rest of the way to the tank, veering well away from the community garden likely ready with the slightest brush of air to alert those sleeping that I have come to steal their most precious resource like a shameless thief in the night.

Like a coward, Ava's ghost whispers beside me.

No alarm sounds. I hold up my empty bottle, self-destructively optimistic. I leave my four-inch blade sheathed in my pocket. I won't need it. The tap will turn, the water will pour, and the dreamers behind the walls will go on dreaming of their fifteen-hour shifts.

I keep up this visualization as I squat on my heels beside the tank, willing it as prophecy. I grip the knob. To my amazement, the tap turns beneath my fingers, and the water pours. *How? Why?* Vague answers form inside my head, but I let them all disappear, strangely uncurious.

With one last check at every window and shadow to make certain I am alone, I tilt my head below the spout and fill my stomach until it swells, and then until my bottle overflows.

The steel lid from my water bottle, a thin string of rope, five sticks, a wad of kindling, a piece of flint, and the scrape of my blade.

It took half my patience and all my resolve to make the water boil inside the lid. And to *wait* for the water to boil. But under the teepee of my jacket and over the steady flame, the liquid reached 212 degrees Fahrenheit, and the surface turned bubbly, telling me it was dinnertime.

I added half a cup of the boiling water to my freeze-dried chicken. The instructions said to let it stand for five to seven minutes. I let it sit for thirty seconds and ate my meal in one meager mouthful.

The flame gone, I toss aside my jacket and breathe in the balmy country air. I pack up my supplies, drape my taupe cotton scarf around my head and shoulders, and recline across my rigid bed.

I lie inside an old wooden rowboat I found abandoned in a field. Its splintered, rotting shell rests in the center of a shallow depression, wide enough to have once been a pond. Spiked ends of grass peek out above the stern, their wave-like movements creating the illusion the boat still floats on water. I flick my eyes up, settle in, and gaze at the night sky.

The clouds have cleared, revealing a blanket of a thousand stars, and I wonder whose fault it is I am here. The crippling guilt I've carried within me my whole life has told me it was, is, and always will be my own. *Or is it yours, Father and Mother, for conceiving me? Or is it the universe's, biology's? Some cruel creator's?*

My fingers twitch as sleep pulls me under. My eyes close, my muscles relax, but before I fall too deep, a warm flash of light snaps my lids back open. All at once, my muscles clench and I'm wide awake. The stars dim as four beams of light slash across the sky.

Spotlights.

"Everyone outside, immediately!" a harsh electronic voice commands.

I wrap my arms around my rucksack and slide my hand inside my pocket. My fingers slip through the brass rings of the knuckle duster and crush my fear into the handle of my knife.

"This is a military sweep!" a Guard yells into his megaphone. "Line up for inspection!"

The spotlights change course, and I sneak a single eye above the chipped stern. The sight overwhelms me.

My fingers clamp tighter around my knife as I take in the community farm besieged by armored vehicles, screaming State Guards, piercing searchlights, and hand-thrown surveillance drones flying above the dreaded silver nose of an unmistakable Scent Hunter. All radiate a lethal, manic energy that burns through the field and ignites my wooden hideout. *It won't be long now,* they taunt. *There are only so many places to hide.*

I duck and cover, the drones circling above the surrounded farmhouse. Quickly, silently, I scatter the ashes of my measly fire and shoulder my pack. I pull myself overboard and sink to the ground, landing stiff on my hands and knees. A shaft of light passes over my head, and I drop to my stomach. Heat and sweat are trapped inside my clothes and boots, boiling me with the need to run.

My head and ears sting with a sudden chill, warning I've forgotten something.

My scarf.

I scour the grass but find nothing. The drones' search area broadens. Their infernal blades drown out the shouts.

Leave it. Leave now.

I crawl, inch by inch, into the depths of exposed land, like a toddler trying to outswim a shark. *To where? To what end?*

The searchlight's beams return, highlighting the sky above me, hunting, hungry for nocturnal prey scurrying in the dark. Rodents. Sheep. Me.

A shrill cry reaches me as I retreat. "Enough!"

Several voices join in, then I hear the taser guns. The raucous sounds of a scuffle, more stifled shouts, and then the beams of the spotlights disappear, blanketing me in darkness. The whirling hiss of the Scent Hunter falls ten yards behind me. It crashes to the ground right as the thundering boom of a sonic weapon shatters the night air.

I'm too far for its power to reach me. But the people from the farmhouses fall silent. All I hear now are the violent, amplified commands of the Guard.

"Search every house!"

"Search the fields!"

"Arrest any who resist!"

I escaped, leaving the people behind only to delay my fate.

Ava's last words follow me as I run.

You're a coward.

Maybe I am.

AVA

"Spaghetti."

"I'm sorry, please repeat," a serene, robotic voice replies.

"Spaghetti," a voice restates doggedly.

Surrounded by soil—the soft earth a comforting stowaway companion—I lift the black tarp covering the top of the truck bed I'm stashed inside. A drive-thru food printer with a bright sign invites hungry customers to "Dine in Tuscany tonight!"

"I'm sorry, please repeat," the machine says again.

"Spa-ghet-ti," my driver enunciates slowly.

I was forced to abandon my first ride. When I heard the water truck's autonomous system announce an upcoming highway change to I-15 South, I slipped off during a slow left turn. I waited outside another charging station for two hours before this farm truck pulled in.

The company logo across the back windshield told me the truck belongs to a local family farm. The bumper sticker shouting "Proud Father of a Wilson Bulldog" told me the truck belongs to a man from Wilson, Montana. After consulting my trusted map, I saw the route will likely head through land that used to be known as the Blackfeet Indian Reservation. Just east of Glacier County.

And right where I need to be.

"I'm sorry, please repeat," the machine recites once more.

I silently scream with impatience. I can't keep my legs still; my feet keep kicking up the dark soil, and I'm anxious for the truck to keep moving forward. The sun will rise in two hours, exposing me in dangerous light for the last twenty-five miles to the coordinates.

I peep my head farther out from the tarp and glare at the machine. My weary feet halt their simulated march when my eyes catch sight of Halton Roth's face.

Wearing an elegant military uniform—a diminutive clone of his grandfather—he has Mckinley Ruiz's arm tucked neatly into his elbow. She's dressed in an elaborate ball gown, diamonds on her throat. Together, the couple looks absolutely regal. And powerful. With a royal wave, they greet the crowd assembled below. The advertisement excitedly invites the listener, "Join us live. A celebration seventy-five years in the making. One Child, One Nation."

I watch Halton's smug smile play again and again on loop. The prince of the ball and his second-place princess. White-hot anger blazes through my body. Anger that this unworthy boy brought down my family, anger at myself that I didn't see it coming. Anger that my biggest problem used to be getting out of attending a stupid Gala with the arrogant governor's progeny. I'd give anything to be back in that basement with Father and Mira right now.

That life doesn't exist anymore. Focus on the task at hand.

I bring my attention back to the advertisement. "Join us live . . . One Child, One Nation." And then it hits me.

The Anniversary Gala. The perfect opportunity for the Common to make their first strike. Everyone will be watching. We have to infiltrate the Governor's Mansion. But how?

Together your faces can symbolize a revolution.

Another stab of anger pierces the open wound in my chest. Not anymore. My sister is gone.

A disheveled head pops out of the window, blocking the screen from my view. The agitated man presses his lips against the speaker.

"Spaghetti!" the farmer shouts, all patience ripped to shreds.

"Okay. Risotto. Please scan your wrist."

The man lays into his horn.

"You ill-bred, sheep-biting lout of a robot scum—"

The man cuts his insult short and kills the truck's headlights. Pulls the truck slowly away from the lights of the drive-thru machine. Safely shrouds the vehicle behind a row of bushes. From my hideout I scour the horizon. What spooked this farmer?

Through a gap in the branches, I see in the distance dust from an entire State Guard unit thundering past. Eerie and foreboding in the small hours of the night, the sight turns my blood to ice.

Stay calm, we're hidden.

"Nuh-uh, nope. Not getting myself mixed up in any of that trouble tonight," the man says aloud to himself. "Promised Jimmy I'd be home for breakfast."

We wait in dark silence until the dust finally settles. The man pulls back onto the main road, headed north, abandoning his spaghetti, without any idea of the trouble he has stashed away in his truck bed.

Less than three hundred miles to go.

MIRA

Light on my feet, blending with the darkness in my full-length charcoal coat, I trudge up and down the rugged terrain anticipating the sirens. Every few hours I shed my clothes and change into a new disguise like they can help me disappear. It's the only piece of advice I've taken from Rayla, but it's a superficial fix. I know I am surrounded.

If I can just make it out of Montana, I still have a chance.

Something catches my eye, halting my thoughts, slowing my steps. Flat, orderly squares of farmland disrupt the repetitious hills and draw my attention to a short wooden building that looks scarlet in the moonlight.

But it's what's on this ordinary building that pulls me closer.

I yank the hood of my coat low and lean into the powerful wind that threatens to knock me flat. In minutes, I'm standing in front of a barn, arm's length away from the three words spray-painted casually across the sliding door.

White. Reflective. Clear.

SAVE THE TWINS

My brain struggles to catch up to my eyes. It's not possible.

"A woman came by an hour ago and wrote that," a soft voice says behind me.

My knife is out before I fully whip around. A boy in nightclothes emerges from the shadows—he must be ten or eleven, with messy hair and a chipped front tooth. He aims his pocket knife in my direction, his blade as small and thin as my pinky finger. He doesn't look afraid.

A swift scan assures me he's unaccompanied, and I put away my weapon. He pockets his too.

"How old was the woman you saw?"

He shakes his head. "She wore a hood."

I quickly study the painted words. The yawning arcs of the two *S*s, the slanted cross of the *T*. It doesn't look like Rayla's handwriting. But then again, it wouldn't.

"Are you her?" the boy asks. He moves forward, peering up to get a better look inside my hood. "Are you Ava?"

"No." I keep my face calm. Unreadable. "You better clean this off before the Guard comes. They'll arrest your parents. And you, if you don't hurry." I move to take my leave. I shouldn't be here. I'm endangering us both.

"I won't help the government hide the truth."

His words give me pause. His passion makes me turn.

"They're saying Ava really does have a twin," the boy maintains, electrified, his wide pupils fighting to see me in the dark. "They're saying the twins are here in Montana. They're calling on us to help."

"Who is saying this?"

The boy shrugs his flannel shoulders. "Everyone."

He removes his pocket knife again, mutters a command, and instantaneously the curved edge of his handle casts a light, projecting a video onto the barn door. My face. Ava's face. Pressed together inside the open trunk of a car. The night of the checkpoint. The night we lost Rayla.

The security footage zooms in, focusing on the two "Ava Goodwin" facial recognition tags hovering above our identical features. "There are two of them!" a Guard shouts. "There are two Ava Goodwins!"

My disbelief leaves me numb. *The whole country knows.* I should run and hide, but my legs are powerless and unresponsive. I can't feel my feet.

The boy swipes to a new website.

An extreme close-up of Ava's nose and my nose. Ava's cheekbone, my cheekbone. Ava's chin, my chin. "Numerous analysts have authenticated the footage as the twin daughters of Darren Goodwin," a distorted voiceover states, "inspiring thousands to rally in support of the Goodwin family . . ."

And another site.

Four people of even height stand together in prosthetic masks. Homogeneous with their average features and matching stubble beards, their brown eyes peer out eerily from their illegal disguises as they call for the people to resist. "Cut the wires on every surveillance. Distract the Guard. Save the twins!"

The boy swipes to a fourth site. Then another. And another. He swipes so quickly, all I see are a blaze of blurred lights—my face and Ava's face, digitized, multiplied, shared across the underground webosphere for millions to bear witness to our secret.

"Every site the government shuts down, a hundred more pop up in its place," the boy says, his gaze fixed on me.

I stagger back, intoxicated by the images, his words, and the sudden surrealness of what is happening. A wail of sirens in the distance rouses me. The hologram vanishes, and "Save the twins" glows once more on the sliding door.

"Take my bike!" The boy sprints into the barn and, panting, wheels out an electric bicycle. "It's fully charged," he says.

I stare down at the thick, knobby tires and full-suspension frame. The boy stares up at me.

"The military took my mom," he says, his chipped tooth gleaming in the darkness. "She cut out her microchip and tried to free me of mine. One night the Guard came and just took her." I wonder if there was a scuffle, if his tooth broke in the fight.

Spotlights flood the sky.

"You have to make it," he tells me, looking under my hood, straight into my eyes.

With no time to spare, I climb onto the low seat of the e-bike and speed away, leaving the lionhearted boy standing beside the defiant message. SAVE THE TWINS.

Since I left Rayla's I have been awake, running and hiding, for over forty hours.

The consequences hit me all at once as I cruise through the even farmland on the motorized bicycle. My head dips and bobs, my grip slackens and slips. The terror of the sirens and the never-ending panic that has nipped at my heels and kept me on my feet cannot suppress my body from now taking what it craves.

Delirious, asleep at the wheel, I hit something hard. The motor stops, the bicycle pitches me over, and I land on the sharp ground, useless and disabled.

The boy's request echoes in my ears. *You have to make it.* What is *it*? Make it to where? There's no safety anywhere. No hope. Roth is everywhere.

Behind my hazy, cross-eyed vision, I see a dozen skyscrapers closing in around me. *I've been captured and returned to Dallas.*

A scream dies in my throat as I tuck my useless legs into a fetal position, seal my lids shut, and drop into a comatose state. A lamb for the taking.

They're only trees, my dreams tell me. *You've made it to a grove of trees.*

My lids rip open.

The panic returns and jerks me upright. My forehead smacks into a snapped tree branch, which sends drops of dew raining down on me. I ignore the pain and scramble to gain my bearings in the early morning light.

The land before me is a forest of matchsticks. Stripped, limbless trees and mangled stumps poke out from the charred undergrowth like gravestones. Ashes shroud this cemetery. Layers and layers of ashes.

The aftermath of a wildfire.

Gently, so as not to disturb the silence, I rise and pat my coat free of the powdery remains. I grip my rucksack with one hand, uncover the boy's e-bike with my other, and pick my way through the blackened forest where nothing green could live.

I keep my compass in my bag. Keep the persistent, nagging thoughts out of my troubled mind. I look aimlessly around me. However grueling the strain, however punishing the pressure, I must keep my mind blank. Blissfully hollow.

To think is to feel. To feel is to acknowledge hope. And hope is agony. Hope is cruel. I'm too far gone. Roth and his men have me trapped, and when I close my eyes, I see them closing in. The only thing left is to put my hands up and surrender.

I make it five more steps before I see the patch of yellow.

My legs give way and I crawl, wrestling with dead branches and severed trunks to touch what my eyes can't believe: a cluster of black-eyed Susans. Bright, resilient, and growing from the ashes.

My mother's flower.

I reach out, pluck a single stem, and hold on to it with all that I have. Love squeezes my heart. It's painful, but it tells me there is still life. There is still hope.

"Ava," I whisper.

Her name summons a howl of sirens that shatter the stillness of the dawn. They're so close now.

"Wait for me."

AVA

Seventeen hundred miles from where my journey first started, I stand in front of a massive tree line, out of breath and full of muted expectation. It's high noon. Somewhere inside this pristine wilderness is a hole in an impregnable wall that leads to freedom.

I ran the first five miles north after slipping out from beneath the tarp when the truck pulled into the family farm. Even in daylight, it was easy enough to make my getaway unnoticed—the farmer was preoccupied by his lively reunion with his wife and young son.

When my legs faltered and I had to stop, I fueled my famished body with water and mettle, and carried on at a brisk trot, the waning time ever present in my mind.

Tick-tock. Tick-tock. Make it to the border, or you'll be caught.

I take in a lungful of the clean, fresh air and step into the forest.

For people to understand their place in the world, they only have to stand in the center of an ancient forest and surround themselves with huge western red cedars, hemlocks, and cottonwoods that soar so high their expansive canopies absorb nearly all sunlight. No need to look to the immensity of space. Looking up, my breath taken from me, I know my humble place beside these centuries-old trees.

I clamber to the top of a fallen log, wider than my five-foot-six height. From my high ground, I can see that the dense network of deep-green foliage—speckled with bursts of yellow flora—goes on for miles. No hint of a border in sight.

Thin rays of sunlight penetrate the trees' shade like little spots of encouragement. Then a sudden jolt of alarm floods my body, rushing down to my feet, urging me to run.

Military spotlights.

Our intention—*my* intention—of crossing the border must be clear to Roth and his men; why else would we travel all the way up to Montana? These woods might be packed with dozens of drones and Scent Hunters scouring the area overhead, a hundred watchful eyes on me right now.

I stand motionless and listen for noises: a footfall, buzzing, barking, an alarm, a shout—anything. After a few silent moments, I realize my eyes were deceiving me. It was a ruse of the sunlight. I dig my nails into my palm—they've grown long and sharp—and press on, determined.

Tick-tock, tick-tock.

My progress is slow as I pick my way cautiously through the tightly packed vegetation. Half an hour later, I'm staring at two huge white signs nailed into two trees.

RESTRICTED AREA. DO NOT PROCEED.
DANGER OF DEATH AHEAD

Using a thickset cottonwood trunk as my shield, I scan the forest around me in vain. All weaponry will be expertly hidden. I'll be dead before I even know I've tripped an invisible wire, detonating my own demise. I've heard of videos online showing groups of people mowed down as they attempted to cross the border into Quebec. I'll never make it past the ground sensors and automated guns.

Propaganda, Rayla assured us in the car.

I leave the protection of the tough outer sheath of the trunk and grab a jagged fist-sized rock from the ground. I lob my decoy ten feet in front of the tree like a hand grenade and brace myself, waiting for gunfire or an explosion in response.

No gunfire. No explosion. Stillness.

Maybe Rayla was right. The signs, the videos, all the horrifying rumors were just propaganda peddled by both sides to dissuade the masses from storming the border.

I gather a pile of rocks together and place them into a sling tied around my neck, fashioned from my jacket. Facing north, I seize a rock and toss it twenty feet in front of me. Stillness once more. I take a few steps forward. I reach for another rock and repeat the process.

Better safe than blown to pieces.

I've been walking over an hour with nothing to show for it. Discouraged, hungry, and dehydrated, I raise my water bottle to my lips. My sore shoulders sag in defeat, but I quickly straighten up to my full height.

I've hiked at least four miles north into the wilderness. I'm not lost. I can't be. According to my map, the coordinates should be no more than five miles from the start of the tree line. I'll have to run into the border eventually.

A relentless obstacle of trees stands in my way, a secondary defense before the corrugated steel wall. Along with whatever else the Canadian Border Services Agency has protecting the International Boundary Wall. Antivehicle trenches. Double or even triple fencing with a no-man's-land monitored by bright lights, armored trucks, and cameras. Autotarget sentry guns that use motion sensors. Gray wolves.

Rumor has it that the uninhabited sections of the border are patrolled by vicious wolves who attack anyone who manages to slip past the defenses. They're leashed to a system of implanted chips and shock sensors that stop the wild animals from wandering off their line of duty.

America wiped out most of its own endangered animals decades ago—grizzly bears, bighorn sheep, mountain lions, bison, elk, red foxes. The list is extensive, so I have no fear of meeting anything wild on this side of the border.

Humankind is everything's and everyone's most dangerous predator. Blindly killing its own planet, slowly wounding it over the centuries. Forcing my generation to mop up the blood.

I stash my empty water bottle in my bag and push forward.

Endless green and brown, green and brown. Everywhere I turn, no matter how far I walk. Over six miles by now. I sigh, frustrated and exhausted.

You're going to get caught before you ever find this damn wall.

I wipe the sweat dripping into my eyes with my shirt and reach out to remove a drooping branch with flat, pointed leaves from my path.

I suddenly stop short. Metallic gray.

A twenty-five-foot galvanized-steel wall, angled at the top to prevent climbing, stands guard in the middle of an open forty-foot swath cut into the forest.

I step slowly out from the cover of the trees, my heart pounding in awe. I face east, then west. The limitless wall stretches on to infinity.

But there's no hint of a trapdoor. No hole to slip through to the other side.

I look up, craning my neck back so the hood of my jacket slips from the crown of my head. No rope to help scale the rigid steel plates. I study the foundation of the solid structure below. No tunnel dug into the likely concrete-filled ground.

There's no way through in sight.

For thousands of years, societies have built walls to keep their adversaries out or their populations in. But history tells us they all eventually fall. Stone, brick, wood, concrete, barbed wire, and tamped earth cannot keep a sharp mind and a desperate determination at bay forever.

My fingertips lightly touch the rough edge of a hole in the wall before me, just big enough for a body to crawl through.

When I first found it, I anticipated a siren, gunfire, or a rebellion member shouting my name—but it's just me, the silent trees, and this colossal barrier that I was trained to think was impassable.

I've sat facing the opening for a full hour now, staring into the hollow space, an arm's length away from freedom. It's right there, waiting for me.

But my body won't move.

Thoughts of Mira—she's suddenly in the center of my heart again—weigh my entire being to the ground like a stone. For the first time since our separation, I look behind me, scanning the tree line, thinking every dark shape is her.

My blood pounds in my ears and I feel dizzy. Tears fall unbidden down my stained cheeks. *Where is she now? What if the military captured her?* She could be on a plane headed for Texas at this very moment—lost to me forever. Or she could be lost in the forest, looking for me, almost two days without water.

I will not leave without her.

I briskly swipe the salty liquid from my chin. Turning from the wall, I face south.

The way back to my sister.

Prompted by the late afternoon sun, an orchestra of chirping birds and buzzing insects accompany my mad dash through the forest. Heedless of everything but my urgent need to find Mira, I fly over fallen trees as thick as cars and charge through sharp bushes that cut into my ankles.

My head constantly swiveling, I scan my surroundings, penetrating the dense layers of vegetation and towering wood, hoping somehow my sister will simply appear.

"Mira, tell me where you are," I say aloud like a prayer.

In answer, a small hummingbird dives down from the branches and hovers in midair directly in front of my face. Hypnotized by surprise and the soft hum of its furiously flapping wings, it takes several seconds before I register the telltale hole in its glossy purple throat and the silver needle-like beak. *You're not a bird at all.*

A Scent Hunter.

I thrash at the drone, frantic with the certainty that its nose has already sucked in and identified my scent. The drone ducks and weaves, easily avoiding my jabs, and I see its body flash a threatening red as it zooms in for an attack.

I lurch away wildly and lose my balance. Tripping on a root, I tumble hard to the forest floor. The drone's on me again before I can rise, but this time I grab hold of its tail feathers and launch the bastard into a tree.

I scramble to my feet and hurl myself past the tree line into an open clearing, listening for and confirming the drone's tireless winged pursuit. The more I run, the more I sweat, leaving an easy scent track for the Hunter to follow.

But if I don't run, it's all over.

I see the outline of a small town on the horizon. *Keep running. Get to the town. You can throw off your scent in a crowd.* But I slow down as I struggle to breathe, a stabbing pain just below my ribs. Malnourished and dehydrated, I can't keep up this pace.

The hummingbird swoops down again and floats effortlessly above my head. I exert all the power I have left in a final swing of my arms. Before my fist can connect with anything, a tranquilizer dart shoots into my neck, and my eyes roll back.

I careen to the ground like dead weight, and the last conscious thought that fires off inside my brain is *Mira*.

"You've changed your hair."

Groggy and confused at where or who I am, the baffling words slowly reach me as if I'm leagues away, drifting at the bottom of the sea. *Why does my neck feel so swollen?* I try to move my arms to investigate, but I can't—they're caught on something. With momentous effort I open my eyes.

A blurry figure sits in front of me, panting heavily like a dog. I struggle to blink the details into focus. A dark-blue military uniform. The insignia of captain on the shoulders. Slicked-back dark hair and wet lips parted into a smug smile.

Halton Roth.

I spring to life, gulping for air, but I'm instantly thrown back, my wrists and ankles bound to a chair, thwarting me from wrapping my hands around his throat. A powerful rage ignites every fiber of my being. Half-crazed, I desperately fight my restraints. Triumph in his eyes, Halton waits on his silver folding chair, patiently waiting for me to finish my useless attempt at escape.

In one panicked sweep I evaluate my circumstances. My location hasn't changed—I'm thirty yards from the tree line and several miles from the small town. But there's now a military SUV parked sixty paces to my right.

No Guards or agents, however. Halton appears to be alone.

If Halton is in fact a captain in the military now, where is his company? Governor Roth would never trust his ineffectual grandson to capture his infamous fugitives all by himself, without Guards or Special Operatives to babysit.

But he did *catch you, didn't he?*

I suddenly stop my violent thrashing, a hot shame rippling across my skin. Deflated, I hang loose on the chair, supported only by the cable ties that bind me.

"You've created quite a fuss out here in Montana," Halton says almost casually, like I'm not tied to a chair in the middle of the wilderness, forced to listen.

He waits for me to speak, but I stare at the patchy grass, my mouth a hard, closed line. Refusing to meet his eyes.

"You are very, very lucky I'm the one who found you, Ava."

Leaning forward in his seat, he searches my face for a revealing twitch, a tightening jaw, or a flickering eyelid. Any acknowledgment he correctly identified me from my sister.

I keep my face purposefully blank. *I will give you nothing.*

"Oh, I know you're Ava." He holds a fingerprint-scanning device under my face, making sure I see. "You are unquestionably Ava Goodwin. I have to say I'm impressed that you and your sister never once put a single finger out of line. Eighteen years you were both perfect. But that imitation microchip . . ."

He trails off, clicking his tongue. "Your father must have known there was no real solution for that hiccup in the plan. No trick to fool the machines. Or me. How unfortunate for your twin. That must have been difficult for her, being the second-born. The secret. What is her name? I bet I'd be only the fifth person to ever know it."

I snap my gaze up. If I could weaponize the venom in my eyes, Halton would be dead where he sits.

"I want to impress upon you again, Ava, how fortunate it is that I captured you. The unit that took your sister captive, however . . ." He leans back against his seat, calmly clasping his hands in his lap. Taking his time, a habit picked up from the elder Roth. "It's better if you don't know what my grandfather has authorized them to do."

He's lying. An interrogation tactic.

I will not break for you.

236

"After the soldiers are through with her, your twin will publicly take the fall as Ava Goodwin. Whether she's made to confess or not, evidence will unquestionably link her to your father's involvement in a foiled terrorist plot with the Russians . . . or the Saudis. The options are endless. All will be believed."

A sudden gust of wind muffles Halton's threats. But the respite is brief, and I clearly hear his next tormenting promise.

"Both will be executed as traitors."

I lose all sense for a moment, lost in heartrending visions of my father and sister lined up against a blank wall, blindfolded and shot.

"My grandfather will kill you, too, of course. Privately, without the public's knowledge. He'll shoot you himself and have your body incinerated, destroying the definitive proof that the Goodwin twins ever existed."

I'm drowning again, hit with a wave of absolute fear. *He's right.* Governor Roth has the power to make my entire family disappear, erasing the Goodwin name from all memory and time.

The silver bars on Halton's shoulders catch the sun and shine, signifying his command.

"I'm going to save you, Ava."

He knows what he wants, and he knows he's going to get it no matter what.

He wants me.

My thoughts swim in maddening circles, going nowhere. I'm empty, drained dry, and I float disoriented between denial and belief. My anchor—my sister—is gone.

Then I remember my swollen neck. I shake my head, attempting to clear my muddled mind. *You're drugged. He's manipulating you. None of this is real.*

"You're lying," I fire back. My voice sounds heavy and strange, my tongue thick in my mouth.

Halton releases a disappointed sigh. Pursing his lips, he reaches into a bag next to his chair and pulls out some sort of cloth. He spreads it carefully across his knees; it's a taupe cotton scarf.

Mira's scarf.

"I was hoping I wouldn't have to show you this. I wanted it to be a surprise." He looks at me closely, his fingers lightly grazing the fabric.

All at once I break.

I thrust forward, my body writhing with frenetic abandon, an aching cry pouring from my chest.

"I've been ordered to burn this." He lowers his eyes, his thumb and forefinger seizing hold of two frayed corners. Gently, he folds them together. Again, then once more. "But I've kept it for you as a gift. To remember her by."

He places the neat triangle on my lap like a burial flag.

"What was your sister's name, Ava? I'd really like you to tell me. We can remember her together."

Mira. My sister's name is Mira, and she will live inside me even if we are separated by death.

The chair groans as Halton rises and stalks toward me. He kneels, inches between us, his warm breath like thunder on my skin. He searches my stained, hardened face. I jerk my head away, protesting his closeness.

"I can protect you, Ava. I can save you." He reaches out to wipe a tear that falls down my cheek. "No one has to know. It can be our own little secret."

I lift my chin, and Halton leans in closer, our lips almost touching.

I spit solidly in his face. He stumbles backward, his pale blue eyes wide with surprise.

"The people will know," I promise. "The blood of my family is on your hands. The Common will come for you."

I watch with dull satisfaction as his neck and cheeks darken to a deep crimson, my saliva dripping down his narrow chin. He wrenches

Mira's scarf from my lap and wipes his face clean before discarding it on the ground.

He stands, refusing to meet my eyes, and turns abruptly toward the tree line. I follow his slow, stiff withdrawal until he disappears into the trees.

The moment I'm alone, I sink into my chair, all life escaping from my shackled limbs.

Something moves suddenly in the shadows. I flick my eyes to the right and see Halton's agent materialize from behind the military SUV, hand on his gun. His lips lift into a smile.

"You'll pay for that," Agent Hayes promises. *"Glut."*

My eyes fall to Mira's scarf.

There's no part left of me to hurt.

MIRA

I stand as still as the trees, rooted to the forest floor, cultivating my plan of attack.

It's been twelve hours since I drank the last drop of my water, ate the last morsel from my protein packs, and showered the last ounce of my live-or-die antidrone spray onto my body until my skin shone and my latest disguise reeked with the potent pine odor. My ankle throbs again beneath its soiled wrappings, the stabbing pain so ruthless I'm certain my foot will soon fall off. My lungs are stripped, and I fear my eyes will go blind from never closing. But I am here. Just south of Rayla's coordinates.

And so is Halton.

Even through the dense woodland, its leaves and foliage soaking up all sound for miles, I heard it. Ava's scream. I ran, her cry reverberating in my head, guiding me to her in this labyrinth of a forest. Just when I thought I was lost, I heard the manic shouts of a young man's voice.

I found Halton in a frenzied tantrum. Cursing and hacking at the thick, sharp trees with his fists and boots. Hidden inside a hollow trunk, I watch him now as he paces between two logs ten yards from me. Twenty yards from the forest's perimeter.

"Just do it. Just do it—prove to him you're not weak," Halton mumbles distractedly to himself, mopping the sweat from his forehead with his elbow, his entire body shaking.

My own muscles vibrate with a powerful adrenaline no spray could hope to mask. I mute my energy. Hone it. Reserve it for when it's time.

Halton tries to pull himself together, tucking in his uniform, slicking back his greasy hair. He slumps down on a log matted with moss. A hologram pops up in front of him, and I see the moment that caused the downfall of my family. Me, Ava, my father. Our living room in Trinity Heights. He studies the image stolen by his tablet's camera like he's watching a film.

I barely catch his whispering, "They all think I'm weak."

I throw it back at him. "You thought I was too." I raise my weapon and move for him.

Halton whips around to find me six . . . five . . . four feet from where he stands. His face lights up, astonished.

"It's you!" he blurts out.

Before he can say another word, I jab the pointed end of my umbrella into his throat. He doubles over, choking, his mouth opening and closing like a landed fish gasping for air.

"I . . . can't . . . breathe," he rasps, clawing at his neck.

Quickly dropping my umbrella, I grab my knife and pull Halton up by his hair, shoving the blade to his Adam's apple. His panicked hands swat at the knuckle duster protecting my grip as I grope at his duty belt and seize the gun above his right hip. I point the barrel to his temple.

"You don't deserve to breathe."

I zip-tie his wrists tight enough for his hands to swell and stiffen. In a last-gasp effort, he attempts to wrench loose, but after two violent spasms, his limbs slacken and yield. He feels the fury of my strength. Understands that I am ironclad, and he is but bait in my grasp.

His body weightless, I drive him forward, my blade and his gun forcing his dragging feet into a march. Wheezing, floundering, frantic to suck in air, Halton coughs and gags strangled cries as we edge in tandem toward a clearing where I spot Ava's lifeless body.

I hear the click of metal. My eyes focus on Agent Hayes, his weapon drawn and aimed at me. He shoots his eyes to my forehead, left shoulder, my right leg, and my stomach, searching for a clean shot. I stand unflinching behind the governor's grandson. My human shield.

"Drop your gun!" I shout, my order as steady as my hand that holds the pistol to his charge's head.

My voice jolts Ava awake. "Mira!" she howls, flailing and twisting against her restraints.

I keep my focus on Hayes. He moves three steps toward me, but I stand my ground as he locks his eyes with mine, sizing me up. Working out my vulnerabilities. He grins like he's found one, and with cocksure composure, he points his gun at my sister's chest.

"No!" I yell savagely. My blood surges, and my finger stiffens around the trigger. I dig the barrel deeper into Halton's temple. "Tell him to drop his gun, or I swear I will blow your goddamn head off."

Terror trembles down Halton's spine. A hideous gurgle bubbles up from his throat, and his voice cracks as he pushes words past his damaged windpipe. "Drop it . . . That's an order . . . Agent!"

The gun remains trained on Ava's heart. Halton hears my trigger click. "Drop . . . it!" he shrieks, the veins in his neck bulging. "Or I'll have you shot!"

Reluctantly, the agent lowers his gun. His eyes throw daggers as he tosses it to the ground beside my foot.

"And your mouthpiece!"

He opens his mouth wide, rips out a tiny communication device, and flicks the mouthpiece into the weeds alongside the gun. *Did he already send out a call?*

Hurry.

I stomp hard on the device with my heel. Shove the firearm into the waistband of my pants.

"Put your hands behind your head and lie flat on your stomach!"

The agent fails to comply, so I ask him again with my pistol. He bends slowly, glaring all the way down, but his bulk finally hits the ground, and I sprint for my sister, dragging Halton with me.

"I thought they had you, Mira," she whispers when I reach her. Immobilized, Halton watches, a captive audience, as I kneel before Ava, making certain she is whole. Ava's eyes are puffy and dazed. I graze my finger over the angry dart wound below her ear, just above the star-shaped scar on her neck.

"How?" she asks me. I don't need to answer. She really doesn't care how. Just that I am here.

"Mira . . . Ava . . ." Halton tries to clear his throat. It sounds like a garbage disposal grinding up his voice box. "I can . . . help . . . you both," he continues to croak. "Come with . . . me."

He pushes closer, but I fix the barrel to his forehead, warning him not to move.

Hurry.

I cut the cable ties that bind Ava and hold out my arm to help her stand. "Can you run?"

Just as Ava grabs my hand, a flurry of motion snaps my head to where Agent Hayes was lying. Too late, I see a knife launch from his fingers. It spins like a razor-edged wheel, cutting at me through the air. I close my eyes—*what a stupid thing to do*—hoping it will be quick and clean. I hear a sickening thud. The cry of agony.

I open my eyes to find the six-inch stainless-steel blade sunk deep into Halton's chest. His face slack with shock, he staggers, then drops limp to the ground. Before I can think or move, Hayes hurtles toward Ava, his bare fists swinging.

Instinctively, I lift the gun and fire.

Two explosive shots burst from my hand, releasing a deafening ring as a bullet finds my target. The agent lurches back. He collapses to the ground, legs sprawled, eyes empty. He doesn't move again.

Ava releases the weapon from my grip, and I peer down at a white-faced Halton, uniform soaked in blood. He tries to raise his zip-tied arms.

"I . . . I . . ." His voice comes out in halting spurts as he struggles to speak. I can't hear his last words. I can't bring myself to listen.

"That knife was aimed for Halton," Ava says in astonishment. "It wasn't a mistake."

She gazes down at Halton's feeble fingers swatting at the blade's handle, buried inches from his heart.

He's trying to pull it out.

"His own agent. Roth's man."

Halton's movements wane, and his eyes dim. The bleeding is so immense, it's clear he won't last much longer. I bend to cut the plastic tie that binds Halton's wrists. There's nothing more we can do for him.

"I . . . I . . ." Halton gurgles, choking on his words.

Sirens blast their familiar song. The piercing alarm is so loud, it feels like it lives inside me.

"We have to move," Ava says, gathering our bags and shoving the gun inside her waistband.

Dust rises in the air from the town, only miles away. From the pocket of my jacket, I remove my mother's flower. I place the crumpled black-eyed Susan beside the blade lodged just beneath his collarbone. Heavy-eyed, Halton looks at the flower, then up at me, a shadow of a smile on his colorless, cracked lips.

Ava spares him a final glance, and we flee into the forest.

I . . . I . . . Halton's voice haunts me through the countless trees. Disappears when I glimpse my first jarring sight of the border wall. Despite myself, my mouth drops at the pure spectacle of it.

"The entrance is farther down—forty yards," Ava tells me.

A drone hums overhead, hunting somewhere in the distance. The Guard must have found Halton's body by now. *Don't think of what's behind. There's only forward.*

By Ava's side, I push past the tree line into the unsheltered clearing. My hood slides down my tangled hair, but I do not move to cover my face. *I don't have to hide anymore.*

I crane my neck, trying to see how far the barrier stretches. It's endless and dominating. A steel monster guarding an imaginary line. A made-up boundary we're not supposed to pass.

Ava crouches next to the hole in the wall they said was impenetrable.

"It's really true," I breathe.

My sister looks to me, her arm extended, inviting me to freedom. "You first."

I shove through the narrow crevice, Ava following close behind.

The other side. Canada.

The sun sets behind the trees. Brilliant rays of orange and red ignite everything around me, beckoning us.

Ava rushes to me and embraces me hard. Her fingers dig into my bones as if to check that I am real. Our bodies release a mountain of tension, and our fast breaths harmonize.

"The people know," I say, searching Ava's eyes. "They're rising."

She smiles. She somehow already knew. It's written on her face. Beautifully clear.

"We made it, Ava," I tell her.

She pulls her forehead to mine.

"We made it," she tells me.

Together we turn to face the vast new country, our hands locked as one.

We run. Not because we have to. But to willfully embrace the unknown.

And to prove we're still alive.

PART IV
THE COMMON

AVA

Forty miles past the wall.

After breaking through the Canadian forest and trekking all night across grassland, Mira and I survey a highway in the distance. Soft morning light illuminates the two-tiered structure, the top layer a series of interconnected parks and walkways, while the bottom bustles with autonomous cars. The four-lane road is designed with colorful trees and flowers flanking rows of streamlined buildings. The great suburban sprawl of Lethbridge, Alberta, lies beyond. Despite the congestion, the energy is calm. Almost peaceful.

Calgary and the Common are less than two hours away if we can get one of those cars.

Side by side, we set out toward the road, me still keeping my hood up while Mira keeps her bare head exposed, her scarf left in the dirt next to Halton. *Another person dead.* And the toll will just keep rising.

Mesmerized, we walk down the raised pedestrian passageway, glancing at the local shops and restaurants. The paths are clean and orderly, decorated with plants instead of garish advertisements and propaganda. I see no cameras or surveillance of any kind. No one uses umbrella shields or masks to hide. No Guard stalks the streets.

I suddenly realize how dirty we must look. How wild. Lowering my hood, I smooth down my hair.

"Ava, look." Mira points to a family of five walking by: a mother, father, and their two sons and daughter.

My heart twists for what could have been for my own family. But I also see the future in that united family. The Rule of One oppressing us no longer.

A flashing blue light catches our eyes. It's a kiosk with a bright digital sign: "Ride Center." Two single-file rows of sleek compact cars are parked along the edge of the street, simply waiting for riders and destinations.

I approach the first car and circle it, looking for a way in. There's no door handle or obvious way of unlocking the car.

"Door, open," Mira commands.

Nothing happens.

"How do we wake it up?" Mira gives the car a quick kick.

"Car, take me to 968 Paramount Point," I try.

Suddenly the pavement lights up below our feet with a mat blinking the word "Welcome." The entire left side of the car yawns open, inviting us inside.

"My name is Sylvia. Please make yourself at home."

It's like I just stepped into someone's living room. The seat wraps around the interior like a sectional couch, and there's a small foldable table on each end. I scan a large screen and find endless professional and entertainment resources. There's even a miniature food printer in the corner. You could run an entire country inside this car.

"Please select your method of payment," Sylvia hums.

"Cash?" Mira ventures.

A cash slot lights up. So does our amazement.

"The citizens aren't microchipped," I say, taken by surprise.

I slide in the dollar amount owed, and the car seals itself closed. I take a seat across from Mira, and our eyes meet as we soundlessly glide toward a place where Rayla promised we would find friends.

"Sit back and enjoy the ride," the car tells us.

Mira and I stare out at the trees that blur into buildings as they speed by our glass window.

This past week, the longest of my life, races by in my mind, one event after another, just as quickly as the miles to our destination. The car settles into a quiet stillness.

Sylvia must sense our moods, because she asks, "How about some tunes?"

An upbeat rhythm fills the car. Soft red and purple strobe lights dance in quick, joyful circles.

I smile. It's so surreal.

"You have arrived at your destination," Sylvia says.

The music and lights cut off. Mira and I look out the window at Paramount Point in silent expectation. I find an elegant ten-story early-twentieth-century building staring down at me. A white sign reads "Paramount Point Hotel" just above a yellow door.

"The rebellion's based out of a hotel?" Mira says, doubtful.

Sylvia's left side opens, and we step onto the mildly trafficked sidewalk. Before I can make sure we're in the right place, the car drives away with a cheerful good-bye.

Mira and I turn to face the brick building. As if on cue, the yellow door unlatches and a woman walks out. She's tall, simply dressed, with dark curly hair and features that project intelligence. A young man, about my age, pops up behind her, and another man gathers at her side.

All wear expressions of anticipation. Of hope.

"Ava and Mira Goodwin," the woman says. "We're pleased to finally meet you."

A glass ceiling towers high above the lobby atrium. My eyes quickly take in what must be a hundred doors, ten hotel rooms to each level. The design and furnishings are neat and efficient. Unassuming.

Dozens of people walk about the lobby, entering and exiting a bank of elevators at the far wall. More stroll along the various corridors up above. Those near us glance at Mira and me with curiosity. Are they all rebellion members or merely guests? How many are American refugees like Mira and me?

"So the hotel's a front for the Common's headquarters?" I ask, turning to face the small group gathered loosely around us. The woman introduced herself as Emery, who appears to be the brains behind everything; Pawel, the young-but-eager man who appeared at her side; and Barend, who must be the broad-shouldered muscle of the group.

"This is more like the war room, really," Emery answers. "The nerve center is much farther away."

I give Mira a side-glance. *A digital war, I hope. We need to get inside that Gala.*

"Is Rayla Cadwell here?" I ask, searching the numerous faces in the lobby. "Have you been in contact with her?"

Pawel steps forward, his innocent brown eyes shy. "I sent word of your arrival the moment you pulled up to our doorstep. Your grandmother knows you're safe."

"How did you know Rayla is our grandmother?" Mira questions.

Emery simply shrugs. "I would recognize Lynn's daughters anywhere. Even with your disguises."

"You knew our mother?" I say.

"She was my best friend when we were young back in Denver," Emery reveals. "We trained together under Rayla. I was to be Lynn's right hand when she took over the cause. When she left, it fell to me."

I glance at the rebellion leader's right wrist. A lion's head with a sword running through it covers most of her forearm, the blade's point dipped in yellow.

"Did our mother have one too?" I ask, motioning to her tattoo. Mira examines the others' wrists, also inked, a look of intent in her eyes.

Emery nods. "Of course. Tattoos are a mark of the Common. Lynn's was a black-eyed Susan."

Our mother must have gotten hers removed. There was no hint of it in the hologram videos.

"I wonder if our father had one too," Mira muses out loud. "A blacklight tattoo, maybe, with ultraviolet ink?"

"If Darren marked himself, I never saw it," Emery says.

"Is there any news of him?" I ask, fearing the answer.

"Roth had Darren moved to a new location after he blinked his coded message. We haven't been able to locate him since," Barend says. He wears thick combat boots, and there's a pistol at his hip. "But finding him is a top priority for our members down in Texas."

I nod stiffly. *Stay alive until we find you, Father.*

"Let me show you to your rooms. You can clean up, and then we can all talk more," Pawel suggests helpfully.

"No," Mira and I say in unison.

"Do you have anyone here capable of hacking into the Emergency Alert System?" I ask.

Emery twists her lips into a dangerous smirk. "Paramount Point houses all sorts of useful people."

"Good," I say.

My eyes sweep over the group standing in front of me and the hundreds of hotel room doors, each one potentially occupied by a man or woman with rebellion in their hearts.

More players in this larger game.

Let's make our next move.

MIRA

Ava looks at me in the mirror with her green eyes. Her contacts are gone, and so is her raven-colored hair. Her locks are a fiery red once more, like an alarm. Like a beacon.

"There I am again," Ava says evenly.

Music seeps in from the other room, echoes of our university choir floating around us like ghosts.

One child at a time, we built a lasting nation.

Stability!

Prosperity!

Family Planning is our foundation.

"It really is a catchy tune," Ava says, patting down her stubborn bangs. "Too bad the lyrics are garbage."

I fix my own green eyes on my reflection. I kept my blonde hair, wearing it loose and wild. It just feels right. *Here I am, finally.*

"We can write new words," I tell her.

I smooth down my shirt and pluck off any lint or wisps of rogue hairs the camera might pick up. Ava clasps the high collar of her yellow jacket, looking every bit a bright flame. We both wear our faces bare, hiding behind nothing. Our identical features on full display.

I glance at my watch. 7:45 p.m. Almost show time.

Turning away from the mirror, I move to a set of chairs beside the door. I gaze soberly around the bedroom, which feels like a waiting room for an appointment long overdue.

Ava paces up and down the tiled floor, repeating a silent recitation.

"How's your wrist?" I ask her.

"Healing quick." She stops her marching and slowly peels back the bandage on her right arm. A snake curled in the shape of an infinity symbol marks her skin. Pops of gold and yellow adorn the scales, just like Rayla's tattoo. "For renewal," Ava told me when she chose her emblem. "A rebirth."

My own tattoo itches and burns, like my growing intensity. I rise from my seat and move for the door just as the singing stops.

"I'm ready," I announce and give her a strong nod.

She returns a grin. "I don't know how else to say it, but I'm proud of you. Father would be proud too."

"Father *is* proud," I correct her. "He knows."

Ava turns the handle, and we move from our quiet room, shoulder to shoulder, down the hall and toward the waiting rebellion.

I fold the sleeve of my shirt above the shiny pigment inked onto my right wrist, just over my microchip. I chose an eye as my emblem. Beautiful, bright, and solemn. The bottom row of lashes are the petals of a black-eyed Susan, the yellow curves shaped like tears. The government is always watching, but now so am I.

As we enter the first door on the top floor, the radiance of a dozen screens flash and scream at us. Dallas. The Governor's Mansion. The Anniversary Gala.

The Common is watching you now, Roth.

Three lights illuminate two stools placed before a white background. Emery stands beside the camera, messing with the lens. I take a deep breath. I hear Ava take one too. We step into the flood of light and take our places.

Fireworks electrify the screens to my left. To my right, I see close-ups of stately guests strutting and cheering as they make their way toward a platform the length of a football field. I spot the president, his wife, their son. And directly before us on the screens, center stage, I see Roth, his mansion and opulent gardens behind him. Two screens the size of houses flank his regal shoulders. His bloated, severe face leers down on the crowd. Two gigantic eyes. Ever watchful.

Ava keeps still. Placid. Poised to strike. I breathe deeply to stop my rage from bubbling to the surface.

Roth moves to the front of the platform, a badge of mourning strapped around his uniformed arm. He stands soaking in his power, waiting for the smallest noise to settle. It takes only three seconds for a deafening hush to fall over the governor's garden. Over everyone in our room.

His thin lips move, but I can't hear what he's saying. He motions to his wife and the empty chair beside her. A hologram of Halton, idealized and glorified in his noble Strake uniform, fills the seat where his grandson should be. I spot Halton's former Gala date, Mckinley Ruiz, hovering behind his chair, making a show of her fake sorrow.

Roth moves his hand over his heart. A sharp buzz emanates from speakers in the ceiling above us, and Roth's voice suddenly comes blaring through.

"Today is a celebration of the power of one."

His eyes bore into mine. But I feel no fear. Only resilience. Grit. Strength.

"One Child, One Nation. One people."

"Save the twins!" rings out from somewhere in the crowd of ritzy guests, an unexpected intrusion.

A perfect introduction.

"Now!" Ava calls out, sharp and strong.

The camera flashes red. Emery nods. Pawel flicks a switch, and it's show time.

"My name is Ava Goodwin," my sister begins steadily.

I see our outlawed faces displayed and magnified on every monitor across from us. Every jumbotron inside the Anniversary Gala has been hijacked. From Pawel's command panel, I see videos of our twin image towering over the streets of Denver, Chicago, and Seattle, the skyscrapers blasting out our message.

"My name is Mira Goodwin," I announce, my voice finding power. "We are the twin daughters of Darren and Lynn Goodwin."

I stare straight into the lens, trying to see the people behind it. Millions are watching. Millions are listening. *The entire country. Hell, maybe the world.*

"Tonight our country celebrates seventy-five years of the Rule of One," Ava declares. "Seventy-five years of oppression."

The president, the governors, the Guard. All of the nation's most important leaders watch in horrified silence.

"We speak to you now, on this symbolic day, to affirm that we exist. We went against the system"—Ava grabs my hand—"and we survived."

Dwarfed by our identical faces, Governor Roth glares up at his screens. A captain runs to his side. "Turn off the power, you half-wit filth," our speakers betray Roth's rabid whisper.

He can't. He's powerless.

Defeated.

"We are the rank and file, the discontent, the Common. We are labeled Gluts, marked rebels. And we are many." I repeat the last words as a threat. As a summons.

"Revive the rebellion," Ava tells our country, echoing Father's appeal. "And the Common will rise."

Ava stands. I stand. We hold down our wrists, fists clenched, exposing the tattoos that smother our microchips.

"Resist much."

"Obey little."

The screens go black, and the camera turns off. I exhale.

"Was it enough?" Ava asks.

The question hangs in the air, then sinks into an extended silence. It sits there, waiting for someone to pick it up.

To answer the call.

ACKNOWLEDGMENTS

Thank you foremost to our parents. Your untiring support and belief in us made it possible to chase our dreams. From the very first steps of our journey to become writers, you never once told us to get "real jobs." It's all for you and we love you.

To our best friend and beta reader, Brandon McKay. This book would never have been written without you. You never doubted this story and our ability to tell it. For nearly a decade you've been our sounding board, our lighthouse. Your time, feedback, and friendship mean the world to us. We're lucky to have you, Hopscotch.

To our editor, Jason Kirk, the giver of dreams. Our captain. Thank you for saying yes to Ava and Mira's story. Your energy, ideas, and enthusiasm are priceless. We are forever grateful.

To Lacy Lynch, our agent extraordinaire. Thank you for taking us under your wing and sharing with us your inexhaustible talent and wisdom. Your guidance has been invaluable. Our deepest thanks to everyone at Dupree Miller.

To Ginger Sledge, our biggest champion. Thank you for your steadfast belief in this story over the years, and for putting us in front of the right people. You've been irreplaceable in our lives. Lauren O'Connor, thank you for taking the lunch meeting over tacos that changed our careers. To our grandparents Daddy John and Nonnie, thank you for your support and for giving us the tranquility of your beautiful lake house to write portions of this novel. It was both an escape and a gift. To Allen Ho, the first person to hear our logline seven years ago and the first person who asked, "And then what happens?" Your encouragement kept us going.

To our developmental editor, Amara Holstein. Your expert notes and support throughout the editing process strengthened our story. You consistently pushed us while being a complete joy to work with. Thank you also to our copyeditor, Kamila Forson; our proofreader, Amanda Mininger; and our cover designer, David Curtis.

To the incredible team at Skyscape and Amazon Publishing: Courtney Miller, Colleen Lindsay, Brittany Russell, Kelsey Snyder, Haley Kushman, Rosanna Brockley, Amanda Clark, and Kristin King. We could not have found a better home.

Lastly, we would like to thank our dogs and writing mascots, Wyatt and Winston. They were with us through all the long days and nights, giving us the best encouragement and laughs when we needed it the most.

About the Authors

Photo © 2017 Shayan Asgharnia

Hailing from the suburbs of Dallas, Texas, Ashley Saunders and Leslie Saunders are award-winning filmmakers and twin sisters who honed their love of storytelling at the University of Texas at Austin. While researching *The Rule of One*, they fell in love with America's national parks, traveling the path of Ava and Mira. The sisters can currently be found with their Boston terriers in sunny Los Angeles, exploring hiking trails and drinking entirely too much yerba maté. Visit them at www.thesaunderssisters.com or follow them on Instagram @saunderssisters.